Cut and Run

Alec Marsh

Copyright © Alec Marsh 2024.

The right of Alec Marsh to be identified as the author of this work has been asserted by him in accordance with the Copyright, Designs and Patents Act, 1988.

First published in 2024 by Sharpe Books.

In memory of Irene Spouse, née Farnsworth (1907–2000).
She remembered the Tommies going off to fight.

CUT AND RUN

Chapter One

Wivenhoe, Essex coast, England, March 1916

It was just past low water and the boats that lined the dried-out waterfront at Wivenhoe lay askew, their masts and idle rigging a confused bird's-nest against the cold white sky. Several of the boats were held between taut ropes, braced like flies in a spider's web. Others squatted in the soft muddy beds whichever way the receding waters had left them, their ropes sagging to the shore, draped in green weed. Around them the riverbed was coated in marine and human detritus: the neck of a bottle protruded here, the iron hoops of a shattered barrel there. The damp air carried a pinch of salt that tickled the nose.

I pulled once more on the oars and the bow of my dinghy pushed through the water. For several minutes now I'd felt the change in the river; the tide was turning and the sea was once more claiming back the territory lost over the previous six hours. The tides made me think of the war: the constant advance and retreat of the sea not unlike like the frontline of battle where ground is taken and then yielded by well-matched opposing forces. A seagull swooped low over my head – I ducked. Its flat call scraped the air like a violinist hatching his bow across his instrument's sharp strings. The dinghy glided along under the power of the current...

I looked back out along the estuary towards the curve in the distance and the low line of trees on the horizon. As far as the eye could see the terrain was grey-brown; the low river banks, fringed with tall grasses, giving way to the gentle incline of the exposed, glistening mud. Then, finally at the centre, the narrow channel: a chaotic, choppy sea of continuous undulations, where the shallow brackish waters remained a briny brown, no matter how blue the sky or brilliant the sun. But the sun was not shining today; instead the whole seascape was leaden, dense, faintly forbidding. It was just as I liked it.

I pulled on my left oar, allowing my right blade to halt, and water to spill over it. The dinghy obediently turned to port, and with a

1

heave of both oars, I arrived at the varnished stern of my b[oat] *Nancy*. I shipped my oars and tied the dinghy to the bigger bo[at]. A glance told me that *Nancy* was just as I had left her.

I unloaded the wooden tender; placing a pair of metal bucke[ts] each piled high with oysters, onto *Nancy*'s teak deck, a[nd] depositing a hessian sack containing two good-sized soles tha[t I] had caught that afternoon beside them.

I arranged a pair of oily rags over the tops of the buckets [to] conceal their cargo and took them ashore. As I stepped down on[to] the jetty, a hot pain coursed through my left leg, stopping me mi[d]-stride. The burning sensation was not unexpected; it sharpened an[d] then dulled into a numbness, not unlike an episode of pins an[d] needles, as I knew it would. I drew a breath, recovering mysel[f] and looked across at the Rose and Crown, my destination. [A] glance told me that the waterfront was clear – and pressed on.

Passing the post office, I noticed that someone had scrawle[d] several jagged black lines across the peeling recruitment poste[r], scarring Kitchener's steadfast face. That would have shocked m[e] once. Now, I simply couldn't fathom why it hadn't happene[d] sooner. I picked up my pace. None of that meant anything to m[e] anymore.

The rain had eased off and two soldiers stood outside the pu[b] with tankards of beer, smoking cigarettes beneath the old gold sig[n] and dripping hanging baskets of spring flowers. I saw from the[ir] castle and sphinx cap badges that they were from the Esse[x] Regiment, which was my old lot. I didn't recognise either of the[m] but then, why should I? In the months since I had left ne[w] battalions had been formed bolstering the ranks depleted by w[ar]. They were both young and didn't appear to notice me. And th[ey] wouldn't. Increasingly in a world at war, civilian dress render[s] you invisible.

Inside the Rose and Crown, I was hit by a wall of heat and t[he] drum roll of male voices – and stamping feet. At the bar, Sam[my] Keep, the one-eyed publican, was locked in an arm wrestle wit[h a] burly stranger. The landlord's straining face glowed puce a[nd] glistened with perspiration at his recessed temples. The grip

CUT AND RUN

...ts wavered over the varnished counter. Left they went – then ...ck right. They hovered: Keep sensed victory, his bicep swelled ...r one last effort. Then the publican's good left eye spotted me ...d the buckets – and twitched. It blinked, this time with obvious ...itation and his arm crashed down onto bar. The onlookers roared ...d coins changed hand. I pushed through the knot of gamblers to ...e small, enclosed garden at the back of the pub.

Keep exploded from the side door, his imposing girth reined in ... a tatty leather apron. He glared at me.

'Damn you Champion, you just cost me five shillings.' His ...eaty hand flexed towards the buckets. 'And what in the Lord's ...ame is that? I told you I needed four buckets – *at least*. There's ...n army of weekenders coming for tomorrow's regatta. I can't be ...ort of oysters, not this weekend – not tonight!' He leaned in, his ...oice falling to a whisper, 'These people pay London prices.'

'Don't they know there's a war on?'

The scarred lid clenched over the defunct eye.

'Folk still need to enjoy themselves,' his finger stabbed my ...hest. 'And mark me, they will do. Cometh the hour, cometh the ...ustomers. This place will be heaving and now I've got no ruddy ...ysters.' I looked down at the haul, feeling less pleased with it than ... had. I scratched my beard.

'There's a pair of sole you can have,' I suggested.

'Damn your sole,' he growled. And he meant it.

'I'll bring you some more oysters first thing, once the tide's ...wn.'

'Don't bother –' He snatched up the buckets and kicked the door ...en.

...I grabbed the handle of the nearest pail and the eye glared back ... me with Cycloptic ferocity. I tugged the bucket back towards ...

You've forgotten something, Keep.'

...He cursed, his shoulders falling and set the oysters down. 'There ... He thrust a slim brown bottle into my hand. 'Don't drink it all ... once,' he sighed, his tone softening. 'See if you can get two ...re buckets. This weekend is going to be murder, mark my ...rd.'

3

The door slammed behind him and there was a moment of peace. I twisted the cork free and tilted the bottle to my lips, letting the smooth whisky fill my mouth. A sensation of wellbeing passed through me, offering a moment of calm – until I caught the ripe tang of fish on my hands, still tacky from the soles. In the same moment I glimpsed my reflection in a fragment of broken mirror on the wall: the weary, cold eyes of a stranger stared back at me. I took another slug of the whisky and felt better. *Look at the state of me.* My beard was a disgrace – like the hedge of an abandoned house, and dark fish blood streaked my cheeks. Damn you, I thought. I wiped my face and stomped to the waterfront.

Outside a pair of empty tankards stood on the table where the soldiers had been. A breeze pressed against my face – the race would have a good day of it tomorrow if this kept up. But there was rain coming. The clouds were high in the sky, spanning the heavens in a great arc that was blushed salmon pink.

'Red sky at night,' announced a voice. I turned, seeing the silhouette of a man in army uniform against the bright red evening sun. He added, 'Shepherd's delight.'

The lyrical note of the voice unlocked a memory, and I peered closely at my interlocutor.

'Nathaniel Kennedy,' I exclaimed, breaking into excited laugher. I moved forward and shook his proffered hand heartily. Then a cold realisation overtook me. When we last saw each other in Nairobi in 1910 we had not been friends. I let his hand go...

'What do you want?'

He scanned my face, noticing the missing lobe of my scarred left ear, and the ridge of an angry cut on my cheek that disappeared into my ragged beard. Then that smile I remembered came to his face.

'I had a hell of a job tracking you down, Champion –' His voice carried the soft, beguiling lilt of County Cork, his eyes twinkled with possibility. 'Is there somewhere that we can talk? I have to admit, I'm rather parched.'

Inside *Nancy*'s cramped saloon, Kennedy leaned back against one of the narrow cushioned benches as I lit the oil lamp. He removed his hat, giving me a view of his bald head, which when I'd last seen it, still had plenty of coverage, albeit in retreat. After a moment, a yellow flame glinted off the varnished interior. I unhooked a brace of duck that hung by a string from the bolt of a porthole rather too close to his head and laid them on the chart table. The evening light from the hatch fell across the jade neck and head of the mallard and caught a streak of vermillion on his yellow beak. I poured a couple of whiskies and went to add a dash of water.

'I won't, thanks,' he said, removing his glass.

I splashed some in mine and plonked down opposite him.

'Cheers,' I said, raising my glass. But the grey eyes weren't looking at me. They were reviewing the book shelves behind my head – and assessing my narrow library: the slim volume of Freud, the broader spines of Marx, Macaulay and Gibbon, and then the behemoth of Bosworth-Toller's magisterial *Anglo-Saxon Dictionary*. These oughtn't to have surprised Kennedy, as he knew my reading tastes. He raised his tumbler and drank.

'What happened to you, Champion?'

I chuckled at him, 'What do you mean?'

'Come on, man,' he threw up his hands. 'You look ruddy awful and this place *stinks*. If I didn't know any better I'd say you've been reduced to poaching.'

I snorted and looked down at the gloom to my feet. He wasn't that far from the truth.

'It's not meant to be funny,' he added belligerently. 'You could have made governor.'

I shook my head. 'That was always your ambition, not mine.'

Kennedy gave his glass a loud sniff and, evidently satisfied that it was uninfected, drained the vessel in one go. With my fingertip, I pushed the bottle towards him.

The three pips on his shoulder told me that he had been made a captain, not bad after only a couple of years' service, though somehow I doubted that he had done an honest day's soldiering in that time. His lapels carried red flashes, showing he'd been put through staff college, so someone reckoned he was a horse worth backing. And above the pocket on his left breast, among the three inches of multi-coloured decorations, he also wore the distinctive narrow blue, broad red, and narrow blue ribbon of the Distinguished Service Order. So he'd done something brave, or got the credit for something brave someone else had done. As Kennedy poured himself a good double measure, I saw a distinct shake to his hand, which was telling. He had not been a 'proper drinker' before.

I smiled at him.

'You look like you're having a good war.'

He nodded back, knowing it not to be an unalloyed compliment. There was also a price for his adornments: the white strokes at his temples, where the last of the hair still clung on. I'd also reckon, conservatively, that he was the wrong side of a couple of stone heavier than when I'd last set eyes on him in East Africa.

I wondered if it was just the war that had so altered my old comrade from our days together in Africa, when we had both been fresh-faced, naive servants of the empire. Or was it merely weariness owing from the march of time?

Then Kennedy's fat, brown moustache twitched – on the left side, with the corner of his mouth rising as though half-smiling. It gave me a flash of recognition of the younger, boyish, man I'd known. I also realised that he was about to get to the point.

'I've just come from France,' he said. 'A young woman was murdered in Béthune last Monday. She was a prostitute. Her body was left in the bandstand in the town's main park. Her throat had been cut.' He glanced down at his drink. 'She was twenty.'

The words hung in the air for a moment – but not without effect. In the pit of my stomach the acid rose and a hungry space appeared, like the mercury falling in a barometer before the storm.

Apart from the obvious question – *why*, precisely, was Kennedy telling me any of this, a second and rather more pressing point confronted me. Why did he and presumably the British Army give a fig about a French prostitute, dead or alive? I pondered this as I lit my pipe. He was about to continue when I cut him off:

'The Blue lamp or the Red Lamp?'

He brightened.

'Good to see that the old Frank Champion is still there

underneath it all.' He smiled, 'The Blue Lamp.'

The Blue Lamp was the unofficial name given to the brothel for British Army officers; the Red Lamp was the establishment, usually on the less salubrious side of a given town, frequented by 'other ranks', so the vast majority of private soldiers and non-commissioned officers.

'So you think a British Army officer is responsible?'

He nodded solemnly. 'Now, I won't insult your intelligence, Frank. You'll already know why I've come here. But I'm going to ask you properly: will you do it – will you come to Béthune with me and find the man who did it?'

'Why on earth would I do that?' I looked down at my pipe to evade his insistent stare.

'Because you can.'

'Really?' I replied, momentarily surprised. I stared into the warm glow of the pipe's bowl, at the tiny furnace of the countless spidery flakes of tobacco.

He leaned forward.

'Champion, I haven't forgotten the Morgan case.'

'Nor have I –' I glared at him. 'You left me high and dry.'

'You left *yourself* out to dry, Frank. You bit off more than you or anyone could chew – and you know it.' He smiled, 'But anyway, we got what we wanted, didn't we? Word got around. Page was quietly moved on – you know he was punished for what he did.'

'Not as much as he should have been.' *And not as much as I was.*

'That's as maybe,' Kennedy hesitated. 'But Frank, that was then, this is now. I need your help. We need your help. I'm probably not overdoing it to say that the people of Béthune need your help.'

I shook my head, 'I can't do it.'

'The Morgan case–'

'I was lucky with the Morgan case.'

'That's rot!' His finger stabbed the tabletop. 'I know you better than that. You don't believe in luck.'

'Don't bet on it,' I shot back. 'A stint in the trenches teaches you a lot.'

'What about right and wrong? Are you going to tell me that life in the trenches changed that, too?'

'You'd be surprised.'

He raised his chin with something approaching distain, the lips set hard. I could only hazard at what was going through his mind. Recriminations over a wasted journey would be the least of it.

'Look,' I sploshed another dose of whisky into my glass – 'while it's a bit embarrassing for King and Country to have a British officer in the frame for this killing, why do they really care? They don't care about the thousands of their own men that they kill through their own gross neglect and stupidity, so what's this poor woman to them? Come on, level with me.'

Kennedy viewed me hard through the eye of a slowly revolving, baroque swirl of pipe smoke. He took a deep breath.

'Whatever you might think about losses on the battlefield Frank – and I think we all accept that mistakes have been made – we cannot permit even the possibility of a British Army officer going around killing prostitutes. Discipline, especially among the officer corps, is paramount. If that goes we've lost it. That means this man has got to be stopped. And the last thing we want to do is to involve the French authorities – they're a pain in the damned neck as it is. We need to solve this internally – and *fast*. And I know you can do it.'

'Call in the Royal Military Police; that's what they're for.'

'Damn it Frank,' he growled. 'We no more want the RMP involved than we want the French blundering about. It needs to be handled delicately and it needs to be off the books. But it also must be handled by someone who will stubbornly follow the evidence – and that's you.'

Kennedy lit a cigarette.

'You could just close the brothel? No more prostitutes, no more murders; simple.'

'Out of the question; the place is essential for morale – and you know it. Our chaps need somewhere to go where they can let off some steam.'

That was one way of putting it. Young men confronting death deserved to have the comfort that a woman could bring, all the more so if they'd not experienced it before. Even if they had to pay for it.

'That's why it's imperative that you come to France with me immediately.' He leaned forward, his head was bathed in the light of the lamp – turning his eye sockets into skeletal, black holes. 'I know you're not interested in money – but we'll make it worth your while.'

I tapped my finger along the straight stem of my pipe and asked: 'What actual evidence do you have that a British officer is responsible?' Kennedy sat back, his eyes coming into the light. 'This woman will have had other clients, won't she – French clients? She will have had numerous French connections, from family to lovers and estranged lovers. Why are you so certain that it's one of yours?'

He lowered his gaze and rotated his glass between his hands, gently swirling the liquid.

'A British Army issue condom was found with the body,' he said distastefully. 'It was still in its foil packet, I hasten to add. It was gripped in the girl's hand, rather as if it was put there deliberately by the killer.'

'I'm sure it was.'

Kennedy cleared his throat. 'What we know for sure is that we don't want another one turning up. We're getting enough flack from the frogs as it is for – as they see it – our not pulling our weight in the war effort, so going around knocking off their civilians doesn't go down very well. We can't let it happen again.'

Smoke tumbled from my mouth and I permitted myself a smile.

'And who are "we" these days?'

He looked at me sharply.

'I have a liaison role at Saint-Omer,' he explained, his eyes shifting momentarily over my shoulder. Saint-Omer was the location of the headquarters of the British Army of France, so I understood him to mean that he was involved in some form of military intelligence, from which I supposed the case was generating some political heat. Perhaps they hoped someone on the outside would be able to get where those on the inside couldn't, and ask awkward questions. Of course, outsiders could be silenced more easily, too, particularly if they came across the wrong information.

'Who would I be working under?'

'Me. But you're a free agent as far as I'm concerned. It's been properly sanctioned, that's all you need to know.'

'Sanctioned by whom?'

'General Risborough.'

'I don't know him.'

'And you don't need to.' He smiled, 'The general will be my problem – I promise. You'll deal with me.'

Which was fine, if only I could trust him. I looked up at the flickering candlelight reflecting in the planked ceiling and thought of a poor dead woman left in some cold bandstand. The last thing I wanted to do was go back to France. I sighed and shook my head.

'All right. I'll do it.'

Chapter Two

We made landfall in France at Boulogne after a rough night aboard a Royal Navy frigate. It was rough in several senses of the word; from the attitudes of the officers whose company I was forced to keep while aboard, to the seas under us, which tossed the warship about as though she was the size of *Nancy*. I was seasick from start to finish, which at least gave me the excuse I needed to leave the wardroom and be on my own without causing offence to the sensibilities of my hosts.

Safely restored to dry land we then caught a train packed with British soldiers to Béthune, arriving shortly after eight o'clock in the morning. We were then met on the steam-filled platform at Béthune Station by Kennedy's batman, Private Greenlaw. He was an untidy-looking Yorkshireman in his early twenties, with sandy hair and a ruddy complexion that was best described as 'medium rare'.

On sight of us, he flicked away a rolled up cigarette end and pounced on our bags. I grabbed my old Gladstone before he could get to it and then let it be known that I'd no truck with being called 'Sir' by him either. This was a bolt from the blue for the Yorkshireman – prompting him to glance uncertainly towards Kennedy, who emitted a disapproving nod to authorise my request. He thereby subsumed what I would describe as the honest appeal of one working man to another beneath the towering pyramid of military orthodoxy. Greenlaw then looked back at me, frowning in disbelief, before referring to his officer.

'So what should I call him then, sir?' he asked.

'Champion,' replied the Irishman, flashing me a tepid smile with just the hint of humour. 'He likes that, because that's what he thinks he is.'

We walked along wet, slippery cobbled streets to our digs, located in a small frowsy-looking hotel on the town's large medieval market square. I smoked a pipe in my room as I unpacked my few items of kit. This included Murray's British

Army issue Webley Mark VI revolver, a memento of my service days, which I had inherited. It was useless at anything other than point-blank range but – if discharged in such circumstances – pretty lethal, thanks to its 0.455 inch calibre round. I hid it behind the wardrobe, wrapped up in a canvas rag.

I had remembered that when I was briefly in Béthune eight months before, most of it as a crippled casualty, I had heard about the girls at the Blue Lamp; they were said to be far prettier than those at the Red Lamp, and cleaner too. They even bathed, it was said, between callers – of the rank of major and above, that is. It struck me as perverse that even in such a thing as prostitution the British class system was so unassailable. Of course, it was utterly unthinkable that gentlemen officers and the working man could enjoy the ministrations of the same women of the night. It reminded me of that piece of good domestic folklore: good fences make good neighbours.

I wondered if Kennedy had tasted the pleasures of the Blue Lamp, but doubted it. He hadn't gone in for that sort of thing in East Africa. It wasn't my cup of tea, either, and never had been. Paying for something that ought to be freely given – and for love, let's not forget – offended my sense of propriety. But in this I was knew I was in a surprisingly small minority.

From my window I had a good view of the enormous square, a broad uneven rectangular expanse of cobble, probably the size of half a dozen football pitches. The main event was a stone tower which stood off-centre some hundred feet or more tall and was capped by a handsome belfry beneath a pointed spire. It could have been a piece of Scottish Gothic transplanted from the imagination of Walter Scott in Aberdeenshire. Beneath the stone crenulations were arranged dark, heraldic shields, interspersed with protruding granite gargoyles, their mouths contorted and teeth bared. Several, I had noticed earlier, possessed broad clawed hands and, not for the first time, I wondered what purpose such architectural adornments served. Were they there to frighten demons away or to ward off more earthly evils?

Apart from this tower the square was empty, saving for knots of churchgoers in their Sunday best heading towards the red brick church tower at its northern end or, presumably, one of the other spires I could see over the rooftops. The scores of shops, cafés and restaurants that lined its perimeter were shuttered and blank; across the way was the imposing steep-roofed town hall, grey, ugly and like everything else, closed. Few things in the world are as shut as France on a Sunday.

The first time I laid eyes on the place had been last September. My regiment stopped here after a three-day, fifty-six mile hike through northern France in the rain in full kit. We didn't know it, but we were just hours from the Battle of Loos, the correct pronunciation of which was loss, and which was precisely what happened. But first of all, we arrived here in Béthune, soaked to the skin and already exhausted. There was a hasty breakfast, then we went up to the lines to be dragooned to our deaths. Three-quarters of us, anyway. The lucky ones survived, but luck has its price: guilt for surviving when better, braver comrades died. I knew I ought to be grateful, but I was too sick of the whole thing to feel gratitude and then I felt guilty for that, too.

There was a knock at the door and Greenlaw poked his ruddy face in through the gap.

'Captain says he'll see you downstairs in ten minutes.'

I thanked him and spotted him pause in the doorway.

'Begging your pardon S–' He broke off, shutting his mouth to stop himself from using the banned 'Sir' word. 'I wanted to ask. Captain Kennedy said you're a filthy Communist.'

'Did he now?' I chuckled. That was just like Kennedy. 'Do I look filthy to you?'

Greenlaw beamed, showing his teeth.

'I wouldn't say so.'

'Good. And what about you? Are you a filthy Communist, Private Greenlaw?'

He exhaled. 'I don't think I'm anything, Champion.'

'Ah, so you're a nihilist, are you?' I smiled.

Greenlaw held my gaze for a moment and then grinned, 'I'm more of a Liberal-Unionist, if I'm anything.'

'Very sensible.' I realised I liked Private Greenlaw. 'Tell the comrade Captain Kennedy that I shall be down directly.'

He disappeared and I gathered my things and then quickly finished my pipe at the window, pondering the buildings on the far side of the square. They were grey, just like the sky, with angular, stepped, mean Flemish roofs. My thoughts went back to a conversation with Kennedy during the crossing. He had reminded me of the visit he had made to stay with my family at the rectory in Northwich in Cheshire when once our leaves coincided long before the war. I had recalled his reaction to Dorothy, my middle sister. Over the following days it became clear to everyone else, if not quite Dorothy herself, that Kennedy was smitten. When she did discover it, she remained cool towards him. Perhaps uncharitably, at the time I felt a relief over this because I had already begun to suspect differences between Kennedy and myself that I feared might have led to division between my sister and me, had their relations blossomed. Of course, if I had known that she would go on to marry the Reverend Charles Newnes, with whom she now shared the rectory at Wivenhoe, I would have taken a different view. I sighed.

Movement caught my eye: in the foreground I saw a man in the square, hands buried in his overcoat pockets. He was alone in the vast wet space and faced me. Some fifty yards off, he wore a beaten bowler hat and what was clearly a Royal Navy-issue overcoat, distinctive by its long cut and shade of dark blue. I would have known it even if we hadn't just spent the night aboard a frigate. And he was very blatantly looking at me. I turned to reach for my binoculars but when I looked back, he was gone.

Without further preamble, Captain Kennedy led me to the park, the one where at six o'clock in the morning the Monday before, the body of a young woman named Marie-Louise Toulon had been found. It was, I discovered, a neat square of green surrounded on four sides by imposing mansions and town houses in the French style. Over the top of the trees, I saw attractive stone and cast-iron balustrades, and tall windows flanked by gaily painted shutters below steep slate-grey mansard roofs. Even on the grey day the architecture offered a glimpse of colour.

'The body was found in the bandstand by a chap walking his Bichon Frise,' observed Kennedy. 'The dog found her first, of course.'

The aforementioned structure had an ornate conical roof and was the centrepiece of the park. It was surrounded by a perimeter of lawns, encircled by a ring of benches, ornamental flower beds and shrubberies and cherry trees. Around this was an arboreal border with manicured foliage and gravelled walkways interwoven to engender a sense of bucolic seclusion. As we followed the wending path to the centre it occurred to me that was a privacy exploited by the killer too.

At the bandstand Kennedy pointed out the precise position of the body and the way it laid. The pathologist had concluded that Marie-Louise Toulon was killed by a deep, curving cut to the throat. It was the only injury that could be determined. Very little blood has been found at the scene, indicating that the murder had likely taken place elsewhere and that the body had been transported here for discovery. As more discreet options for disposal will certainly have been available to the killer, this was therefore a statement of some sort.

I pictured the body laid out on the stone floor, overlaying the photographs that Kennedy had supplied with the physical reality. I imagined the dark figure of her killer laying her down and arranging her limbs, prior to closing the condom in her right hand, which was then placed over her heart, for additional emphasis.

Marie-Louise Toulon was five foot, three inches tall and weighed at death about seven and a quarter stone, giving her a weight in life of something rather over seven and a half stone, so barely 100 pounds of weight. This meant that a man of average stature could be expected to port her body alone, thereby possibly eradicating the need for accomplices. This meant there could be less planning or organisation and might even, therefore, lessen the degree of premeditation, if it came to it. The post-mortem examination report noted that Toulon had not been sexually interfered with prior to death, which denied the obvious sexual motive for her murder.

The rain intensified so we lingered under the bandstand. Why would you bring a body here? Why expose yourself to the unnecessary risk? And what purpose did the condom serve? I looked up towards the large detached houses, my eyes probing their dark upper storeys. If Marie-Louise were murdered in one of these properties then the bandstand was a close, anonymous place to rid yourself of the corpse. But might it also be a challenge or declaration: was the killer throwing the gauntlet down at someone, or the community as a whole? Was not the bandstand adorned with gilded dragons, the emblem of the town? And what of the condom? Was it part of a warning, but to whom, and what could it signify? Was it a protest against the lax sexual morality of wartime? Was Marie-Louise a victim of a moral outrage? It hardly seemed likely. Kennedy lit a cigarette and interrupted my thoughts.

'The squat lump over there is the home of the mayor, Monsieur Chambord.' He pointed to a handsome, three-storied bastion in the south-west corner of the square. It was painted a pale shade of lemon yellow and had a pair of spidery apple trees in the front. 'You'll get to meet him before long – I daresay you'll get on like a house on fire. He's right up your street.' Kennedy grinned mischievously. 'Shall we?'

We walked back up the hill taking a different route through the narrow lanes until we arrived at the rue de la Délivrance. This was a quiet, brick-paved back-street several rows removed from the main square on the east side and home to the Blue Lamp. The little road was made up of distinctly French terraced townhouses, each rendered and painted ochre or grey, the shades of Hastings in the rain. The windows were damp dead sockets, closed from peering eyes by rotting brown shutters, giving the street a dejected, taciturn appearance. Dogs had been at the bins and rotting litter was strewn across the yard, adding a piquant tang to an already ripe atmosphere of sewage that had been accumulating since arriving in the street. We entered an archway into a house and went up to the first floor where Kennedy knocked loudly at a tall varnished door.

After a moment, we heard the sound of approaching footsteps and then a heavy bolt was drawn on the far side of the door. A shrill voice barked at us.

'Nous sommes fermés!'

There was a second 'clunk' as another bolt was shifted and the door jerked open six inches to reveal an elderly face, supporting a mass of dark hair.

'We're shut!' The woman's haughty brown eyes glared up at me beneath arched, razor-thin, eyebrows. She went to slam the door, then spied Kennedy. 'Ah –' her tone softened and she gave a smile. 'Come in, gentlemen. As a rule we do not work on God's day, but there are always exceptions, no?'

The woman led us into a large, jade-green salon, the wallpaper faded and lifting. Dusty cobwebs straddled its cornices. We sat on a pair of grimy velvet sofas which were arranged before tall windows, their tattered, floor-to-ceiling curtains only half drawn. I was trying to place the smell. It reminded me of the pungent, unhealthy aroma of an elderly maiden aunt's pantry in which fruitcakes and other household staples are very slowly petrifying. A black lacquered baby grand piano, splattered with red candle wax from two burned-out candelabra, occupied one corner. Yellowing pages of sheet music were strewn across the floorboards, wine-stained Chopin waltzes mingled with Gilbert and Sullivan operettas. Empty wine bottles and glasses dotted the floor and surfaces of the room.

'I am Madame Lefebvre, proprietress of the Blue Lamp,' the old woman declared, her jaundiced eyes addressing me unforgivingly. 'I assume that you are here for poor Marie-Louise?'

For the next five minutes, as Kennedy introduced me, her gaze kept vigil on the dark, jagged scar that announced the missing lobe of my left ear. In return I noticed she had a slight overbite which gave the impression that she was endeavouring to retain a large boiled sweet in her mouth. She appeared to reposition this confection as she surveyed me one more time and I decided to begin.

'How long did Marie-Louise Toulon work for you?'

'Deux ans.' She looked away from my ear, the eyes swivelling beneath the Norman flying buttresses of her highly plucked arches. 'It was two years, give or take.'

'How did she come to be here?'

Madam Lefebvre exhaled, causing her bottom lip to vibrate.

'Like any other girl.'

There was a pause and Kennedy and I exchanged a glance.

'Please explain.'

Her expression flashed with irritation and she spoke hastily.

'She arrived one day, and needed work and somewhere to live. We gave her a home. It's that simple.'

'Where was she from?'

'I have no idea; the south, I think.' Her gaze temporarily referred to the scar on my left cheek, the one hidden by my beard. 'I never asked. I don't as a rule.'

'Which of the women here was she closest to?'

'You will have to ask them.' Lefebvre bobbed her chin upwards, indicating a space upstairs. 'As far as I can tell, they're all thick as thieves. It is a family, no?'

And families had their secrets.

I asked, 'Did Mademoiselle Toulon have any regular clients?'

Lefebvre's left eyebrow arched.

'Monsieur, they *all* have their regulars – until they get killed.' She flicked her bony hand across her throat and made a high-pitched whistling sound, followed by a flutter of the fingers, imitating a bird in flight. 'Your gallant young officers that is, *mon Dieu!* They are the ones who die, usually.' She crossed herself and then settled the nimble hands in the lap of her black gown. I momentarily contemplated the pearl choker that retained the grey folds of her throat. Every now and then it was obscured by her chin, which protruded like the parson's nose on a lightly roasted chicken. Lefebvre must be knocking on eighty.

'Have any of your girls said anything about any of the clients – are any of them violent?' I asked.

Lefebvre coughed, her head rocking back.

'Monsieur –' Her eyeballs widened with emphasis and she spread her bony hands. 'You must not be naive. Many of our gentlemen have peculiar requests. That is the nature of the work. Many of them have been in battle, sir.' She took a deep breath, her nostrils flaring. 'That is the life, sir. You must know that, you are a man; you have been in war, no?'

Lefebvre held my gaze and sucked the sweet in such a way that somehow conveyed suspicion.

'Many is the man who visits here; we have French, English, in times gone by, German even; I remember 1871.' Her gnarled finger admonished the air imperiously. 'The Germans were animals, but they paid! The men who visit here often want things that their wives will not do – things they will not volunteer at confession, but these are not killers, Monsieur, they are just men, being men.' She gave a deep, weary, chocolaty laugh. 'That is what they do.'

Kennedy cleared his throat.

'How many women do you have here, Madame?'

'C'est dependant.' She offered him a warm smile; she liked him. Her shoulders bobbed, 'Six, seven; once we had twelve.' She looked at me and the corners of the mouth fell. 'We are six now.'

She crossed herself urgently.

Contemplating our pool of potential suspects, I ventured to ask how many regular clients they had.

She paused, the black outline of her head still.

'Perhaps fifty, sixty,' she suggested.

I exhaled and saw the toe of her patent shoe protrude slowly from the hem of her black dress.

'When was the last time you saw Marie-Louise alive?' I asked.

She shrugged.

'Sunday afternoon. That is when I left.'

'And no one has any idea where she went?'

'No.'

I exchanged a glance with Kennedy.

'Do any of the girls give you trouble?' he asked.

'Of course,' she said, tilting her head to one side. The hands came together. 'But we manage things. It is what 'appens. If it is a big problem we have to let nature take its course. But that is what nuns are for, no?'

I asked, 'Did Miss Toulon have a lover, a sweetheart?'

Lefebvre craned her head towards me, as though straining to hear, and I raised my voice…

'A sweetheart!' The claw went to her breast and she appealed to Kennedy. 'God give me hope.'

'How can you be so certain?'

'Non!' She raised her fist, anger rising within her. 'It is not allowed. The girls know it is forbidden and it is an iron rule. It always leads to trouble.'

I cleared my throat.

'Does the Blue Lamp have an enemy, anyone who would wish you harm, someone who might have done this … to hurt you?'

'Non.' She shook her head defiantly. 'Non!'

'What about rival brothels?'

'Non.'

Kennedy cleared his throat and rubbed his hands together, reminding me of a land agent deflecting by an awkward question over boundaries. Once she had calmed down a little, I gave her something else to chew on.

'Out of interest, Madame, why haven't you closed the brothel?'

Her eyebrows lifted.

'Why would I do that Monsieur? Do *you* suppose that one of my gentlemen murdered Marie-Louise? *Non*, Monsieur.' She shook her head as though I was a fool. 'Our clients *need* the girls alive for what they need them for.' The mouth hardened and she regarded me with scorn. 'And let me say this, Marie-Louise was not even working the night she went missing, so how would closing the brothel be of assistance? It would be better to insist that the brothel never closed, eh?'

Lefebvre's eyes glistened with triumph at her display of logic.

'Madame,' cooed Kennedy. 'We cannot discount entirely the possibility that the killer is a customer of the Blue Lamp, and whoever has killed once, may kill again.'

'And what do we do while we wait, *Capitaine*? Starve? Freeze to death?' Lefebvre shuddered and shook her head with contempt. 'Non Monsieur, we must go on. There is a war on. We are doing our duty for France!'

The madam reached into the folds of her dress and drew out a black Crucifix and rosary. 'I will continue to pray for the death of the man responsible. I believe that God will work his justice soon enough.'

There was a sharp knock and a young woman stood in the doorway. She was plain-looking and wore baggy cotton trousers and a large blue Breton jumper. Her chocolate brown hair was pulled back from an oval, watchful face that was overshadowed by a pair of round glasses.

'Ah, Celine – ' Lefebvre's tone was proprietorial. 'Fetch the girls down to the salon. The British detectives wish to question them about poor Marie-Louise.'

For a moment I had the impression that girl was appraising Kennedy and me. I couldn't be sure, then I saw her fingers fold into her palms. Defiance.

'The girls won't take kindly to being woken at this hour, Madame,' she said.

'I don't care,' barked Lefebvre. 'Bring them down this instant.'

Celine bowed her head and departed. The fists remained.

Chapter Three

First, I inspected Marie-Louise Toulon's room. It was situated at the very top of the house and occupied a small triangular-shaped wedge in the attic immediately beneath the roof. The only light came from a small hinged window, which was about the size of hardback book – perhaps an atlas or gazetteer. It offered a view across sloping roofs of weathered slates in various states of repair and a busy society of domestic chimneys belching charcoal-coloured staircases of smoke into a steel firmament. Just visible were taller chimneys of factories and looming shapes of warehouses near the railway station in the distance.

The room carried the pall of damp, mingled with a faint odour of perfume, possibly all that was left of the former occupant, her personal effects having been removed by the police. I perched on the edge of the single bed, springs croaking under a mean mattress and felt them dig into my backside. This space, barely eight feet long and five feet wide with its acutely angled ceiling wasn't much of a home. I sighed and decided to look under the worn hessian rug, just in case. Having done so, I flipped the scrawny mattress and even pulled out the bed to check nothing was hidden by it. I then did the same for the narrow chest of drawers and the flimsy wardrobe. Wispy spools of dust and hair grimed in along the wainscot were all that remained of the late occupant. I could only imagine that whatever clues it might once have contained were either now with the police or lost to the world for good. I took another look out of the window. Beyond the choppy sea of slate a weathervane – a distant iron cockerel – on top of the square tower of the church of Saint Vaast at the far end of the main square showed that the wind had moved to the south-west. It would doubtless bring more bad weather.

Downstairs, Kennedy excused himself on account of urgent business unrelated to the case, and left me to interview the women of the Blue Lamp. Over the course of the next hour and a half, I spoke to six of the Blue Lamp's 'girls' about Marie-Louise, their customers and the workings of the brothel. 'You see the same faces returning for a few weeks at a time,' said Rebecca, a lanky if buxom woman from Normandy who gave her age as twenty-four and was fighting an unequal battle with a heavy cold. 'Some talk about themselves,' she added, followed by a sniff long enough to drain a wine glass. 'Most don't know how to talk.'

If the men did not have an appointment with a specific girl or know which they wished to see, Celine, who in Lefebvre's stead acted rather like a maître 'd'hôtel in a restaurant, would ask questions to channel the clients towards whomsoever she considered the most appropriate girl for them. If it went well, the client would be encouraged to ask for the same girl on return. Some men became regulars, but not for long. 'Then they go back,' sighed Rebecca. 'Maybe they return on their next leave a month later…' She shrugged and left the sentence unfinished.

Another of the girls, Annette, a blond of perhaps thirty, sat twisting her hands in her lap in the shadow of her compressed cleavage. 'Many of them are virgins,' she confided seriously, shaking her head. 'This would never happen in France.'

'Are any of the men violent?' I asked her.

'Non. Well,' she reconsidered, gently shifting the mass of her right breast with the crook of her elbow. 'Not particularly.' I wondered out loud what 'particularly' meant and she waived the question away. 'Some of them ask for their mummies in their sleep, Monsieur, others for their nannies. You have to wonder.'

I asked her if she could fathom any reason why someone might harm Marie-Louise and she shook her head. 'Marie-Louise was just unlucky.' Annette nodded, deciding that that was true. 'She was just unlucky.'

The next woman, who gave her name as Heloise, was profoundly miserable and told me that she and Marie-Louise had barely exchanged a word. 'I don't know anything about Marie-Louise, Monsieur,' she insisted. 'We were never friends; she wasn't a very friendly person – not to anyone as far as I could tell. She was a cold fish. A cold fish! The other girls will tell you the same.' She took a truculent drag of her Gauloise, and then shook her head, as if shaking off the subject.

'Do you like living here at the Blue Lamp?' I asked. 'Non.'

'Well, why don't you leave? Surely you could if you wished?'

'Of course –' Her eyes fired at me. 'But where would I go?'

Next, Celine showed in Francine, a young woman with a feral, harried look to her. Slim-hipped, with short raven black hair, she had attractive green eyes, but they were ringed darkly and her complexion was drawn. It gave the decided impression of a person requiring several heavy meals and probably a period of rest in the soothing environs of somewhere like Lyme Regis. She was nervous, too, and I realised it wasn't the circumstances of the interview that made her this way, rather it was her natural state, or perhaps the state that life had left her in. Her large eyes made no direct contact with me for longer than half a second, and, between heavy drags on her cigarette and consumptive wheezes, she did little more than confirm Heloise's assessment, before asking to be excused. 'Marie-Louise barely spoke to me – or anyone,' she sighed. 'Now, if you don't mind, I'm extremely tired and would like to go back to my bed. I have a dreadful headache…'

Another of the women, Rose, who brought a glass of wine into the interview with her, agreed – 'Marie-Louise was obnoxious' – and after providing little additional intelligence before departing for her bed. I had almost given up all hope when Fabienne was shown in.

And she was quite different. What confronted me was an evidently attractive women in her mid-twenties with luscious blonde hair, tied loosely at the nape of her neck. Immediately, I realised, she had an energy about her, a sense of lifelines. Perhaps, I wondered, she had just had a better night's sleep than the others, but it was more than that. She wore a pale lilac tea dress which showed the narrowness of her waist, the curve of her hips and the swell of chest. Her perfect cupid's bow mouth was as shapely as her figure, and brought to mind a Botticelli nymph. She lowered herself onto the cushion next to me, and I felt the need to edge away.

She had been at the brothel for six months, she said, and had nothing bad to say about the customers – nor Marie-Louise. I asked her what she had been like?

'The truth is I could not say, not properly.' She had pronounced after a thoughtful pause. 'Marie was a very private person.'

This statement struck me as interesting. You have to know someone to describe them as private. Otherwise, like previous interviewees, they might be thought haughty or cold or ascribed some other disobliging adjective. 'Private' requires observable insight.

'How do you know that she wasn't just rude?'

Fabienne smiled. 'It is a possibility, of course.' Her lips pursed, 'But I don't believe it to be the case.'

'So, you were friends?'

For a moment her fingers hooked into the small hole at her throat and took out a thin golden necklace with a hanging cross and small medallion, like a Saint Christopher.

'Yes and no –' She pushed the necklace back inside her collar. 'I knew her a little. Places like these are transient Monsieur Champion.' Her blue eyes held mine, 'half the time it's like the Gare de Lyon here. No one really makes friends because such a friendship cannot be real, because there's no pause, no intimacy; everyone moves on all too quickly. But also, friendship has its price.'

That it does, I agreed wearily.

'And you grieve for Marie-Louise?'

'But of course.' She nodded and swallowed, her eyes falling to the floor. She took a deep breath and dabbed at her eyes which were brimming with tears. I waited for her to compose herself before continuing.

'Did Marie ever mention her family or where she grew up?'

There was a blank shake of the head.

'What about a lover – did she ever mention a lover?'

Another shake, this time more rigorous.

'Was her behaviour at all unusual or did anything unusual occur in the days or weeks preceding her death?'

Fabienne looked up at me, her expression one of appeal. 'I have positively wracked my mind, Monsieur Champion, to try and think of anything that she might have told me, but in truth she said so little about herself. We lived in the moment, Monsieur. We kept reflection at bay. This is all we have, no?'

Her comment prompted me to remember a line of wisdom from Marcus Aurelius, one I used to repeat to the boys at the school I had taught before the war. 'Man lives only in the present, in this fleeting instant: all the rest of his life is either past and gone, or not yet revealed.' I quoted this and Fabienne looked at me, a keen frown on her brow. Her lips widened into something resembling a frank smile.

'We were friends, Monsieur. You're right. Yes we were. And that was my mistake.' Her tone became more certain. 'I did allow myself to know her better than I normally do. Than I should. And now she is now gone –' Fabienne glanced at the clock, and I saw that tears rimmed her eyes. She pressed them away carefully with a folded handkerchief, and looked at me with those piercing blue eyes. 'I fear the truth is you are wasting your time, Monsieur. This killer will never be discovered.'

'What makes you so certain?'

Her gaze immediately broke from mine and I realised – for whatever reason – that she knew she had misspoken. She sprang from the chair, a gasp escaping her mouth and made for the door, erupting with apologies. At the threshold she stopped and turned back to me. I was moving towards her and she held up her gloved hand, silencing me.

'You are cleverer than the French policeman who came to question us, Monsieur Champion. I like that.' She held my gaze. 'But it is impossible to answer your question because what I describe is a feeling. I am sure of it, that is all.'

She spoke with newfound firmness.

'You're sure?'

'I am positive, Monsieur.'

I wasn't convinced.

'Who are you afraid of?'

The eyelids lifted – ripe with calculation – and the mouth fell open with silent indignation.

'I mean it,' I said. 'Who is it?'

Fabienne was about to speak but instead she gave up and exhaled. She shook her head. 'The truth is I don't really know.' The corners of her mouth compressed and she nodded, 'It's just what I believe. People don't care about people like us.' Her voice felt more certain now. 'Marie and me, we are whores. We are doing words that have become nouns by dint of our occupation and the judgement of society. No one cares about us, and that is why Marie-Louise's murder will never be solved.'

In the distance the belfry chimed the hour – and she swore under her breath.

'*Mon Dieu* ... Apologies, Monsieur. I'm late –'

A moment later she was gone and then I heard the front door slam shut. Half a minute later I saw her emerge into the street below, hurrying beneath a black umbrella up the street avoiding the larger puddles and heaps of litter. A couple more agile sidesteps and she turned the corner, taking the truth and her fears with her.

I half turned from the window, but instantly moved back...

A sodden figure stood in the doorway on the opposite side of the road; his head and shoulders were obscured by the angle of my line of sight by the doorway, so I could only see his shaded feet and lower half of the long, navy coat. Then he moved and I saw the narrow brim of his bowler hat; it was the man from the square.

My heart pumping, I burst into the street, stamping through the puddles and detritus. But the doorway across the road was empty. The man was gone. I cursed, took one judging, scoping glance left and then right – before hurrying to the end of the road that led towards the square. I knew I had an equal chance of getting it right, or wrong. Arriving at the square, Bowler Hat was nowhere to be seen. I stood in the drizzle, the raindrops splashing heavily against my face and caught my breath back.

Chapter Four

Shaking water off my tweed cap, I knocked purposefully at the door of the large, yellow-painted house which stood on the corner of the park where Marie-Louise Toulon's body was found, and belonged to the mayor of Béthune, a Monsieur Chambord.

A ginger-haired manservant with a severe side-parting dressed in a morning coat, wing collar and striped waistcoat, answered and deposited me in a narrow sitting room just off the hallway. It was furnished with overly stuffed chairs, fussy silk covered sofas and occasional tables, and dressed up with prim ceramic ornaments of dogs. Above the cream marble mantelpiece was a landscape of peasants harvesting apples in a sunlit orchard. Béthune, I recalled, produced a rather distinctive cider. It was a drink I had avoided, I remembered again, since getting drunk with two friends – Masterman and Rounce – at school, when we were in the lower sixth. Masterman had been sick violently in the chaplain's garden, and looking back it now dawned on me that the way his eyes had bulged from their sockets with the force of each convulsion reminded me of the face of a man being gassed. The chaplain's sunflowers never really recover. Nor had my taste for cider.

Monsieur Chambord arrived, bringing the fragrant smell of roasted meat with him, his full face flushed with wine and protein. He was younger than I'd envisaged, perhaps forty, but he carried some timber which aged him nonetheless. The eyes behind his wire spectacles were at once observant, shrewd and far from genial. In fact, my first impression was that rarely have I met an expression as closed as his in that moment. Moreover, it was clear that he regarded my presence in his parlour on the sabbath as an affront, and I readied myself for him to say so. A slim black Labrador with a velvet and leather collar bounded in with him and came to meet me, its paws trotting on the tiles. Chambord gave me a nod as I introduced myself and sat opposite, keeping his distance, as I apologised for interrupting his Sunday.

'Where I come from,' I explained, 'mayors are often weak officials, armed with all-too limited authority or imagination to affect the public good. In France, you have an altogether different system where individuals such as yourself wield great power in your localities for the furtherance of civic good. That is correct, is it not?'

I paused, hoping that I'd not overdone it, but the mien of self-satisfaction that visited his face told me I could have gone further without arousing suspicion of flattery. 'To that end, I've come to ask you whether you will consider using your authority to close the Blue Lamp and the other "maison tolérées" in the town – until we have found the killer of Marie-Louise Toulon?'

Chambord removed his glasses and chewed thoughtfully on one arm of his spectacles before his mouth located a curious grin. 'Have you got any idea of what would happen if we tried to do that, Monsieur?' He paused a second before answering his own question. 'It would be a disaster. There are a hundred thousand British Empire soldiers within a twenty-mile radius of here –' His hand swept about the room. 'You understand? It is a question of civic calm, Monsieur. The brothels keep your men happy and that means my town is happy. It's as simple as that.'

'It's not quite so simple for the women who work there.'

'Monsieur –' His tone was emollient but iron. 'You must respect the way we do things here. Alors, no one is forcing these women to work at the Blue Lamp or other such establishments. They are at liberty to act as they wish, no? That is what we are fighting the war for. These women are patriots, playing their part in supporting the war effort, no?'

He clasped his hands around his knees and raised himself from the chair, drawing our conversation to an end.

'And what if the killer strikes again?'

'Well, all the more reason to ensure that the brothels remain open.' His tone hardened as he adjusted a strand of his hair in the looking glass. 'If we deprive this deranged individual of these women, he may target other females – the wives or daughters of decent, honest townsfolk. And we cannot have that, can we? Now,' his spectacles performed a twirl, 'if there is nothing else?'

I got to my feet.

'Honest, decent townsfolk?' I met his grotesque, insouciant gaze. 'For God's sake man, this woman was murdered on your doorstep! Where is your compassion?'

'Compassion, Monsieur?' There was a growl to his voice and he spoke through gritted teeth. 'How dare you lecture me compassion, on a Sunday of all days. You know nothing, Monsieur. The Gendarmerie is investigating it – and I have faith in them,' he ticked off this point on the little, ringed finger of his hand. 'Now you are investigating it,' another finger, another tick. 'I daresay there are others investigating it that neither you nor I know about but who have an interest in such an enterprise, because that is the way of these things.' A third tick. 'So what are we to do? The world keeps spinning, Monsieur. The war continues – the Germans are still ten kilometres away, your men have needs, the women who work in the brothel have needs. We all have greater things to concern ourselves with – namely half a million Germans just over there …. You understand? Compassion has nothing to do with it. This is a question of necessity.'

'So, why do you think the killer left her body out there – on your doorstep?'

Chambord shrugged, 'How should I possibly know, Monsieur?'

'You must have asked yourself that question?'

The Frenchman turned to leave, the dog following him.

'For why?' He shook his conceited head slowly at me. 'As a matter of fact I have *not* asked myself that question. And nor shall I dignify it. Let me say this, I am gratified that the British Army is investigating this crime. That is right and proper. But nothing about your visit is those things. If you wish to see me in future, Champion, you must come to my office and make an appointment like everyone else.' He swept from the room. 'Good day to you, Monsieur.'

I strode out into the rain, my hands curled into tight fists in my overcoat pockets. Damn him. Damn his arrogance, damn his grotesque want of basic human compassion. I welcomed the cold rain; it was refreshing to my senses and rinsed away the odour of roasted meat. At the gate of the park I turned back and looked at the yellow house. I had met men like Chambord before – they were everywhere, these people. They were people for whom life was a series of expedient calculations, people who paid little heed to individual cost, unless it was their own purse that would be lightened. My father, an Anglican vicar in a provincial town, had been obliged to socialise with people such as this and I had despised him for it. Until I had understood.

I shook my head at the proud façade of Chambord's house and turned away. I had not found out much yet during my short time in this town, but I now knew something for sure. Whatever else, I knew it in my bones that Chambord was guilty of something. It was just a question of finding out what it was.

And I would.

I intercepted a pair of duelling pigeons as I cut across the sward to the bandstand. The haggard birds lunged at each other with their beaks outstretched, fighting over at the same small, curved bone. One had it clasped, lopsided, in its bill, the other snatched it free, sending it scuttling away. They both dashed at it, tumbling into my path. I stepped away.

I exited the park to the far side, and then made my way through empty streets of shuttered shops to the Gendarmerie. It was surely not unrealistic to hope that the local police authorities would give me a warmer welcome than I had received from the mayor.

A splayed trio of dejected-looking Tricolours hung above the entrance to the Gendarmerie, their vibrant, revolutionary hues dulled by the rain and sooty grime. Like the town, the place was pretty well shut up too. After bashing on the front door for several minutes I was about to give up when a sleepy, half-dressed Gendarme arrived and let me in. Reeking of stale wine, he led me into the interior of the building and showed to me to a door, which he knocked at and pushed open before walking off without further explanation.

Through the open doorway, a serious face greeted me from within. It was dominated by a broad dark moustache that concluded with points like the curved talons of a bird of prey. The chin was lost to a vast waxed tuft, streaked with white, which could also be seen in the long hair that was swept back from the thick, chalky face. This hard-featured Velazquez conquistador sat at a tall black typewriter, surrounded by disordered stacks of paper and folders, his fingers poised above the chrome keys. A yellow cigarette hung from the corner of his mouth, and his eyes pinched with recognition.

'Monsieur Champion? I didn't expect you quite so soon...'

Inspector Catouillart drew heavily on his Moroccan cheroot and then emitted a pair of slow, curving spirals of black tobacco smoke, like snakes curling from his nostrils in perfect, synchronised symmetry.

'The regrettable truth, Monsieur, is that we don't have much information to follow, apart from the most obvious. We have made the relevant enquiries; no one has seen or noticed anything. There is no evidence from the scene. All we have is a set of assumptions that we can make from the location of the body and nothing else. It is rather limiting.' He extinguished the cigarette in the powdery heap of the ashtray. 'The only point of interest is the infamous British Army regulation condom, which is – *well*, a fascinating adornment or addendum, if you will, but of no obvious use to furthering our inquiries. Just because it is English it does not mean it is an English killer.' He reached for the box and slowly removed another turmeric-coloured cigarette, which he lit with careful deliberation. 'If I had to speak entirely plainly, Monsieur, I would say that the killer has been meticulous in his execution of this crime and the best chance the authorities have of catching him is to hope that next time – and mark my words, there will be a next time with a crime such as this – he isn't quite so careful. Some crimes, I fear, are insoluble.'

'That's not a very optimistic prognosis, is it?'

'It is what it is, Monsieur,' he lifted his thick hands into the air in an expression of helplessness. 'You can only detect what is to be detected, no?'

I wasn't quite sure if this meant anything, not really, but I wasn't about to contradict him. It was too soon for that. He pushed his ivory cigarette box towards me.

'Are you sure you won't smoke? I find it helps me think.' He seemed mildly affronted that I should deny myself such an exquisite luxury. Instead I moved my hand through the small box of items that had been brought up for my inspection: what remained of Marie-Louise Toulon's earthly possessions. There wasn't much to show for her life; some cheap jewellery, a plain silver ring, some bottles of perfume, and clothes, of course. 'What about the picture?' I asked, lifting up a small empty oval silver frame. 'Where's the picture?'

'That,' the Frenchman conceded, 'is most vexing.' He raised his eyebrows, 'The authorities have been unable to establish *why* that is missing or indeed *if* there was anything in it to go missing in the first place.' Catouillart's face was pale and heavy and creased, like loaf of bread prior to baking. The heavy tortoise-like eyelids dipped thoughtfully.

'Do you think it's odd that she has no family to speak of?'

'No.' He spread his hands. 'Many people are without families.'

'But has anyone fitting her description been reported missing?'

He shook his head. 'War has thrown everything into the air, Monsieur. These days there is a multitude of missing people, many of whom do not wish to be found, which is most inconsiderate.' He went over to the window and gazed out at the rain. 'No one fitting Marie-Louise Toulon's description has been reported missing, but all that signifies is she has no one who will miss or mourn her. The women at the brothel said she was from the South or South-west and arrived from Paris about two years ago. With her mixed-race background it is easy to speculate that she might be from Marseilles or one of the ports on the south coast. My brother has married a woman from North Africa. It is not uncommon in France as it is in England.'

'All it suggests is that her family don't know she is dead.'

'You are presuming that they would care if they did.' He offered a frosty smile and I nodded. I decided to reward his cynicism by trying one of his cigarettes. He bowed solicitously at me as I lit it.

The tobacco was strong – I coughed on the first drag – but it was smooth, with a chocolatey finish like a good cup of coffee, and not at all unpleasant.

'Do we know anything about her; what she did? where she liked to go? who her friends were?'

Catouillart sighed.

'She had been seen in the town, reported in some of the local night spots, but that signifies little. She was a very private person. A little aloof. That is what everyone has said.'

His choice of words echoed Fabienne's, and was unlikely to be a coincidence. I had merely followed the same path followed by Catouillart and his ilk and, like them, I had turned up nothing. He passed me one of the black and white photographs of Marie-Louise taken at the bandstand. It showed only her face, her brown hair drawn back, revealing her attractive features; brown eyes – a luminous mid-grey in the photograph – evenly divided by a straight nose and her mouth, if anything, a little too wide for her rectangular face. She had, I noticed, a cleft chin. There is no doubt that she could have earned quite an income as an artist's model or as a mannequin. I wondered why she hadn't done that instead.

As I left, Catouillart apologised that he could not be more helpful. 'Here –' He scribbled down the name and address of someone for me to speak to. 'This man takes a close interest in all that happens in Béthune. He has the Red Lamp – not quite officially of course, but he does. If there's anything worth knowing about the murder of Marie-Louise Toulon, he'll know it already. They call him the Eagle.'

'And what do you call him?'

Catouillart sighed and spread his hands.

'As little as possible.' He smiled, the points of his moustache lifting. His heavy eyelids dipped thoughtfully. 'His real identity is not known to the authorities, Monsieur. Nor is he someone that a police officer such as myself can hold easy conversations with. You, however,' Catouillart clicked his tongue, 'are neither French, nor a policeman.' He smiled. 'So perhaps he might speak to you…'

CUT AND RUN

Chapter Five

That evening I dined alone at my lodgings, Kennedy having left a note to explain that he was going to be away till the morning on an errand. After dinner I went for a stroll through the quiet streets of Béthune to see what it looked like on a Sunday night. This was partly to familiarise myself with the town a little more, but I also need to think. The clouds had given us all their rain for the day and left a sticky, wet residue on the cobble stones and darkened buildings, which dripped from every eve as though the place was thawing out after a long winter.

Every now and then I'd hear the cry of a baby, a harsh cough or the growl and bark of a dog and I would realise that life existed behind the tightly shuttered windows. After a few minutes the tone of the quarter changed. I left behind the proud, perpendicular streets of the centre, with their tall, proud, uniform houses, and the roads became less regular, narrower, more winding. The buildings and houses became imperceptibly smaller, closer together and the intermittent cloud of effluent lingered in the air, rather as I imagined it had done in Tudor London, when people discharged their waste from the upper-storey windows. Eventually the pavements gave way to compacted earth and rubble, now reduced to a thick mush thanks to the rain.

Under the dim halo of a street lamp a dog hurtled out from the shadows in pursuit of something unseen, but I could hear it scuttle. On the far side of the road, a broad structure turned out to be a grimy-looking boarding house, with rotted shutters hanging askew from their hinges. Further down the street I heard laughter and merriment as the door of a bar creaked opened.

I decided to try it, feeling thirsty after what felt like a very long day.

Inside it was hot. The patrons, their faces glistening with sweat, were Frenchmen and locals at that, though seemingly oblivious to another foreigner. Ribald and homely chatter reverberated off the wooden panelled walls and as I waited to be served at the counter

– no doubt in variance with local custom – I spotted four British soldiers in the corner. They would be on leave from the front line and devoured the few women in the bar with their eyes. It was hard to imagine Marie-Louise Toulon or Fabienne Thomas passing unnoticed in such an environment. I shook my head. They wouldn't. What's more, it was perfectly possible that either of them would expose men such as this to an intensity of thirst that they might find surprising. And rather like Homer's Lotus-eaters, once tasted the flavour would never be forgotten. That might explain what had happened to poor Marie-Louise. Perhaps she had awoken an ungovernable jealousy in a man unhinged by war?

I took out my pipe and contemplated speaking to the soldiers in the corner. Experience told me they would be amenable to the company, though they would naturally prefer it if I were the robust-looking young French woman who showed three inches of cleavage at the table by the fire. These men were from the Buffs, the Suffolk Regiment, which had fought alongside my unit at Loos the previous September. I wondered if they knew any of my lot – Warren, Cartwright, Cowan... names from the shadows of my past. A sense of foreboding passed over me. I was distracted by the barman and I ordered a glass of wine. He frowned at me but went to fetch it nonetheless.

The door swung open, sending the candles fluttering, and I turned to see Private Greenlaw swagger in, his arm draped around a dark-haired girl of about nineteen or twenty. She was of greater than average build; buxom with a pale complexion and not unappealing at first glance. The soldiers in the corner broke their conversation to appraise her. I quickly turned back to the bar, to spare Greenlaw's blushes. A moment later I heard him order two glasses of wine in passable French and I could contain myself no longer.

'So this is what passes for civilised entertainment in this town,' I growled, 'is it Private Greenlaw? Why aren't you in your digs?'

He turned, horror overtaking his formerly easy relaxed demeanour. I smiled and pressed him on his shoulder before nodding solicitously to his guest,

'Mademoiselle.'

Greenlaw's rustic face was the colour of claret but he rallied admirably.

'There's not a rule against it, Champion,' he piped, grinning, composure recovered.

'Of course not.'

'They can't ban human nature can they?'

He smiled, as did we all, as their wine was served.

'You're a character, right enough Champion,' he chuckled, as he paid. He handed the girl her drink, and we clinked glasses. 'Nay doubt about it.'

'Is that what Captain Kennedy says?'

'Aye, an' the rest.'

'You'll have to fill me in some time.'

'Too bad. He swore me to secrecy.'

I noticed Greenlaw's lady-friend glance over at the table of Tommies in the corner. She was already getting bored. As I had no interest in spoiling his night – I daresay he'd earned whatever was coming his way – I drained my wine glass and got my cloth cap.

'A question –' I lowered my voice to Greenlaw's ear. He cocked an eyebrow.

'Point me in the direction of the Red Lamp…'

Attending two brothels in one day was going to be something of a personal record for me. This thought occurred as I ventured along a darkened lane towards the southern end of the town. The road then opened up into a cobbled courtyard, on the far side of which lay railway lines. Dozens of men, mostly in forms of disordered uniform, stood around the place, warming themselves at flaming braziers, chatting loudly, laughing, singing, smoking, rowing and clanking bottles. I saw revelry, gossiping, boasting, joking, mockery and misery all at once in the flickering flames of a handful of fires. There wasn't a queue at the Red Lamp, as I had perhaps imagined, of polite Britishers lining up outside for their moment, for their ration of life. But they were still waiting their turn. A summonsing voice called out: 'Next!' I heard a low cheer go up and saw a figure stumble his way through the crowd. The men knew their own order.

I made my way through the boisterous knot: around me, seemingly, there were soldiers of every regiment in the British Army – it was like a Saturday afternoon in Aldershot. There were lads from the Essex Regiment, there were some Buffs, even a smattering of Guardsmen, and a cluster of Welch Fusiliers. At the far end I even spotted the neat, steep turbans of a trio of Sikh soldiers from an Indian Army unit.

'Champion!' boomed a voice, and a powerful hand landed on my shoulder like a house-brick dropped from a balloon. I turned in alarm.

'Good God! Private Warren!'

'I know,' he grinned, showing me his teeth. 'Still here after all these years. And they made me a sergeant.' He stroked his fingers over the three stripes on his arm.

'Well I never –' I gasped. If there's fifty thousand soldiers within ten square miles what are the chances that you'll bump into some you know? But there he was all right, and all in one piece, and he hadn't changed a bit, excepting a scar here or there. And a sergeant, too. I grabbed his stripes. 'Richly deserved, I'm sure,' I said, suddenly remembered the overgrown, toothy butcher's boy that I had met on the first day of training in Essex in November 1914. That felt like several lifetimes ago.

He drew me into the gang of men I'd seen moments before. 'Lads –' His voice was deep, broad Chelmsford, mostly agriculture but with an occasional London word thrown in for good. 'Let me introduce you to one of our old comrades in arms – Private Frank Champion, late of this parish.' I found myself looking into the gazing faces of half a dozen eighteen-year-olds. They wore thin, new moustaches, grown for the Army, and eager expressions as each shook my hand and bobbed their heads readily. Warren reeled them in. 'Private Champion 'ere was in our platoon at Loos and what's more – he saved our skins. Got us home, didn't you Champ?' I gave a spectacularly mistimed laugh of self-deprecation and then felt Warren's strong arm round my shoulder. 'Come on Frank,' he squeezed my shoulder hard, 'tell the lads the truth.'

'Ah, there's nothing to tell…' Then seeing their faces, I hammed it up: I didn't want to let them down, nor Warren. I grinned: 'Really, it was nothing.' He laughed, clapped my shoulders and jammed a cigarette into my mouth: a lad lit it quickly with a burning stick from the brazier and a bottle was passed to me. I asked after Private Cowan.

Warren's face darkened and the lads bowed their heads in respect.

'What happened?'

'An infected wound. It was slow.'

Poor Cowan. Never a better fellow to have alongside you.

'It's the way it goes.' Warren gazed up at the sky. 'Though it might have been better for all concerned if he'd gone quickly. Poor sod moaned like anything.' He spat. 'Cartwright didn't get a chance to moan, or much else.'

I passed him the bottle and he took a swig. He wiped the back of his mouth and handed it on. 'Would you believe it?' he sighed, nodding at the gang. 'This is the old crew now.'

I mustered a weak smile at the lads, their faces glowing like Victorian urchins in the flames. Warren, meanwhile, was showing signs of age, I now noticed. He was few years my junior so he'd be thirty by now, or as near as damn it and the dusting of age was beginning to fade his hair. He was no age really, but this war left its mark.

Warren cleared this throat, drawing in the attention of his crew.

'Now, have I told you about the day we went over the top at Loos?' It was a rhetorical question judging by the eyeballs being rolled about me. 'This fellow you see before you, is a ruddy hero. He won't admit it, mind, but he saved my life at Loos – and what's more he saved the lives of everyone in our platoon – Cartwright, Cowan; the whole gang.' Warren's gaze settled on mine, 'the whole gang.' Half his face was lost in shadow, the other shifted in reflection of the flickering flames. I could smell liquor on his breath. I did not know how much he remembered of that last day of innocence – as I saw it, the day when we careened into the deepest depths of hell and became animals once more. The day we de-evolved to the condition of early man, forgot fire, unlearned the dictums of civilisation and fought with our teeth and fingernails if we had to. I subsequently learned that of the twelve hundred men who I went over the top with that morning, eight hundred died, a historically high record of failure, even by the standards of our own general staff. Our battalion got its fair share. Most were killed – blown to smithereens or maimed beyond rescue in a lethal lottery of incessant German machine gun fire and mortar bombardment. I didn't remember much of it. Thank God. And what little I did I tried to forget. It went beyond terror, really. But then some men fall better than others. Some men like the taste of the apple.

'We all just did what we could.' I looked around at the moustaches. 'You'd all do the same.'

'That we would.' Warren's mighty arm once again gripping my shoulders tight. The odour of wine and spirits permeated my face from his breath. He was drunk. 'But you went beyond the call of duty my son, and I'm eternally in your debt for it. And I'm not the only one.'

I met his gaze; which he held with intense gin-soaked certainty. He had never discussed what he remembered with me, a fact I was grateful for. All I knew was that just trying to recall the day provoked a nauseous flush of fear in me, one that would make my heart beat with erratic fury and my hands and knees tremble. I couldn't explain it. It was a visceral taste, perhaps, of a greater sensation that awaited me should the full burden of knowledge be placed upon me. Even then I felt the swelling sickness in my throat, as I nodded my thanks in my acknowledgement of Warren's kind words. I had to get away... I flicked my cigarette into the brazier, and issued my farewells, promising to catch up if not before then after the war and waved goodbye to the lads.

'Thank you Champ.' Warren clutching my hand in his. 'God be with you.'

I extricated my fingers and moved away as gently as I could, retreating by moving forwards, pushing through the mass of Tommies, grateful to be away, but knowing that what awaited me was not without its hazards too. Entering the dark doorway from which I had seen sated comrades emerge, I arrived moments later inside the notorious Red Lamp.

Sheltered beneath the remnants of a glazed, cast iron ribbed roof, was an enclosed campsite the size of a football pitch of motley tents, irregular canvas structures and improvised marquees. They were patched and stitched and of varying colours and states of decay, and from within glowed dozens of warm lights, with low oscillating shadows. Sullen bunting and lanterns hung from the ceiling above, which dripped water on the camp below. The cobbled ground was strewn with rubbish and muck; a stray dog cantered past on its own business. And all around were the overlaid sounds of myriad exertion, ecstasy and occasional completion. In return I heard a high pitched Gallic cackle that registered surprise in any language. Elsewhere there were the short gasps of thin encouragement. Lastly, from somewhere close by, I heard a giggle of sincere excitement.

From one perspective, this was a vision of hell. From another it was democracy in action; after all, hadn't officers enjoyed such privileges for centuries? My thoughts were interrupted by a guttural-baritone cry emanating from a tent not far off.

'Keep it down Bill!' fired another voice. 'Or I'll make sure it stays down!'

The groaning subsided and I looked about for someone who might know what was what. In the corner sat a burly fellow, a Frenchman, who had evidently just clocked me because he was getting to his feet and heading over, an irritated cast to his face. He was decked out in what appeared to be a monk's habit, except that instead of a rope waistband with three hanging knots indicating his vows of chastity, poverty and obedience, he had a leather belt with a wooden bludgeon dangled from it. I deduced therefore that his vows, if he had any, were not the sort you would hear from the pulpit. As he approached he growled at me in a thick French-accented English.

'You're not allowed in here without an escort.' His eyes narrowed and a hand the size of a serving platter went to the handle of his club. 'Come on, you know the rules, Tommy –'

He saw my expression and didn't like it, but something in it caused him to pause.

'I'm here to see the Eagle,' I said, looking him in the eye. He unclipped the truncheon, so I name-dropped: 'Catouillart sent me. He said the Eagle would have information for me.'

I was led through one of the anonymous doorways off the side of the enclosure, along a dark corridor and into a broad chamber illuminated by a lone lantern hanging from the ceiling and a roaring fire. The flames licked the burning logs aggressively, snatching the air and firing out angry spits. They also reflected off the bowed shaven head of the room's sole occupant, a man who squatted in the shadows on a three legged stool. A steel plate was on his knee, and he tore at a leg of lamb with his teeth. The door behind me shut, the monk had gone.

Now I noticed something else about the bowed head: it was tattooed with an image that changed its attitude constantly as the man ate and the sides of his scalp swelled and contracted with his robust mastication. He turned to me, the eyes that surveyed me shaded from sight, but I saw a set of teeth that looked too big for the jaw they inhabited. I realised that apart from the fire the only sound I could hear was the moist destruction of roasted lamb as it was ground down between his jaws.

'Step into the light so that I can see you,' he said by way of introduction. His voice was arid and several octaves deeper than you would expect. What's more, it carried menace, like the sound of a corpse being dragged along a gravel path. He snatched again at his lamb and chewed as I did what he asked. 'You're not the normal type we have here,' he talked over spongy, wet, hard chewing. 'Vermin, most of them.' He swallowed. 'All of them, actually.' Another hard swallow. 'But the good thing about vermin is that they're utterly predictable. Rodents, like soldiers, have simple needs that you can see written on their pathetic simple faces, but not you.' He tossed the bone into the floor and wiped his face with a long sweep of the back of his forearm. A muscular dog with a pink, bald snout darted over to his discarded bone and started gnawing on it noisily.

'You should count your blessings that Brother Christian let you in. He's not that partial to strangers. Not normally.'

'I'd be intrigued to know which monastery he's escaped from.'

'He was a monk of sorts once. A Benedictine was it? I didn't know they had them anymore but they do, apparently. Big on burning heretics they were, once upon a time. It is said that he murdered a man in Vienna. I've never found out the truth of it. As you can imagine, it put paid to his monastic aspirations. They'll forgive most things, won't they, priests? But murder is pushing it, even for them.' He gave a hard laugh. 'Turns out Brother Christian has a surprisingly short temper, you see. Just to warn you.'

The man went to the table in the middle of the room and poured himself a drink from an earthenware jug, so that his head was bowed under the light. And I saw it: the eagle, its mighty tattooed wings spread and its head turned down to the young chicks in its nest. Blood drained from its sharp black beak. It was devouring its young.

'So –' He looked over. 'What do you want?'

'Catouillart sent me.'

'He did, did he? What does that po-faced bastard want?'

'He said you might be able to help me with Marie-Louise Toulon, the girl who was murdered –'

'I know who she is.' He nodded sombrely and ventured slowly back to his stool. 'But she was nothing to me, not one of mine, thank God.' He pointed to one of the wooden chairs by the fire, telling me to sit down. 'No, stranger. Not my problem.' He smiled, showing all those teeth again. 'Robecq's your man if you've a question about the Blue Lamp, I would have thought, wouldn't you?' He gestured to the chair. 'Go on.' It was an order, not a request.

I sat down.

'Of course Catouillart would know this. So I wonder why he sent you to me?'

'All he said was that you were very knowledgeable.'

'Is that what he said?' The Eagle smiled. 'I like that. And it's true: I am. But I'm no snitch, understand? There's no love lost between me and Robecq, sure, but we have our boundaries. Good fences make good neighbours.' He peered at me. 'You say that in English, stranger? Of course, you do.'

'Perhaps Catouillart thought you would offer an independent insight?'

'Perhaps he did.'

Because of the darkness I still hadn't seen the eyes but I knew they were working hard, sizing me up, verifying me, categorising me, checking.

'You a policeman, stranger?'

'No.'

'A private detective?'

'Of sorts.'

'Interesting work, I should imagine. Fulfilling?'

I gave him a nod.

'What about you? Looks like business is booming.'

'Put it this way; the war is not all bad.'

He showed me his teeth, like he was proud of them.

The sound of the dog's gnawing grew louder and the Eagle gave it a sharp punt, sending him on his way, the bone pinched between his jaws.

'The truth is,' he declared with a grimace. 'I've no information on who was responsible for Toulon's death. If I did I might be inclined to act on it myself because girls like Toulon don't grow on trees – more's the pity. Those men of yours out there can get a through a new girl in six weeks. Trust me. So girls like Toulon can't be wasted like that.' He cleared his throat. 'You should know that I have made tentative inquiries, too – course I have – but nothing has come to light. So far.' He sighed. 'So if you want my advice, speak to Robecq. If he doesn't know, no one will, well…' He chuckled, 'maybe. But be warned, he can be an evil son of a bitch when he wants to be and that turns out to be a lot of the time. But then, ain't we all?'

The Eagle looked down into the pit of his drink. 'I'll tell you this, stranger. You'll know Robecq when you see him: I won't tell you why, it would ruin the surprise. Put it this way, if you think my tattoo makes a statement, wait till you see his handsome face.'

He lifted an eyebrow. 'You know why Catouillart sent you to me? Because Monsieur Robecq is even less partial to curious people, still less detectives. He makes Brother Christian look like a Christian.' He clenched his teeth, prompting his temples – and the eagle – to flex. 'And, of course, Catouillart wouldn't like to have to admit that people like Robecq, people who represent such troubling deviation from the social norms and law and order exist, in his beloved Republic. But they do. They're everywhere, in fact.'

I gave his insight the benefit of a nod and returned to the subject in hand.

'So you know nothing about the murder of Marie-Louise Toulon?'

He raised a finger.

'Now did I say that, stranger?' He spoke sharply, but with a smile of sorts. 'Did I?' I made no reply and the teeth clenched, prompting the eagle tattoo to tighten its claws. 'Of course I have information. *After all*, I have to protect my investment, don't I?' The heavy forehead leaned towards the door and the twenty-plus women working beyond in the tented boudoir. He got up and poured himself another draft of beer and then returned to his seat. 'But you know what, stranger? That's what you should do, go back to Catouillart and tell him I refused to discuss this with you. And ask him to tell you the truth.'

'The truth?'

'That's right, you heard me correctly. Tell him to tell you the truth about Toulon.'

'What's that meant to mean?'

'Now that would be telling, wouldn't it?' He looked up and his eyes caught the light and glistened. I caught the beery whiff of his breath, mingled with garlic. 'Make Catouillart admit that he's deliberately withholding information from you; he'll like that – or rather he won't. But that's your problem, isn't it?'

My mind was suddenly agog – what on earth made him think Catouillart was concealing anything from me? Plainly the Eagle wasn't going to tell me. He was enjoying it all far too much to do that.

'Go on, stranger, you've had enough. Time for you to run along before Brother Christian returns and wonders what you're still doing here.'

I had no intention of leaving yet and had just finished replenishing my pipe which I now lit with a burning stick.

'There is a killer out there who might well kill again. Next time, he might well damage your own business interests. What then?'

The Eagle chuckled. It was a mercenary staccato affair, like someone hammering a nail carefully.

'Appealing to my baser instincts is wise, but that's playing a dangerous game stranger.' He nodded meaningfully, 'You never know where it might lead. We take care of our own at the Red Lamp. Now, I just told you to be on your way, I won't tell you again.'

I drew on my pipe, aware that he was watching me for signs of compliance or fear, but I was determined to show neither.

'This pipe was given to me by the last person to save my life,' I told him. 'It's made of hornbeam, one of the hardest timbers in nature. As a result it's exceptionally strong – as strong as stone some say. My friend told me it reminded him of me.'

'There's stone and there's stone,' he stated dismissively.

I made no reply. Instead I smoked and filled the space between me and my reluctant host with lolling plumes of tobacco smoke.

'It's a handsome enough pipe,' he remarked at last. The fire was now hot against my shins and I noticed that the Eagle had beads of sweat on his forehead. He was contemplating something.

'Between you and me,' I said, 'I'm not sure if I'm quite ready to accuse Catouillart of being a bare-faced liar. So you're placing me in a position.'

'That's your problem, not mine.' The Eagle rolled back the sleeve of his grimy white shirt, revealing a tattoo of Christ being crucified on his broad forearm. The Saviour was grinning, however. I wondered what Brother Christian made of that. When the Eagle made a fist and tensed his arm – Christ twitched as if in agony on the cross. He watched this, fascinated for a moment, and I noticed there were countless scars over the fist in question. Christ contorted as the veins popped out and muscles tensed...

The interview, I realised, was over, so I got my feet and said goodbye.

The Eagle did not look up from the figure of Jesus as he slowly clenched and unclenched his fist. Then as I reached the door he evidently changed his mind.

'Hornbeam –' His voice raked any warmth from the word. 'You have tugged at my heartstrings.' The gravel voice continued, 'If you're a detective, you can find someone for me, can't you?' His tongue probed the crack of the side of his mouth as he chose his next words. 'How about you do that, in return for the information you desire?'

I turned towards him.

'Go on.'

'Another young woman went missing a couple of weeks ago – vanished in a magician's cloud of smoke.' He flicked open his hand to mimic the explosion. 'And guess what, right up until the time of her disappearance on the twelfth of February she was in the employ of the Blue Lamp, which you might find something of a coincidence?'

He raised his eyebrows speculatively and I nodded in recognition of this fact.

'Her name is Suzette Emmolet and for all I know her disappearance may be connected to the murder of Marie-Louise Toulon – or it might not. I hope not for Suzette's sake. I have no information other than the knowledge that she wished to leave the Blue Lamp.'

'How do you know that?'

'Because she told me that she wanted to come and work for me instead. You see I'm not an ogre, Hornbeam. On the contrary I'm a model employer. My girls get fed, a roof over their heads, medical attention. I'm enlightened.' He coughed, clearing his lungs and expectorated generously on the grate. The phlegm hissed before vanishing into a fizzing puff of smoke.

'Suzette's a beautiful woman and has one very significant identifiable mark – a flaw,' he raised his left hand into the air and seized hold of the ring finger. 'Her father was a blacksmith and evidently clumsy with it. One day she was playing in the forge; it

47

was a lapse, he said, he wasn't looking. The hammer came down – and snip – off it went. I thought I'd mention that.'

'And what's your interest, precisely?'

He tutted, 'My interest? Where's your compassion, Hornbeam?' A smirk appeared like an apparition on his face. 'I'm curious, if you must put a label on it, and disappointed. I really wanted her to join me here. If you only saw the happiness my girls bring to the world.'

He flexed his right hand into a fist, causing Jesus to writhe.

'I'll find her, but only if you give me the information that I need about Marie-Louise.'

The Eagle arched an eyebrow at my comment, rose slowly to his feet and strolled to the iron safe that loomed at the back of the room like a tall wardrobe. After a moment its great door opened and he removed a thick envelope which he brought to the table, beckoning me to follow. 'Come over to the light, Hornbeam.'

The Eagle opened the envelope and slid out a small oval photograph, which he laid on the table beneath the light. It was the perfect fit for the silver frame I had seen in Catouillart's office earlier.

'How's that?'

I picked it up and felt my pulse rise. It showed a family of three – father, mother and their daughter, hair in bunches. The girl was plainly Marie-Louise, aged I would hazard perhaps twelve or thirteen. The couple with her were her parents, that much was obvious. She shared the same cleft chin as her father and his nose. But it was from Madam Toulon who was, I would hazard, of Moroccan or North African descent, that she got her looks. The man was in military dress, with golden epaulettes and the grenade emblem on his stand-up collar, telling me that he was an officer in the French Foreign Legion. The three of them wore the same long faces as my family did in our own drawn-out photographs, which required the sitter to remain perfectly still for the duration of the minute's exposure.

'I knew you'd be impressed, Hornbeam.' The Eagle smiled; it felt like someone pouring ice down my spine.

'How did you get this?'

'None of your business, Hornbeam.' He cleared his throat. 'I am in a cash business, one that is prone to change and vicissitudes in general, much of which is by definition unknowable and unpredictable. As a result information is often by far the most useful commodity one can possess. It's far more effective than muscle, for instance, no matter how attractive the muscular option may appear to be.'

I looked back down at the photograph.

'Do you know who they are?'

The Eagle raised his hands. 'Not a clue, Hornbeam. Now, while I'm loath to tell any man his own job, my own route would be to start with the man. If he's still alive, then I'm sure someone will recognise him. And if he was a commandant or colonel in the Foreign Legion seven or eight years ago, when this picture was taken, then he might be rather more important now.' He sucked his teeth, 'Perish the thought. She's not bad looking, either. You never know, Monsieur Catouillart might be able to help put you in touch with someone from the regiment. That'll be the sort of thing he'll be good at, I should imagine.'

The Eagle went to the safe and clanged the door shut. He then returned to his stool, where he sat down and began browsing a newspaper, aggressively throwing the pages over after a moment's perusal.

'Now,' he hissed, still turning the pages. 'In your excitement I don't want you forgetting your side of the bargain. Leave not a stone unturned in your search to find out what's has happened to Suzette Emmolet. Otherwise a certain defrocked gentleman of the cloth will come and administer divine unction to you – and you don't want that. Trust me.'

Chapter Six

The lights were out at the hotel when I returned. Letting myself in with the key they had given me, I sat in the armchair in my room, smoked a pipe and savoured a whisky, my mind reliving and puzzling over the conversations of the long day. The photograph was a breakthrough – undoubtedly – and one I had to be seriously grateful for, not that it came on its own, mind. Moreover, I had to concede that while it might turn out to be substantial, it might not, as the case may be. I topped up my drink and then took out my copy of Marcus Aurelius's *Meditations* and resumed rereading at the start of Book Seven, a section I rather liked. 'What is evil?' the great Roman asked. 'A thing you have seen times out of number. Likewise with every other sort of occurrence also, be prompt to remind yourself that this, too, you have witnessed many times before...'

The next morning I awoke early in the chair, the book on the floor at my feet and I did not, unsurprisingly, feel much rested. For all that I dressed quickly and had a coffee and a pipe for breakfast, before reaching the post office as it was opening to send a telegram to my sister. I had forgotten that she was expecting me for lunch on Sunday and knew she would be worrying about my uncharacteristic absence. Dotty was one of life's worriers, so a telegram was the least I could do.

Back at the hotel, I found Kennedy demolishing a hearty-looking plate of narrow sausages and fried eggs in the saloon. I declined to join him, my appetite wasn't quite there yet, but I had a coffee and smoked another pipe, while I updated him on the case.

He didn't know the Eagle – nor did he recognise the man in Marie-Louise's family photograph. 'I meant to say,' he added, more as an afterthought. 'Greenlaw and the car are at your disposal for the duration of the case.'

He stifled a yawn, the third in as many minutes. I noticed that he had shaved badly, missing a patch of stubble on his chin and I wondered what had occupied him since he left me at the Blue Lamp the previous morning.

CUT AND RUN

'Rough night?' I asked casually.

His answer was lost to the sound of the front door of the hotel crashing open. It was Greenlaw, his face dark pink, his chest heaving. He was gasping for breath. 'Come quickly,' he wheezed. 'There's been another murder.'

Minutes later we arrived at the Hotel du Nord, a mean-looking establishment on the southern side of town. It was not a million miles from the Red Lamp, geographically or in other respects. Tiles were missing from the steep Flemish roof, grasses cracked the tiled entrance and inside the tired floorboards creaked under the threadbare carpets.

Fabienne Thomas lay naked in the midst of sea of blood-soaked bed linen, her flawless face bizarrely serene above an angry cut that bisected her throat. A white cotton bedsheet had been drawn up to her collarbone to protect her dignity but the outline her body was easy to distinguish beneath it.

Catouillart was already there. He looked over, nodded a greeting to me and Kennedy who stood, almost hesitantly, in the doorway. Then the Frenchman's shrewd dark eyes studied me.

'So you know her, then?' He addressed me in English.

I stared down at the body and nodded.

'I interviewed her yesterday.'

All too briefly, I might have added. If you took her face in isolation, it struck me, at first glance the only sign that something was amiss was the fixed gaze of her brilliant blue eyes. Even these had not lost their lustre. But they were opened fractionally wider than was normal, so it was almost as if she resembled a slightly startled waxwork of herself.

'We didn't speak for very long but I was certain that she was the keeper of Marie-Louise Toulon's secrets. I was hoping to interview her again today.' I exhaled.

'An unfortunate coincidence,' remarked Catouillart, whose hand stroked his stubble thoughtfully.

Whether or not it was a coincidence at all, was, of course, the point.

I took a closer look at the cut. The deep wound had now closed up, leaving a woolly, thick red line, almost like crimson icing against a white cake. Catouillart took a step closer towards the bed, his hands linked behind his back.

'As you can see she was almost certainly killed by an incision to the neck in a manner very similar to that inflicted upon Marie-Louise Toulon. Similarly there are no signs of a struggle, so we can hazard that the killer carried out his work quickly – dare I say, before she knew it. Such a wound would have bled profusely – perhaps the killer cocooned the body as she bled with the bedding which, as you can see, is most sanguine.' Catouillart adjusted his hat, revealing his mass of dark, greasy hair. 'Mademoiselle Thomas had engaged in sexual congress prior to death, but there is no evidence of force, of rape. This is different from the situation with Marie-Louise Toulon.'

I looked along the body, following the outline of the sheet.

'Do we have an approximate time of death?'

At the top of the bed a man brushed the headboard for fingerprints. Catouillart cleared his throat.

'Between two and six o'clock this morning.' He referred to his pocket watch. 'Better than that we cannot say.' The note of his voice lowered, 'The hotel alerted the Gendarmerie shortly after nine.'

'Have the other guests been questioned?'

'It is being dealt with. I will have anything of relevance sent over for your inspection, but do not hold your breath. We have already questioned the only other guests on this corridor – a travelling salesman and a temporary clerk who works for the railway – and ascertained that they saw and heard precisely nothing. It is quite common in cases such as this, I'm afraid. As I'm sure you are aware.'

'Was this a routine haunt of Miss Thomas's?'

'I do not think so.' He swallowed, 'At least, the staff do not recognise her, which rules it out since I should think she was rather memorable.'

I'd say. The Frenchman spread his hands and continued his briefing.

'The room was booked in her name and no one, none of the staff or other guests, saw the arrival of the man whom we must assume was her guest.'

I nodded and focused my attention again on the wound.

The terminal cut appeared to begin high on the right hand side of her neck, as you looked at it, with the faintest of grazes. At first it was just a pink line no wider than a thread of cotton, but quickly, within two inches, this line darkened as it deepened, presumably as the curved point of the blade used began to bite. This was interesting. I would need to speak to someone a little more knowledgeable in such matters.

I inspected the skin around her mouth and saw it exhibited a pale blush of mild bruising, confirming that force had likely been applied there. If I was right then in two to three hours the colour would rise further but I was sure that there was enough there already to corroborate my suspicion. That would explain why the travelling salesman and temporary railway clerk had heard nothing; the killer had taken the precaution of silencing his victim with his hand.

Catouillart wasn't finished.

'Mademoiselle Thomas checked in to the hotel yesterday evening for one night only. The killer was evidently an unofficial guest in that he did not register his occupation of the hotel.' He cocked an eyebrow, 'Most inconsiderate of him. He must have met her here as part of a pre-arranged rendezvous, done the deed and then escaped during the early hours of the morning when nobody was awake. The front door is latched precisely to permit the convenient egress of patrons at unsociable hours. It is that sort of establishment.'

It certainly was. The Frenchman punctuated his addendum with a curt lift of his eyebrows.

Four creaks of the floorboards away, a chipped earthenware vase on the chest of drawers contained a bunch of dark crimson roses. They were wrapped in exquisite pink crepe paper which was sodden with water and evidently expensive, just like the roses, which were fragrant, handsome and quite out of sorts with the rest of the room or indeed the hotel for that matter.

'The flowers are from a shop in Saint-Omer,' remarked Kennedy, who so far had made no comment. 'I recognise the paper.' Catouillart looked over as the Irishman added, 'I've been there myself. It's very "posh" as you English say.' I smelled something sweet but it wasn't the roses...

'Chocolates,' announced Catouillart, as my gaze tracked to them. I lifted the flap of the box and the waft of sugar and cocoa was suddenly intoxicating. The packaging declared *La Maison du Chocolat de Saint-Omer*.

Kennedy was at my shoulder. 'That place is always crawling with British officers buying presents for their wives or mistresses,' he lifted an eyebrow, 'and sometimes both. They're not cheap, either.' He sighed, 'I'll get someone along to see if we can identify who the buyer was. The dark roses at least are unusual.' Kennedy's back was turned and Catouillart glanced over at me doubtfully. I made no reply. I noticed that beside the vase on the chest of drawers there was a brush – enmeshed with Fabienne's blonde hair. I wondered what she was thinking and what she had been feeling as she pulled the brush through her long hair in front of this looking glass. Was she inhaling the scent of the roses? Was she deliberating which of the chocolates to eat first? Was she contemplating the future. Was she hoping for better times, for a different life, for children perhaps, for a contented, sunlit old age?

I looked back at her body. Or was it fear? Had she sensed what was abroad, but for some reason or other either accepted it or tragically ignored the voices of instinct telling her to run?

We stood in silence for a few seconds lost in our thoughts, then Catouillart cracked his knuckles.

'Alors,' he announced. 'Are we thinking that this is the same man?'

Kennedy looked at me questioningly.

'Not necessarily.' I turned to Catouillart and slipped my notebook into my pocket. 'It's possible, of course. How many murderers do you think you've got in this town?' Catouillart shrugged. 'There are obvious similarities, but the differences are perhaps more telling. It's hard to know at this precise juncture.'

CUT AND RUN

My gaze jumped around the room, from the body to the floor, to the vase, to the ragged curtains and so on. The location of the body, the fact of consensual sexual intercourse, the absence of the condom, not to mention the gifts; these all indicated that it was a very different kettle of fish.

Just then, I saw a slither of scarlet. I bent down beside the bed and scooped it up. It was a satin negligee, the sort of thing that women wear for the enjoyment of themselves and their lovers. The label identified its origins as Capet & Carr, an upmarket ladies' shop on Piccadilly in London. I lifted the garment to my nose; it smelled of Fabienne's lavender perfume.

Kennedy cleared his throat, 'Scarlet is the colour of the dress uniforms of quite a few regiments of the British Army.'

'So it is –' I turned to Catouillart, 'though it wouldn't have been my first thought.'

'Non,' agreed the Frenchman, who took the garment from me and held it up to examine. 'You don't worry that this is a Frenchman pretending perhaps a little too hard to be a Britisher?'

'I have no idea.'

Catouillart nodded.

'Could you have the Blue Lamp closed while we try and find out?'

He shook his head. 'It cannot be done. And *I know* you've been to see Chambord.'

'Very well.' I gave Kennedy a nod, telling him I was ready to go. 'We have one near-certainty at least. I think it would be unreasonable not to expect more of the same, until we find out who is doing this and stop him.' I made for the door. 'You might want to mention that to Monsieur Chambord when you speak to him again. I don't think this is going to end here.'

The Frenchman sighed glumly and looked over at Fabienne's corpse. 'I'm sure you are not wrong, Monsieur.' He slid a rose from the vase and sunk his nose into its lush black bloom. 'This killer is an unpleasant character,' Catouillart mused. 'There is just enough red in these flowers for Mademoiselle Thomas to have seen romance in them, but for the killer they portended death.' He shook his head. 'Horrible.'

Outside Kennedy left us, without explanation, having first instructed Greenlaw to stay and assist in whichever way I required. Still standing in front of the Hotel du Nord, we watched him stride off towards the main square, which I could see was beginning to fill up with shoppers gathering for market day. Greenlaw evidently read the look on my face.

'He does this a lot,' sighed the soldier, adding a shrug. 'I've no idea where he goes.'

I chuckled. 'Perhaps that's the idea.'

'Oh, I'm sure it is,' he smiled, showing several of his teeth.

'Come on –' I pulled my cap forwards to fend off the rain and set off.

We hurried along the thronging avenues and streets of proud shops, making several more turns before the tone of the urban landscape changed.

After a few minutes Greenlaw, slightly breathless, asked:

'Is it true she had her throat cut?'

I glanced over.

'If you were interested, why didn't you come in? You could have seen everything for yourself.'

He held up a hand, 'That's all right, thanks.'

I cocked an eyebrow at him which he registered with a nod.

'Can't stand the sight of blood, Champion. Never could.'

'Nothing to be ashamed of –' I caught his eye. 'Though you'd be surprised what you can become accustomed too.'

'Oh aye,' he grinned. 'Like that is it?'

He caught my nod as we reached a small frowsy-looking parade. Several shops were boarded up or vacant. I registered a grimy florist that was closed, then a butcher, also closed, and further along a greengrocer's, which was in the throes of opening. Its portly owner was unfurling a tatty red and white awning over the pavement and gave us a surly nod as we walked by. His boy, whistling contentedly, was setting boxes of apples on a trestle table out front. He'd already done the oranges, fresh from Marrakesh according to the sign.

'Has death always fascinated you, Champion?' asked Greenlaw, evidently in a curious mood. I looked over and probably frowned at him.

'Not death. People.'

He looked surprised.

'And have you always done this? Were you a policeman before the war?'

'In a manner of speaking. I was district officer in East Africa for a while. You ended up doing a fair bit of police work.'

A door banged open behind us and a scream filled the air. The note carried long enough for us both to spin round and see a woman rushing out from a shop in the parade. Her bloodied forearms were raised above her head.

As the wail cut through the air, I saw the green grocer's boy freeze, his mouth open and the box leave his hands. The cheerful green apples crashed to the ground and scattered across the pavement.

Everywhere doors and shutters swept open, faces appeared and neighbours closed in. Amid the sudden hubbub of voices someone shouted, 'Get the police,' and an arm of support was stretched around the woman's bowed shoulders, along with a blanket.

We pushed our way through the knot of people towards the woman. They were already whispering, as I had seen the Kikuyu do in similar circumstances in the Ngong Hills. 'It's her sister,' said a voice, loaded with judgement. A pinch-faced matriarch clutched a crucifix hanging at her breast and shook her head.

I signalled to Greenlaw and we made straight for the doorway the woman had emerged from – the butcher's shop. Inside it was in darkness, the floor cobbled and solid beneath a tacky layer of sawdust. All around were lighted slithers like prison bars from the vertical gaps in the shutters. Fat bluebottles danced around the white muslin-covered cuts of meat. On the far side of the counter a serried rank of jagged and irregular steel knives jutted from a wooden block, within easy grasp of the doorway leading into a room beyond. I slid one out and stepped into this darker recess.

Parting the tacky rubber curtains, I entered a primitive chill room. It was cooler in here but the air was thick. Behind me Greenlaw caught his breath. I jammed a handkerchief over my mouth and nose, and continued, entering a short corridor formed by hanging sides of beef and assorted animal carcasses. It was dark, but a grimy skylight cast enough light to see by. The clawing odour of fresh and decaying meat made the air toxic. It was like the putrid smoke from a bonfire made of things you shouldn't burn.

In the quarter-daylight my gaze confronted the fixed eye of a bull staring at me. Then I saw the rest of its head, severed, a ring protruding from its seeping nostrils.

I turned the corner and stepped down to the threshold of a second, wider room. A soft shard of light streaked in from a window, like the projector at the cinema. It illuminated a row of recently slaughtered pigs and sheep, each suspended from hooks mounted on the ceiling. My foot slid on the bloody cobbles – I caught myself before I went over. And then I saw her. Across the room, lying on her back, a viscous, dark streak running from her chest, the handle of a meat cleaver standing from her sternum. Behind me, Greenlaw coughed and started to retch. He'd come a long way for someone who couldn't stand the sight of blood. I covered my mouth. The air was ripe.

I committed the situation to memory, making a mental note of the condition of the victim's dress and apron, all the way down to the soiled clogs on her feet. Tacky footprints led towards a rear door, which was ajar. I motioned for Greenlaw to follow and peered out.

A grassy, muddy alleyway, just wide enough for a cart, was strewn with litter and debris. A stray dog chewed on a bone, which knocked against its teeth as it gnawed. I pushed open the door to get a better look. The dog must have heard because it jealously snatched up his bone and skittered a little way off down the lane.

The trail of bloody footprints led to the foot of a cast iron staircase, which provided access to the first floor of the adjacent shop, the florist. I could see where the metal was flecked in blood.

CUT AND RUN

There was nothing for it. I glanced over at Greenlaw and silently ascended the stairs, taking care with each step. At the top, the door was open. I paused, waiting for Greenlaw to stop moving behind me, and listened. There was silence, the only sound coming from the street out front. I eased the door open, seeing another faint red footprint just inside. Feeling my heart beat fast, I stepped into the hall, careful not to disturb the door further, lest it should creak and alert someone within. I passed the knife back to Greenlaw and slid out a stout walking stick from the stand. If it came to it, I'd rather hit someone with a piece of wood than shove a knife into them. I advanced in short, controlled steps. A slice of the sitting room came into my line of sight: a battered armchair and gramophone, a stationary disc on the plate beneath its copper fluted trumpet. The fragment of a red footstep marked the rug here, like the last innocent potato print on the wall of a primary school classroom. I glanced at Greenlaw and raised my eyebrows questioningly. He nodded, I nodded – and pounced into the sitting room, ready to strike...

Lying on the rug was a British Army officer, his head presented at an angle from the torso that does not exist in life. His teeth were gritted together, the lips pulled back and eyes squeezed shut in an expression communicating fear and pain.

A neat, scorched, blackened hole in the middle of his forehead showed the cause of death, a fact confirmed by the shattered mass of blood, hair, bone and brain that was splayed from the rear of his cranium. In his right hand he gripped a Mark VI Webley service revolver of the type issued to British Army officers. His first finger was lodged inside the trigger guard. I pressed the barrel; it was stone cold, as was the man's face and hand.

Greenlaw coughed – and I looked up in time to see his face erupt in a violent convulsion and his hand go to his stomach. He bolted for the door. Moments later I heard him vomit forcefully against the cast iron staircase. He heaved and went again.

The Webley's tan leather holster lay open on the desk by the window. Next to it a glass paperweight held a note in position. In blotchy handwriting, it declared:

ALEC MARSH

I have sinned and so I pay the price. God have mercy on my sinful soul.
Captain R. Bradbury

I looked at the dead man, now mentally addressing him – *Captain Bradbury* – and wondered at his story. There was only one way to find out.

I searched the room. The relative stiffness of the hand that held the gun told me that rigor mortis was only just beginning. This indicated that death had occurred at least four hours before now, possibly six hours at the outside, giving an approximate time of death of about six to seven this morning. In other words the trail, like the gun itself, had long since gone cold.

An ink stain on the first finger of the dead man's right hand matched the note. His tunic pockets yielded a wallet and identity card. This confirmed his name and told me that Bradbury was in the 2nd Battalion, the Royal Surrey Regiment. This further told me that – if he was married – then in about forty-eight hours from now (once someone official had decided what on earth they would call this mess) that a certain Mrs Bradbury living in the vicinity of Dorking or Camberley was going to receive a house visit that she would never forget. Greenlaw returned, apologising. I sent him to the kitchen to get himself a glass of water and to check it over while he was there.

The tread of Bradbury's boots, I noted, were embedded with blood and sawdust, consistent with a foray into the slaughterhouse. Bradbury's jacket was only half buttoned up, as though he had been interrupted dressing. The trouser pockets yielded a pair of theatre stubs for the local music hall from two nights before. They also contained some low denomination French banknotes and a small photograph of the man himself with a woman and two children, both under ten. On the back, the picture bore the signature and address of a firm of photographers from the high street in Camberley, the Surrey home to a good portion of the British Army.

I put the photograph in my pocket and had another look around.

CUT AND RUN

In the captain's bedroom were some personal items, underwear and so forth, as well as Bradbury's disordered bedding. You couldn't be sure, but it wouldn't have been surprising if whoever had escorted him to the theatre hadn't also joined him here. Either that or Bradbury was an extremely restless sleeper. There was also a box room which contained a narrow bunk which would have done for his servant. The man's kit was there but he wasn't, which posed a question. Greenlaw reappeared, wiping his mouth. He looked better, if not quite restored to his usual medium rare complexion, and about ready for an update.

'Bradbury had a sweetheart, who may or may not have been the butcher's wife. His servant will know the truth but may require an obol or two before he's prepared to sully the memory of his late master.' I saw from the expression on Greenlaw's face that he wasn't following me. 'Silver,' I stated. 'Obols are what the Athenians paid their jurors in.' Greenlaw's hand went to his stomach again, and the mouth flinched. He lunged for the door.

While Greenlaw was sick I took one more look around, dwelling over the body. Something about it bothered me and it was only now that it dawned on me.

It wouldn't have been easy for Bradbury to kill himself like this. The Webley had a six inch barrel and he was not a tall man with long limbs. In fact, quite the opposite. So to have pulled the trigger with his forefinger and delivered the shot to the forehead might have been impossible. It certainly would have been easier with his thumbs. A more natural posture still would have been a shot at his temple.

I found Greenlaw at the top of the stairs, recovering. His face was grey but he was rallying admirably and forced a smile.

'Find Bradbury's batman,' I told him. 'He'll know what's what and then speak to the sister of the dead woman. She'll know for certain if there was anything going on between her sister and this Captain Bradbury. Also find out if he was ever a customer of the Blue Lamp. The servant will also be able to confirm if the handwriting is his or somebody else's entirely. Got all that?'

Greenlaw grinned and stood upright.

'Aye-aye,' he declared with gusto.

'Good man.' I gave his shoulder a hearty slap and then cantered down the iron staircase. Before I reached the bottom, a thought struck me.

I about turned – and called up. 'But whatever else you do, Greenlaw, find Bradbury's pen.'

'His pen?'

'Yes, the one he used to write that note. It's got to be here somewhere.'

And if it isn't then we know this whole set-up is even more fishy than it already appeared…

CUT AND RUN

Chapter Seven

As I turned the corner the stink in the rue de la Délivrance hit me like an elderly French cheese suddenly liberated from captivity. I barged through the odour, through the heaps of rubbish, deep puddles and into the anonymous door of the Blue Lamp, giving a cursory glance over my shoulder – just to check that I wasn't being followed.

The mistress of the house answered my knock, her face heavily powdered and resolute.

'I thought we had seen the last of you,' she declared by way of welcome, as she led me into a small windowed side room that was her study. We seated ourselves facing each other across a small writing desk and I saw that in the cool light from the window the lines on her face showed through the thick powder.

'I assume you have seen her.'

'I regret to say I have.' I took out my pipe and searched my pockets for my tobacco and matches. I intended to have a conversation with Lefebvre and a pipe would help facilitate that. 'I've come straight from the Hotel du Nord. I had hoped to tell you the news myself.'

Lefebvre tugged opened a drawer and took out a packet of cigarettes. Her hands were shaking.

'How was she?'

'At peace.' I lit my pipe as I considered my further response. 'There were no obvious signs of a prolonged struggle. I don't think she suffered too much.'

The heavy eyelids rose and blinked at me. She was about to say something but thought better of it, prompting a lopsided, half smile to fleet across her face. 'This may sound odd but I'm positive she will have made the best of it,' said Lefebvre, 'because that's what she always did, in any situation. It was her way.'

The eyelids lifted against the weight of the mascara and we shared a moment of mutual sympathy. I offered a nod of sorrow.

'When did you last see her?'

'Yesterday morning.' Lefebvre was almost whispering now and looking up at the corner of the ceiling above my head. 'She dropped in briefly before you spoke to her. I was in here looking at the paperwork. She said she was going out for the evening. She was in good spirits. But, then, she was habitually in good spirits. You know that, you met her. It's the way she was.'

'Who was she seeing?'

Lefebvre's bony shoulder lifted.

'A friend... I don't know. I did not enquire. Of course, now I wish I had.' She glanced at me before restoring her gaze to the ceiling. This raised her pointed chin, an act which stretched the loose flesh of her neck. 'And I know what you're thinking. She did not have a lover, as far as I know. Nor is her family or its connections known to me, or to my knowledge any of the girls here. She was a blank canvas, no?'

Something else she apparently had in common with Marie-Louise Toulon, I realised. I told mentioned that the evidence from the scene at the hotel pointed towards a British killer, quite likely a lover.

Lefebvre dismissed this.

'How can you be so sure? She must have had many admirers, and she must have *wanted* a lover?'

She sighed irritably.

'Of course, it is impossible to be certain.' Her hand sliced at the desk. 'What I can say is that I did not *know* of a lover – certainly no one came here, but what she did with her evening off was her own affair.' She eyed me glassily. 'So to speak.'

I showed her Bradbury's photograph and asked if she recognised him.

'What does it matter?' she said, shaking her head.

Frustration welled up in me. 'Madam Lefebvre. This morning I have followed a trail of blood to your door, of which this man was but one stepping stone, the first being Fabienne. So be sure when you give me your answer. Somone must know *who* she was seeing last night.'

Madame Lefebvre shook her head and straightened her back in protest, 'I tell you that I did not, Monsieur.' The old woman hung her head. 'I wish I did.'

'Could she have been moonlighting?'

'Most definitely not! Fabienne was a good girl.'

'So it must have been a lover?'

Lefebvre allowed a weary smile to form on her heavily dressed mouth. Clearly she thought there were other options still, but was unprepared to divulge what they might be. She interlocked her jewelled fingers together, the claws forming a gnarled union.

'Monsieur, while we have rules here, I recognise that there are limits to the reach of my authority. All I can truthfully say is that it has never happened but it is possible, yes.' The finger wagged at me. 'But love is not easy for girls such as Fabienne Thomas. It is hard enough for normal people, is it not? But in this life... it takes a very unusual man.'

'I understand, but I'm interested to know why you are opposed to your girls having lovers. Lovers, after all, might potentially lead to marriage – and marriage to escape.'

Lefebvre's lip curled at me as cigarette smoke emerged listlessly from her long, crocodile nostrils.

'And why would they want to "*escape*", as you put it?'

I shook my head and went to the window. The panes of glass were caked with soot and in the street below – I cursed – I saw the foreshortened brown hat, and navy overcoat on the far side of the road, the Bowler Hat had found me.

I moved away from the window, but already knew that he must have had the pleasure of spotting me. I would address that problem later.

Taking up my seat, I changed the subject.

'What can you tell me of Suzette Emmolet?'

'Suzette?' The eyelids widened. 'Don't tell me something has happened to Suzette as well?'

'Do you know what's become of her?'

Lefebvre shook her head, an act which caused her shoulders to shake from side to side. 'No, she just packed up and left one day. There was a rumour that she was going to the Red Lamp, but she has not – I know this for a fact. We do not like to encourage girls to switch between brothels but sometimes it cannot be helped. Where Suzette went I do not know, sincerely. I was sad, naturally, to see her go. She was highly prized by the gentlemen.'

'Was she allowed to leave like that?'

'We could not stop it, could we?'

'When did she leave?'

'You will need to check. Ask Celine. My memory is not good for dates.'

'How long was she here for?'

'Two years or three, I think. Time passes so quickly I find now.'

I wasn't entirely convinced by Lefebvre's apparent lapse of memory but let it pass.

'Very well,' I said. 'Perhaps you could let me see your records?'

She gave a sudden throaty laugh that was both defensive and calculating.

'Records, Monsieur? What makes you think we keep records?'

'Because this is a business, Madame, and like any business there are shareholders. And shareholders mean there's accounting. I'd wager this business has better accounting than most.'

She regarded me icily and her lined mouth formed a grim, inverse semicircle. 'As you wish, Monsieur. The harm has already been done and, as you say, we can have no secrets. Not anymore.' She moved to the door and paused, half in, half out of the room. 'I will fetch Celine.'

But first I searched Fabienne Thomas's room. It was similar in almost every respect to Marie-Louise Toulon's humble garret, except that it was still filled with her possessions, such as she had, and smelled powerfully of her lavender perfume. Apart from a few dog-eared French novels (not inscribed), there wasn't much to interest me and certainly nothing pointed towards the existence of anything resembling a lover. After looking under the mattress, behind, inside and on top of the wardrobe, and through the drawers of the small bedside chest, I pulled the bed away from the wall. Feeling along the grimy skirting board my hand met something soft but dense at the foot of the innermost leg. It was a purse. I emptied this out into my hand and counted a dozen sovereigns, each brilliant in the dull, flat light from the small window. I had been assured that the clients paid in French francs, and the girls' wages would have been paid in francs accordingly. So, the sovereigns were definitely interesting. I weighed the heavy purse in my hand. Without doubt they pointed strongly towards a British customer or lover, and one of considerable means. This could readily be the same man who would bring expensive flowers from Saint-Omer or luxurious ladies' undergarments from London.

I restored Fabienne's treasure to its hiding place, confident that it would be safe enough there for the time being, and looked over at the dense piles of clothing. Every surface was coated in bottles and jars of perfumes, powders and other ointments and lotions. These were mostly anonymous or French in origin. I found her nightwear and checked the manufacturers; all French. Lastly I sat down on the bed; the springs sagged and my gaze made one last inventory of her meagre quarters – the wardrobe of fifteen dresses, the underwear drawer, the shoes of unknown number and variety.

It wasn't much to show for a life, was it? My mind turned to the sovereigns; what had she got planned for them? Did she have a plan? Who would know?

I picked up the clothbound novel from the top of the pile by the bed and it fell open, the cardboard bookmark fluttering to the floor. I instinctively pressed my finger hurriedly into the parting pages, forgetting momentarily that I didn't need to preserve the place but this reader was never coming back to finish the book. The broken spine told me it was *Dangerous Liaisons*. Beneath it was small leather-bound Bible. I sighed and replaced the book to the pile.

Celine was waiting for me in Madame Lefebvre's study with the paperwork and talked me through it. Each woman had a page in the ledger to record her work, I discovered. These in turn were ordered in columns by date, with clients marked beneath by a simple cross and nothing more, alongside their payments, which varied. Several of the women would have perhaps four or five callers a night and be drawing sums commensurate to several pounds sterling. No one, of course, was paid anything like a sovereign, in any currency. Over a typical six-day period the Blue Lamp, in recent months at least, was making more than the equivalent in francs of a hundred pounds a week – more than twenty times a typical working wage for a man before the war. Small wonder Lefebvre wanted the place to stay open whatever the cost.

I noted that with the exception of just one date in February when neither Marie-Louise nor Fabienne was working, that the brothel was open every night except for Sundays, when it was customary to be shut. 'Napoleon,' remarked Celine, 'said that an army marches on its stomach –' she lifted her eyebrows and gave a wan smile. 'He was not just talking about food.'

I caught myself laughing.

Her small face relaxed, temporarily losing the stiffness that had cast it as a mask. 'You know what they say about the girls of the Blue Lamp taking baths between clients ranked major and above?' Celine announced. 'Fabienne took a lot of baths.'

'And what about Marie-Louise?'

She nodded.

'Out of interest,' I wondered out loud, 'were there many customers who were clients of both of them?'

She nodded, 'Of course.'

While there was nothing in these accounts to help me identify either Marie-Louise Toulon or Fabienne Thomas's clients, I realised that as the person who received clients and took the payment from them, Celine would know the regulars by sight.

'I assume you would be able to recognise them if they came in again?'

'Yes,' she said, adding a decided nod.

I smiled, 'Thank you.'

I was about to go when another thought occurred to me, 'Do you know why Suzette Emmolet left?'

Celine frowned, her finger, which had been sketching an invisible outline on the desk, abruptly stopped.

'No one knows, Monsieur. She didn't even say goodbye.'

'Was that surprising?'

The finger danced on the varnished desk and tapped twice decisively.

'Yes. Suzette is one of those people who gives you a blow-by-blow account of their lives, whether you want to hear it or not. How would you put it? She is a stranger to discretion. So, was it surprising that she left without saying goodbye or telling us where she was going?' Celine looked up at me. 'Absolutely.'

Chapter Eight

I went to see Catouillart to show him the photograph of Marie-Louise Toulon and her parents. Once again he was sat at his typewriter in waistcoat and shirtsleeves – sprung silver clips around each bicep – and was evidently mid-composition. Two inches of paper curled from the top of the machine. On my arrival he yanked off his wire spectacles as though embarrassed to be seen in them, and when confronted with the photograph, held them before his eyes, like a person at the opera. He frowned intently, blinking, as he took in Marie-Louise, the woman and then the military figure.

'Good God,' he lowered the lenses. 'Where did you find this?' His tone hardened, fear arriving in his voice. 'Please tell me you didn't get this from the Eagle.'

'He had it in his safe.'

'Mon Dieu!' The Frenchman's face crumpled and his hand went to his forehead.

'What is it? You recognise him, don't you?'

'Recognise him?' Catouillart turned to face me and his finger stabbed towards the picture. 'That is General Maximilian Troyon. A blind man would recognise him.' The hostile frown stared at me with increasing disbelief. 'Monsieur, are you telling me you don't know who this is?'

'Pretend I'm from the Moon,' I said, sitting down. 'Tell me everything.'

Catouillart exhaled irritably and flicked open the lid to his box of turmeric-coloured cigarettes. 'Mon Dieu,' he muttered...

'First of all, you should know that General Maximilian Troyon is a Chevalier of the Order of the Legion of Honour.' Catouillart, stood at the window, gazing out and paused for me to acknowledge France's highest honour. 'He received this in recognition of his military service which has been most distinguished in many theatres. But he is more than just a soldier; he is also extremely close to Joffre and as you would expect, he has impeccable connections within the government.' General Joffre was the French commander-in-chief and doubtlessly close to the French President, Poincaré. 'Troyon is also a favourite of the prime minister,' added the Frenchman.

Catouillart returned to his chair, leaned back and crossed his feet on the corner of the desk, next to the French military gazetteer which he had just been referring to. He planted the ashtray on his belly and tapped the end of his cigarette on it. 'Troyon is from Le Gers, deep in the south-west of France. It's more or less Spanish down there, most of them are still Cathars, in secret at least. It's all mountains or rolling hills and nothing in between. Le Gers itself is famous for *foie gras* and *magret de canard*, as I'm sure you know. They even make a passable white wine to wash it down, but the red is undrinkable.' He gave a distasteful squeeze of his mouth. 'Troyon was the son of a peasant, who himself was the son of a peasant, from a line of peasants going back to the year dot, if not before. He's a country bumpkin, pure and simple.' He sighed. 'Nothing wrong with that, except this country bumpkin had ambition, a lot of it. Deciding at seventeen that a life of earthy toil wasn't for him, he ran off and joined the Foreign Legion. You are at liberty to guess the rest. Strong, clever, stubborn, he was willing to do absolutely anything to further his career, so he rose quickly. It wasn't long before he became an officer where he distinguished himself in 1890s in West Africa. On the way, he picked up a beautiful French colonist's daughter, whose mother was a local, and they were married. We can now assume that at least one child was produced, Marie-Louise. It is a matter of public record that Troyon's first wife died when the girl was still young. I remember reading about it in the newspaper.'

By that point, he explained, Troyon was now a colonel in the French army, having transferred from the Legion and moved back to France, where he married again, this time to the daughter of a French aristocrat. 'It was a socially advantageous alliance, bringing Troyon into contact with the military elites as well as a degree of inherited wealth. The family moved to Paris, where they inhabited a substantial apartment in Saint-Germain, *naturellement*.'

'So how did Marie-Louise end up at the Blue Lamp?'

'Well,' he opened his hands, 'if one were to speculate, one might suppose that the new aristocratic Madame Troyon did not much care for the common offspring of the first marriage and that Marie-Louise became the Cinderella of the household, while the wicked stepmother then produced her more socially advantaged children. That is speculation but it's not unheard of, is it?'

'And what of Troyon's military career?'

'It continued to go from strength to strength, assisted in part no doubt by his wife's eminent connections, but also due to his own – he's quite a politician. As you can see,' he nodded towards the gazetteer, 'he was made a general in 1910 and had several notable commands before being appointed to the general staff in early 1913. As we speak he's commanding one of the French Armies at Verdun.'

'So he went from stuffing geese and muck-raking to leading the best France has in under thirty years. He's evidently an impressive individual.'

The depth of Catouillart's knowledge about General Troyon made me reflect on the Eagle's insinuation that the policeman was already aware of Marie-Louise's parentage. Plainly, this was not the moment to probe this, but I did wonder. Instead, I took out my pipe. 'Have you ever had cause to investigate Troyon?'

Catouillart smiled, a flash of pleasure as he saw through my question – perhaps.

'No. I give you my word,' the Frenchman placed his hand over his heart. 'You must trust me on this, Troyon is a man to know about.'

'Does he have any enemies?'

'Many, I should expect, but one who would kill his daughter?' Catouillart blew between his lips, 'and an estranged daughter living in such a fashion? That is a different kettle of fish, Monsieur.' He snatched another cigarette, his mind thinking. 'It's not beyond the realms of imagination, of course. Few things are.'

CUT AND RUN

He took a long drag of the unlit cigarette, his expression alive. 'But it would be quite an undertaking for an enemy agent or someone similar to put it all together. A great deal of chance would be required, I think. Yes, it is much more likely to be a question of chance. An act of opportunism, maybe.'

Perhaps, I thought. I watched him consider this as he puckered his lips on his unlit cigarette. Then I heard the measured rasp of a flint and smoke filled the space between us. He cocked an eyebrow at me.

'What are you thinking, Monsieur?'

'It occurs to me that at the very least someone ought to inform the general of his daughter's death.'

Catouillart raised his chin and looked up at me, not entirely with approval, but evidently he had remembered something. He snatched up his spectacles and then sifted through the piles of documents on his desk. A newspaper slid into view.

'I don't like coincidences,' he stated as he leafed through *Le Béthune Soir*. He flicked his hand dramatically against the corner of a page at an article. 'I'm afraid we need to get to Saint-Omer, and quickly.' Pulling the newspaper towards me I saw a photograph of Troyon – somewhat older than in the family picture, and the headline:

GENERAL TO ADDRESS RALLY – SAINT-OMER

'It's tonight –' declared Catouillart, getting to his feet. 'Come on. We'll take your car.'

Chapter Nine

We bounced along a shattered French highway in Kennedy's Crossley 20/25 staff car, Greenlaw at the wheel and cursing liberally at any other unfortunate French road users. Each pronouncement was quickly followed up by an apology to Catouillart who acknowledged it with a gracious nod.

When not responding to Greenlaw's apologies, Catouillart huddled in the back seat swamped in his overcoat under a car blanket, his black Homburg pulled down low over his face. He said little, but I had seen a scowl growing on his face as we fleeted through the broad, undulating Pas-de-Calais landscape.

It wasn't too difficult to guess what irked him. We both knew that Catouillart was going to have to deliver the news to the general himself. His presence rendered me little more than a spectator at the interview, which suited me down to the ground. The article had briefly stated that General Troyon was giving a speech intended to 'raise patriotic feeling', which I thought was an interesting turn of phrase. I leaned in to Catioullart's ear and spoke over the labouring engine.

'What do you know of Troyon's political ambitions?'

Catouillart stirred, sitting up a little.

'Only that he has them.' He pulled his hand down his imperial, tapering it to a neat point. 'As I said he is close to Joffre and Joffre is close to the President. It is as it should be, no?'

'And he's stationed in Verdun.'

'Correct.' There was a pause. 'Though, *naturellement*, his work will bring him to Paris and Saint-Omer, to liaise with the British.'

A Ford motor van came the other way and its headlights framed Catouillart's face. The beams washed out his grey skin, rinsing away the lines and giving me a view of the man beneath the years. He was probably in his early forties, perhaps just six or seven years older than myself, but the change was marked.

We drove through a dim hamlet, an old man and women ate at a roadside café, smoking, drinking. We stopped at a junction where

CUT AND RUN

a pale blue road sign said that Saint-Omer was now only five miles away. A few minutes later the conditions improved and we were driving at a good forty-five miles per hour along a well-maintained highway towards a broad horizon.

I asked Catouillart about Robecq, the man the Eagle had said controlled the Blue Lamp.

'What you need to know about Robecq is that he isn't a man,' pronounced Catouillart, 'he's a family. They were farmers, but over the years they have branched out. So now they're a form of rustic gangsters who happen to have an interest in agriculture. They've an extensive house in the countryside, on the other side of the village of Les Chopettes. They are unsavoury people, Monsieur, but essentially harmless criminals although they are not harmless – far from it. But they are not something that the state particularly needs to worry about. I would advise you to approach them with caution.'

I nodded.

'Be warned, Monsieur,' his voice rose to carry his point. 'Bernard Robecq has a reputation for casual savagery. The good news is that you can't miss him. He is distinguished by a thick double scar that runs down each cheek on his face in near perfect parallel, the gift of an accident with a threshing machine when he was eight years old. He was lucky not to have been blinded.'

Catouillart gave a wicked smile.

'Which reminds me,' he took a last drag of his cigarette and then threw it from the car. 'Something important that I've been meaning to tell you. Not long before you arrived in my office the results of Fabienne Thomas's post mortem examination had arrived. She was three months pregnant.'

We arrived at Saint-Omer at the very end of twilight and parked, making the rest of the journey on foot. Catouillart pointed out a large stone building just off the main square that served as the headquarters of the British Army. It was walled with sandbags and had white tape criss-crossed over the lit windows, just like home. 'It used to be the best hotel in the city,' he said sadly.

A crowd had already assembled in the main square, before the great green copper domed roof of Saint-Omer's city hall. This handsome bauble was still blushing from the end of the sun as we found our way into its shadow. Around us was a scene of industry: everywhere, people identified by Tricolour ribbons or sashes were putting the finishing touches to a red, white and blue banner that ran length of a temporary wooden platform erected along the top of the steps in front of city hall. Behind the platform hung Tricolours and bunting was strung between lamp-posts, encircling the whole crowd in a patriotic web. Elsewhere, stalls had been set up at the fringes where knots of people were drinking, waiting and eating.

People carried signs with slogans supporting the French president, Poincaré, or his party, the *Alliance républicaine démocratique*, the ARD. Others carried anti-German banners. There was a mixture of men and women in civilian dress, of different social classes. There were military, and former military folk dressed in army surplus and marked out by their injuries, be it missing limbs or bandages. A placard read, 'Death to Briand'. He was the French prime minister. I saw Catouillart spot this and shake his head. 'Mon Dieu,' he muttered.

We heard the sounds of drums and a brass band – the martial syncopation of trumpets, horns and drums playing a quick march with high tempo. Then from the far corner of the square came a column of townsfolk, led by the mayor in his chain of office, followed by a figure in full dress uniform – Troyon. A tricolour sash quartered his torso from the gold epaulette at his shoulder to the sword at his hip.

Around him swelled a group of men in sober coats and black silk top hats, and then there was the band, which was in full voice. Amid cheers of approval, the drumbeat kept up and the cymbals clashed as Troyon waved and shook hands with well-wishers as he progressed towards the stage.

More people were now converging on to the square – unlikely British soldiers in their green fatigues, puttees and greatcoats, French women with their children, Frog soldiers in their navy and red uniforms, and a smattering of sailors, too. Troyon ascended the platform and swept off his red and gold embroidered Kepi. There was a roar from the crowd. The entire square was filled with cheering faces...

'My friends,' he cried, and the assembly replied in deafening affirmation. He raised his arms in embrace of them and the din intensified. 'Proud burghers of Saint-Omer,' he hailed, his baritone carrying across the assembly. 'The brave republic is at a crossroads. We have had a year and half of bitter-fought war and the youth of this land is once again being sacrificed to stave off the German menace.'

After paying tribute to the memory of those who fell fighting the Prussians in 1871, he proclaimed, 'We mustn't just defeat the new Prussian assault, we *must* subjugate them. We must finish the job – once and for all, and compel upon them a peace like none they have seen before. This will be a peace for all time. Alsace and Lorraine *will* be returned to France.' He raised a clenched fist. 'We will have a *Pax Francorum*.'

The crowd erupted in ecstatic applause and the band, which had assembled to the left of the stage, performed a superfluous drum roll and crash of cymbals. I glanced at Catouillart. He watched, seemingly impassive but his lips shifted disapprovingly beneath his moustache. I looked over at Greenlaw; if he had misgivings about the notion of an eternal 'French Peace', he wasn't showing it. His mouth was agape, his eyes staring: he'd never seen anything like it. Nor had I, for that matter. The general relished the moment, beaming down at the adoring crowd.

He motioned for silence and an obedient hush fell across the crowd. The general resumed, 'This time the youth of France will not be sacrificed in vain.' I saw his chin raise and announcing a new refrain, his voice deepened: 'Poincaré will not let the Kaiser go free...'

There was a fresh uproar of applause, which seemed to physically swell Troyon. He now proceeded to the heart of the oration – his unswerving patriotism, the indefatigable, uniqueness of the Gallic spirit – before arriving at his rhetorical destination:

Poincaré's enormous gift for leadership and international relations, and his appropriateness for the role of president. 'Vive la France!' cried Troyon and the crowd shouted it back at the tops of their voices, their hats performing jubilant somersaults in the air. 'Vive la France!' they cried. 'Vive la France!'

You could feel the thrill surging through crowd. Couples embraced, fists punched the air, the eyes of the woman next to me streamed with tears. 'Vive la France,' she cried, her chin held high. An Englishwoman, it occurred to me, would have been ashamed of herself for such a public display.

But Catouillart remained unmoved. His eyes stared out mutely at the man on the stage, presumably thinking of what he was about to impart and how he was going to snuff out the pomposity, justified or not, of our esteemed orator.

As the final applause began to fade and the crowd began dispersing, we headed for the stage, pressing against the flow of human traffic. Catouillart leaned into my ear. 'What a complete shit,' he hissed, from the corner of his mouth. 'He's lining himself up for Élysée.'

Troyon was still shaking hands with the coterie of municipal worthies – the mayor, the bespectacled, frock-coated moneyed-looking men – when we reached the front. They looked like judges, physicians and academics, several rungs up the ladder from the petty bourgeoisie, the shopkeepers and their ilk who in turn stood above the working man with scrupulous care. Troyon next moved on to the ribbon of sign-carrying supporters, who had patiently waited at the platform to add their congratulations to the august martial celebrity. They included several women, whom Troyon kissed vigorously in the French fashion on each cheek and which appeared to delight them. Then it was our turn. The general's focus alighted on me uneasily, as Catouillart spoke. I could not hear what was said, but I could see its immediate impact on the general. His expression of self-satisfied omniscience was swept away and moments later we were striding from the square.

General Maximilian Troyon, Chevalier of the Order of the Legion of Honour and former peasant goose-force-feeder of Le Gers, listened gravely as Catouillart explained of the facts of the case concerning the fate of Marie-Louise Toulon, real name Troyon. The general had shrunk into a polished leather armchair in a private parlour of the Grand Hotel Saint-Omer, and nodded from time to time as Catouillart delivered his efficient exposition, in hushed tones. Troyon's expression had remained frozen, more or less, throughout.

Up close, I noticed that the general had quite remarkably sunken eyes, something that was clearly part of the ageing process. The eyes themselves were of normal size but the sockets were somehow larger than normal, leaving black semi-circles over the top of them. Perhaps it was owing to the anxiety or pressure of leadership? Either way, they lent his face an exceptionally severe countenance.

We stood at a respectful distance from him, in a stance reminiscent of undertakers, I thought. Private Greenlaw had been banished to the foyer. Catouillart confined the information to Marie-Louise and was careful not to mention the murder of Fabienne Thomas, despite the strong possibility of a connection between their deaths. Nor was the killing of the butcher whom I now knew to be called Madame Fortier or indeed that of Captain Bradbury brought into the briefing.

At his conclusion, we stood in silence and allowed the information to sink in. The general said nothing. After about a minute he removed a slim leather case from his tunic pocket and took out a cigar, bit its end off, and leaned into the flame of a candle. Only once the cigar was drawing to his satisfaction and his cheeks had puffed in and out several times, did he speak.

'I am deeply grateful to you, Monsieur Catouillart,' he began, before turning to me and pausing, his eye dwelling on me. I suspect he had only just registered the livid scar poking through the unruly bird's nest beard on my cheek and the shrapnel wound to my ear. He nodded as an old soldier might, adding, 'indeed, indebted to both of you for coming to inform me of this in person. I hope it has not been too much trouble for you. As you can imagine this has been a shock.'

We both acknowledged his comment and offered our condolences.

'And nobody has been arrested,' he appeared to hesitate, before finding his words, 'for this crime?'

'Not as yet, General,' I said, speaking for the first time. 'But we are investigating it.' I took out my volume of Marcus Aurelius' *Meditations*, which was small and leather-bound like a pocket hymnal, and resembled a notebook. With a pencil thus poised, I showed the general that a question was coming his way. 'While we are here, Sir, we would be grateful if we could ask you for certain information about Marie-Louise.'

He nodded readily. 'Proceed,' he ordered.

I looked enquiringly at Catouillart and received a nod. I turned back to the general.

'When was the last time you saw Marie-Louise?'

There was a pause as he gathered his thoughts. 'Let me think,' he said at last. 'It would have been two years ago – no, three years ago, in the September. Paris was beastly hot and the heat made everyone bad-tempered, especially me.' He grimaced. 'We met for lunch, which she never ate, if I remember correctly.' He drew on his cigar, exhaled and said, 'Marie was late, very late, and I absolutely despair of lateness; and she knew it made me cross just to make matters worse, so that made me crosser still.' He raised his eyebrows at this, stretching the skin over the bony rim of the sockets. 'Anyway, after we got over the false start we went ahead with the dreaded lunch, just the two of us. My wife did not attend. She and Marie have never really seen eye-to-eye. At first I hoped it was a question of adjustment for Marie-Louise or a phase, and that once she emerged from adolescence her relationship with her stepmother might blossom but no. It wasn't a phase, it was hatred, pure and simple, and by the end of it pretty well reciprocated.' He gave a weary lift of his eyebrows, which I acknowledged with a nod.

'It was not wrong to hope,' I offered.

He sighed. 'For many years we simply endured the situation. It was easier for all of us that way. I was away a great deal, and so too for that matter was Marie – because I had her sent away to school. But after she completed her education and returned to live in Paris, things quickly came to a head. I was now working in Paris at the ministry and I found the atmosphere was personally unbearable. I didn't know how Gertrude, my wife, could possibly have endured it. So in the end – and with a very heavy heart – it was decided that Marie should leave the apartment and be sent to live somewhere else.'

I enjoyed the psychological disassociation of his chosen grammatical construction – the 'it was decided' for instance – as he continued.

'This was duly arranged. Some people I knew on the outskirts of Paris near Fontainebleau took her in. They had been acquaintances of her late mother, which I hoped might alleviate her displeasure. It did not. She hated it. Of course she did.' He smiled ruefully. 'She was only ever going to hate it. And I knew she would, but I wanted to punish her, you see; to show her who was the chief.'

He swallowed hard and his blue eyes closed most of the way.

'Soon after she wrote to me asking to meet me for lunch, which takes us back to that September day in 1913. You see, she'd come to beg me to have her back in the family apartment. She promised to reform, to be a good girl, to stop provoking her poor, well-intentioned stepmother. She even promised to stop drinking my best Armagnac.' He raised his eyebrows at me again, his composure returning. 'She also promised to be a support and more positive example for her half-siblings. In short, she was to be the pinnacle of angelic perfection. If only she could come back to Paris.'

Cigar smoke occluded his mouth and he gazed at the marble tiled floor as he finished speaking. He now paused, presumably considering how to take the story forward or caught by the emotion of the memory in light of what he now knew.

'So what did you do?' I asked.

He met my gaze, a steeliness in there, before looking back to the floor. 'I told her that it was out of the question. And she knew it was, just as well as I did. Things would be fine for a week and then war would break out again. I told her so – and she exploded with rage, just as I knew she would.'

Troyon looked up again and caught my eye. I nodded. He continued. Did I consider him a suspect, I asked myself as I listened? Could he have murdered his daughter, let alone poor Fabienne Thomas? No. Not this proud military leader, who wowed audiences and filled a leather armchair like Caesar Augustus on his throne. No, I could not see him, trudging through the wet nocturnal streets of Béthune and murdering by moonlight. And, certainly, he would not have murdered his own daughter. Not this old warrior. I couldn't see it. I could see him killing for his country – all too easily, but not his own flesh and blood.

'She raged at me,' Troyon was saying, 'she raged at the injustice of the world – to her and women in general. She said marriage was at best servitude and at worse prostitution. She claimed she was the captive of an ossified, paternalistic, nineteenth-century petty-bourgeoisie mindset. She accused me of being selfish, a chauvinist. She said I'd never loved her or her mother – not properly. She said many unspeakable things, none of which she meant or were true. Then she came to her inglorious, impetuous conclusion: she said my wife was a bitch and a whore, adding that she was fit only to service the needs of the Foreign Legion's enlisted men.' He sighed, 'Finally, she suggested that her stepmother's ill temper was induced by madness brought on from syphilis, contracted from me, of course!'

He reached forward and delicately tapped the end of his cigar against the glass ashtray. Three quarters of an inch of dense ash fell away en masse, like a chalky cliff slumping into the sea.

'She was in tears – tears of frustration, of anger, of love... I suppose.' Troyon sighed, 'Doubtless she was mourning for her dear mother and her lost childhood and fearful for the huge open future ahead of her. She was crying for lots of things, Mr Champion. And who among us has not cried for these things?' The eyeballs flicked towards me. 'I was born a peasant, Mr Champion, but I was damned if I was going to die one. I saw what my grandparents went through. No,' the recessed eyes closed and he shook his head, he'd said all this a thousand times before, if not out loud then to himself. 'I made a decision; I chose my path. And that is what my darling Marie was struggling to do, to find her own path. And she knew it, too.' His faced was flushed but he remained composed. French or not, this old soldier didn't want to show his emotion. He wasn't going to shed a tear and he hadn't. But his voice caught.

'She was a beautiful woman, so like her mother. I could see all this and I told her so, damn it if I didn't. I told her this, too, for which you will understand I have had ample reason to regret. I said to her: "If you really regard marriage as a form of prostitution, then you may as well give the real thing a try".' He shook his head, 'and then I told her that at least then she would have a chance of bringing pleasure to her fellow man, as opposed to misery, which is all she was managing to achieve as it stood. It was unspeakable of me. But I was very angry.'

He briefly held his face in his hands. Catouillart and I exchanged a glance. The general resurfaced and addressed me.

'I put two hundred francs on the table, got up and left the restaurant. It was the last time we spoke.'

Troyon heaved himself from his seat and topped up his glass. For a moment there was just the crack of the fire and the chink of the decanter. 'Not long after that,' he continued, his voice now softer. 'She ran away from the family she was staying with and just disappeared. A month later I received a postcard from Nice. She said she was living with an artist. That was the last I heard of her.'

'How did you imagine she was supporting herself financially?' asked Catouillart.

'I tried not to think about it.' He returned to his seat. 'She has always dreamed of being an actress and she had a talent for it.' His restless fist beat time on the arm of the chair. 'I confess I never thought she'd stoop as low as this.'

Indeed not.

A cast of sad introspection attended the general's gaze and the glass went to his mouth. Was that a tear in the old soldier's eye?

Regardless of what Catouillart, Kennedy or anyone thought, or indeed what my instincts told me, I had one question for the general that I had to ask.

'Forgive me, General, but I must ask you where you were on the twelfth and thirteenth of March?'

It covered the date of his daughter's death, as well he knew. The hooded eyes surveyed me coldly. Silently, he planted the cigar between his lips, tugged out a small pocket diary from his tunic and leafed through the pages. At length he grunted and plucked out his cigar.

'As I thought,' he pronounced. 'I was in Verdun –' He turned the book towards me to show me the pages. 'With my men. You will be able to verify that with my *aide de camp*, I daresay, if you feel it necessary.'

I nodded my thanks and there was a brief pause.

'Any further questions?'

We bowed our heads respectfully.

'Very well –' The general rose from the chair and issued us a curt nod of dismissal. 'To your duty, gentlemen. It's all any of us can do.'

We watched him enter the brightly lit salon beyond. The cheers went up as the door closed on us but not before I glimpsed Troyon's face come alive with charm, acres of it. And more than that: there was an overwhelming look of beneficence, like the Ghost of Christmas Present clasping Scrooge around the shoulders and emitting a vast belly laugh. The door shut, stifling the noise and we suddenly found ourselves standing in what seemed like semi-darkness. I registered Catouillart exhale with relief, but I ignored the invitation to converse. Instead I was overcome by a strong sense of being altogether wrong about the man we had just been interviewing. And as we left through the other door, heading for the lobby, the mental image of his transformed countenance in the other room stayed with me.

Catouillart, I realised not unexpectedly, was far from happy. He snatched at my arm, fury in his voice.

'Was it really necessary to ask the general where he was on the night of his daughter's murder?'

'It had to be done.' I pulled my arm free.

'Did it really? When all the evidence points *insistently* to the culprit being someone wearing the field green uniform of the British Army, *not* the kepi of the army of the Third Republic – and certainly not a Kepi overburdened with gold braid?'

There was some truth to this statement but it was also unavoidable to conclude that a senior general with lofty political ambitions such as Troyon might also have motivation to rid himself of an inconvenient daughter such as Marie-Louise. Regardless of my apparent breach of etiquette I knew that Catouillart would not need that explaining to him. Or he shouldn't.

We emerged in silence from the hotel and I saw that Greenlaw had fetched the Crossley round and was waiting for us. I stopped Catouillart before we got any closer and ignored the look of injury on his face.

'I take it you'll be able to confirm that the general is telling the truth?'

Catouillart hissed and the points of his waxed moustache dropped.

'You are impossible!'

With that, he threw up his hands up and marched towards the waiting car.

Chapter Ten

We drove back to Béthune through a broad empty landscape of black silhouettes. The cloud was fetching in low from the east and concealed the slim moon, stealing what little light she offered. We swept through strange fields, dormant villages and towns, foreign country, altered by the shroud of night and offering little comfort to my churning mind. It was too cold to sleep, although I was exhausted still by all that I had done over the previous twenty-four hours since disembarking. I also knew that there was a long night ahead of me.

It was coming up to eleven o'clock when we arrived in Béthune. We dropped Catouillart at the Gendarmerie, left the car at my hotel, and then we walked round to the Blue Lamp.

There we found that Celine had already delayed one of the men whom she knew to have been clients of both Marie-Louise and Fabienne, with a complimentary bottle of wine. He waited for us in Madame Lefebvre's little study. The chubby officer introduced himself as Major Collins, but quickly revealed his real name to be Clarke. 'I say, this is all completely above board out here,' he insisted, a bead of sweat visible on his neck. 'Isn't it?'

I told him about Fabienne Thomas's killing and his eyes shifted uneasily from mine, to Greenlaw, and back to me again. 'That can't be right. I just spoke to the girl, I'm waiting to see her... Ah –' The penny dropped and the note of his voice changed. 'W-what do you want to see me for?'

'We're speaking to all the men who are regulars of hers and the other woman who has been killed, Marie-Louise Troyon.'

'I would hardly call myself a regular!' he protested.

'According to what I've been told you've visited more than twenty times in the last three months. You're a weekly visitor, I understand.'

'Well…. I like to pop in on a Monday. But, what's this about? Am I in trouble?' Panic was rising in his voice. 'I thought this was all allowed out here.'

'It is,' I reassured him. Clarke swallowed and looked over at Greenlaw before fixing his glare on me.

'And who are you again? Why are you in civilian clothes?' His tone was accusatory. 'You a p-policeman? You didn't say so. Where's your warrant card? I'm a Justice of the Peace at home, you know?'

I signalled to Greenlaw who stepped forward and topped up Clarke's claret. As he dived for I returned to the recent death of Marie-Louise, to draw his reaction. 'I heard,' he nodded furtively. 'A ruddy shame.' He set the wine glass down and clutched his hands together in his lap, squeezing his eyes shut. 'But I hadn't heard about Fabienne. God,' he exhaled, tears in his eyes. 'What a ruddy waste! Who would do such a thing?'

I cleared my throat. 'I gather that you were last here a fortnight ago, when you saw Marie-Louise. Is that correct?'

He nodded. 'Yes.'

'Out of interest, how did you decide on her?'

'I didn't. That sullen girl showed me to her. I just told her what I wanted.'

'May I ask why you didn't come here last week?'

'I had toothache.'

'And last night? Did you have toothache then?'

'No.' He glared. 'I had dinner with a pal who was in town. Then I went to my digs on the rue de Saint Dominique; it's just around the corner from the cinema. It's where I stay when I'm away from the lines. The landlady does everything.'

Well not quite everything, I thought. I took down the details of the pal and asked, 'So, where were you on the night of Sunday, twelfth of March?'

He thought a moment, before answering. 'At my digs. It was a typical Sunday, by which I mean nothing happens. You must know what it's like here. Nothing happens on a Sunday.'

'Can anyone attest to your being there? All night?'

'Of course, well, no... I mean, *yes*, my servant was there, but, theoretically I could have got up in the middle of the night, couldn't I? I can see that.' His tone rose. 'For what it's worth, he's a pretty light sleeper… Yes, he can certainly attest to my being there until eleven o'clock or so before he turned in at least.'

His fat hand wiped a bead of sweat from his face. Clarke was one of those people whose pulse's surge at sight of something they dread, be it a stethoscope or dentist's chair. I almost felt sorry for him and I could not imagine him to be a very competent officer.

'Look here,' he exclaimed, 'where's this going? I go back to the front in two days' time for another three weeks.' His voice took on a shrill note. 'I'll probably be dead by the time my next leave comes up … you can't drag my name into this. I've got a family to think of – a reputation –'

I raised my hand and silenced him, but the eyes glowered at me with fear and injustice. I wasn't about to start moralising. Far from it.

'You are free to go,' I told him, and the chubby major bolted.

I sent Greenlaw to search Clarke's property and interview his batman. Meanwhile, I browsed a French newspaper, contemplated the situation and listened to the sound of the piano being played badly from the parlour. Beethoven, I think it was meant to be. It was after midnight when Celine showed in a goofy-faced lad, who turned out to be a captain named George Rylands who hailed from Staffordshire. It was part of the world I knew quite well since it was only down the road from where I grew up. The relatively unusual surname and the geographical proximity also reminded me of something, which I stowed away for later. He offered alibis that could be corroborated for his activities on both the relevant dates in March when Marie-Louise and Fabienne were killed.

'I told them when I got here that I was a major,' he gave a toothy smile, 'because I'd had it on good authority that the more senior you were, the prettier the girls got. I reckoned I could just about carry it off. You get plenty of baby-faced majors these days and anyway, they don't care. As long as you pay.' His eyes flicked up towards the rooms. 'There's not a law against it, is there?'

He confirmed that he'd seen both of the girls on an off for nearly a year – a couple of times a week whenever he was away from the lines. 'I used to visit some of the others as well, but they were my favourites,' he confided. 'Make hay while the sun shines, I say.'

'It must get expensive.'

He shrugged. 'Not really. After all what else is there to spend one's money on around here? And you can't take it with you. So live for the day, I say – tomorrow might not happen.' He gave a hard laugh. 'I also receive an allowance from my father, which helps with the mess bills. God knows what he'd say.'

I wondered if he received his allowance in gold sovereigns. Then I remembered what it was I had stowed away about his family name. 'Rylands,' I remarked. 'I don't suppose you know of Dr Anthony Rylands, the Bishop of Lichfield?'

His eyes sprang open as if he'd seen a ghost.

'Know of him? He's my ruddy grandfather.' The lad shook his head in disbelief. 'My eye, Champion, you're good at this detecting lark.'

'Not really. My father just happens to be a vicar in Cheshire. Your grandfather ordained him about thirty-five years ago.' The lad looked crestfallen. 'Don't worry,' I said. 'I won't tell him. God forbid.'

Before releasing him I referred to my notes, 'Are you personally acquainted with many other officers who come here?'

'Are you joking?' He leaned across the table. 'I've seen most of the occupants of the officers' mess in here at some point or other, apart from the colonel, obviously. I'm sure the same's the case for most units. This crew must be doing a roaring trade. But it stands to reason – we'd go crackers without this lot, wouldn't we?'

'Are there any officers you'd know who have been here on the same nights as you, ones who have also seen Marie-Louise Toulon and Fabienne Thomas?'

He blew out between his teeth, and gave a cagey smile.

'Well... there's McGregor, a lieutenant I know in C company who I've seen here a few times. I certainly saw him here a few Mondays back. I'm pretty certain he's seen them both, in fact, I know it –' Rylands blushed, 'because we talked about it once.'

'Comparing notes?'

He ignored that. 'But he's not your man, Champion. He's not a killer. Unless you happen to be German and in uniform.' Rylands clicked his tongue, he'd remembered something else. 'And anyway C company is up at the line at the moment so he couldn't have been in Béthune on the night he'd needed to have be, right?'

'It's not inconceivable that he could have travelled back to Béthune on Sunday night, is it? What if he'd had a task to complete – an official letter to deliver to someone important? It's not very far to the lines.'

He frowned, 'Unlikely, but not impossible.' Rylands stubbed out his cigarette, and stood. 'If I'm being honest, I don't think he's your man, Champion. He's too green, too young, but you never know.' Rylands shook his head at the suggestion. 'The good news is, if you really want to question him, I know where you'll find him – sleeping in my dugout as we speak in all probability, though of course you can't really call it sleep. He'll be there for another week, poor sod. All being well, of course.'

All being well. I thanked George Rylands and resolved to pay a trip to C Company, the 2nd battalion, the Staffordshire Regiment without delay.

Celine returned shortly after two o'clock. 'We are closed,' she announced in a voice of weary gratitude. She brought out the bottle of brandy and poured a couple of glasses, and sat down heavily.

'Santé!' She raised her glass and then sent a good amount of it straight down, a real sailor's measure. 'Did you find anything?' she asked.

'Maybe. I think we can probably rule out two of the men who used to be regulars of both Marie-Louise and Fabienne. I've got a lead for a third. That's something. We'll have to verify all their stories, of course,' I added.

As my words lingered in the air, something Major Clarke said returned to my mind along with Rylands' comment – 'All being well' – and it dawned on me that solving these murders was very likely a race between my deductive powers and a German bullet, shell or bayonet. If so, given the rate of attrition on the front and my progress so far I was heading for second place. Celine stared down at the desk, her finger doodling on the surface; just now she was shading in an unknown field with short diagonal strokes. She looked tired in the candlelight but the yellow light softened her features. Whereas some people's faces are a function of their dominant, constituent parts, Celine's was the opposite. Her eyes were small, as was her nose and her mouth was thin and narrow, giving the impression that her open, oval face was sparsely populated. However, give her features something to occupy them and the whole came alive. Granted, she would always go unnoticed among the Fabiennes and Marie-Louises of this world, but there was a discreet charm to her face.

'The brandy's good,' I announced, perhaps a little louder than one would ordinarily if conversing with a fellow countryman. I raised my glass. 'Cheers!'

She smiled awkwardly, an act which caused her cheeks to swell. It lent a transient moment of warmth to her general cast of severity.

I asked, 'How old are you?'

Her eyes squeezed shut for a second, presumably as she decided how to answer. If it was a lack of trust in me in particular or the world in general that prompted her reticence I could not say. At last she said, 'I'll be 20 in May', as though she were admitting to a sinful past.

'Twenty?' I chuckled. 'That's only two months. You should have a party. Twenty deserves a party.' As I said this – and as I saw her resist the proposal with the truculent set of mouth and shake of the head – I remembered where I was twenty years ago, in my penultimate year at Haileybury. I was old enough to be her father. The realisation was momentarily arresting, bringing to the forefront of my mind the untapped potential of my adult years. I sighed and put it all away.

'You should have a party,' I said again.

But there was no softening of Celine's mouth. She lowered her gaze thoughtfully and turned a slim silver ring on the second finger of her left hand. I said, 'I'm sorry. I've been tactless, haven't I?'

She rotated the ring again and said nothing.

'You said you'd been here for a year?'

She nodded gently, sadly even. 'I was in Paris before, but I didn't like it. I struggled with it. I missed the countryside, the open, clean skies; the light. The city was beautiful but the people were ugly.'

I told her I'd felt the same way about London and that for the last two years I'd lived on a boat with none but terns, curlews, coots and thieving gulls for companions.

She smiled at that, this time showing her teeth, which were small, white and neat.

'What took you to Paris?'

'Childish dreams.' Her mouth contracted bitterly. 'It wasn't what I thought it would be. My father was right about that.'

Celine stared into the distance. The index finger of her right hand played on the woodwork, painting small circles. I reached into my pocket for my tobacco, watching her as I did so. She was still blinking into the never-never, stroking shapes onto the desk as I lit my pipe and smoke occupied the space between us.

She said, her voice faraway, 'My father smokes a pipe. He's a farrier.' She looked up at me from her doodling, 'He's an honest man, too.'

'I'm pleased to hear it. An honest father is an honest start.'

She took a drink, self-consciously, furtively, like bird pecking at a bottle of milk.

'Where is he?'

'In a village in Brittany.' She wiped her mouth, 'It's where I grew up.'

'Could you go back?'

'I've thought about it,' she raised her chin, addressing the ceiling. 'I could.'

'I can give you money if it helps. This is no place to spend your life.'

Celine lowered her eyes to the desk and compressed her small mouth thoughtfully.

I asked, 'How did you come to be here?'

She adjusted herself in her seat, crossing her legs and spoke to her glass, 'I was in trouble when I left Paris. I was only eighteen. I didn't know where to go. I couldn't go home. Somehow I found myself in Béthune – a place I had never heard of – and Madame Lefebvre took me in, gave me a home, a job, sorted me out. She's been incredibly kind. The girls are my family now.'

I gave her a reassuring smile.

'Thank you, Mr Champion. Has anyone ever told you that you have very kind eyes?'

I parried her compliment with an awkward shake of the head.

'It's true,' she insisted, giving me a disarming look that felt like it went straight through me.

I took a drink and she changed the subject.

'How confident are you that you will find the man responsible?'

I shrugged, 'I've managed it before.'

She cocked an eyebrow at me. 'That's not the same thing.'

'It's not, is it?' I shrugged. 'Killers kill for a reason. And where there's reason, there's logic and where's there's logic there's a solution, like any puzzle.'

'What if they don't kill for a reason? What if it's senseless?'

'There's always a reason for murder,' I said. 'And if there's no reason, then that's your reason. There's always a trail, whether it's bodies, logic or something else entirely. Usually it's money or pride, or both.'

Celine tilted her head back and drained her glass in one swift movement that was so natural, I guessed it was learned at her father's table.

'You're right,' she said. 'I pray you find this man, Mr Champion.' She got up. 'I relish watching him go to the guillotine.'

Chapter Eleven

Private Greenlaw was sucking on a rolled-up cigarette in the rue de la Délivrance, looking cold and tired, when I emerged from the Blue Lamp. He glanced up at the sky which was showing signs of clearing with a star or two visible.

'It's going to rain again,' he declared belligerently, by way of greeting.

I was inclined to think that the opposite was the case but made no direct reply. Instead I apologised for taking so long, which seemed to cheer him, and we set off in the direction of my hotel. In the few minutes since leaving Madame Lefebvre's study I had resolved above all else to catch this killer before a German bullet or shell denied us the potential for justice. That meant alacrity of action. My pace quickened and Greenlaw hurried to keep up.

'Aye,' he muttered. 'It's definitely rain.'

The tall silhouette of the stone belfry in the square came into view and then the dark shadow of my lodgings and the adjacent building. Béthune was asleep but despite the hour I was not sleepy. Far from it, and – what's more – alarmed at the prospect of imminent failure in my mission. As we arrived at the back, I had reached a decision.

'Greenlaw,' I announced. 'Fetch the Crossley.'

The night sky was clearing now but it was still dark, dark like a well without moonlight. In the Crossley we motored impatiently along narrow lanes and broken paths, driving east, towards the war. If Rylands had told the truth, then Lieutenant McGregor was entrenched with his unit, C company, second battalion of the Staffordshire Regiment. They were up on the front line somewhere the other side of the village of Givenchy-lès-la-Bassée, or what was left of it.

We joined the main road that leads through Beuvry and Annequin, towards the sound of sporadic gun-fire, sporadic in the sense that it was so infrequent that it was surprising when you heard it. We reached a military roadblock outside Annequin, where several rows of empty houses kept company with a derelict steel-works. The Tommies more or less saluted the green military Crossley and let us through without question. From there it was another mile along darkened roads, where occasional houses still seemed to be occupied, but most were not. At first glance they might look complete but then you would catch sight of them from a different angle and you would see that they were merely half-formed shells. A squadron of cavalry galloped up to us and its kindergarten commander demanded to know our business. I told him what we were about and he took his men off. He didn't care. They disappeared into the night, their hooves playing on the road.

We drove through an abandoned village, the buildings were fragments. Single walls and half-formed arches defied gravity, standing reminders of what had been before, amidst a new landscape of rubble and wild brambles. After the village was a supply depot, busy despite the hour. A hoarse-voiced sergeant barked orders as haggard-looking orderlies loaded waiting horse-drawn wagons. The men were dead on their feet.

Greenlaw obtained directions and we continued along the road a little way before stopping. The rest of the journey would have to be made on foot.

A battalion of infantrymen, Suffolks the sergeant had said, were bivouacked among the remains of a woods to our left; the trees were more like stumps now, and you could see the men's faces and clouds of breath illuminated in their low, small fires. A sentry hailed us, asking our business. I looked up and high in the sky – now clear and cold, I saw an old friend Aldebaran, the lightest star of the constellation of Taurus and one of the brightest in the firmament. Taurus was clear, as was Gemini next to it and the vast latticework of stars. Aldebaran had been helping grateful sailors since before the wheel and was a reminder that the answer could usually be found, if you knew where to look for it.

We followed the dark lane, high hedges either side, filtering streaks of moonlight. We passed more stalls of supplies and a field dressing station – serried ranks of circular canvas tents sheltered behind a shattered old farmstead and the broken remains of a barn.

We heard horses and a troop of gunners passed by, coming the other way up the lane. Their horses were spent and the riders' heads bowed, their mud-grimed feet limp in their stirrups, the eighteen-pounders rolled after them. Next we met ambulances coming our way, moving at barely a walking pace, their cargo ominously silent. We passed several more camps and assorted military establishments, including a company of engineers. There were the remnants of two decaying horses by the side of the road. Still tethered together, moonlight glinted on the tack and tackle and showed white where crows had picked their rib cages and hips bare. I could feel my stomach knotting tighter as we approached. Perhaps this wasn't such a clever idea, after all.

Occasionally we heard snatches of gunfire – a few seconds of lead pounding towards the enemy, the crack of a Lee-Enfield, or the explosion of a mortar arriving from over there. We were close. Then I saw it. Up ahead, the earthwork embankment jutted out into the night sky, a blank outline against the glittering stars.

We were at the trench.

It was just as I remembered it. There was that overwhelming smell of damp, so heavy you couldn't help but taste it on your tongue, like a freshly ploughed field after a downpour. The knot tightened sharply.

I remembered entering a supply trench like this on the morning of the battle last September. I remembered the unfamiliarity of it, despite all our training in trenches back home. I remembered the anxiety, the sickness; I remembered suppressing the urgent need to urinate, like I was fit to burst. I remembered how no one spoke, how the two hundred or so men of my company, to a man were silent. All you could hear was the tramp of boots on the duckboards and the occasional squelch as a misplaced foot sank in the mud. The only other noise was the creak and clack of our kit, our filled leather webbing, our rifles and bayonets – all as two hundred glaziers' sons, shipping clerks, bricklayers and burned-out socialists made their way in single file to the fall. Christ, I felt sick.

I remembered the padre trying to raise our spirits by talking about the Salamanca Eagle, telling us – though we all knew only too well – how it had been snatched from Napoleon's troops in 1812 by our regimental forebears. It had since been the regiment's most prized possession and was paraded on the square on high days and holy days to symbolise our invulnerability. Fat good it was out here. When the shooting started the padre was among the first to die.

It had taken an age to weave our way through the access trenches, the supply trenches, then along the zigzagging communications trenches before we finally got to the front line. Still no one said anything. Someone would have whistled, I'm sure, but a shout would silence him. We were mentally preparing ourselves, like a prize fighter before he steps into the ring. We were also the vanguard of a surprise attack, you see. So silence was essential, not that you would have heard the sound of the whistling from six hundred yards, would you?

Looking back, the whole build-up seemed calculated to shred a man's nerves. Three days' hike to get there, the last ten-mile march up to the lines, the handing in of kit and any personal items at the mustering stations, the issuing of ammunition. Then the tortuous, silent tramp along the wooden duckboards to the front line past hundreds of others, all of whom had seen what you were about to see for the first time. And how it showed in their haggard faces. Several even crossed themselves as we passed. That you didn't need.

The countdown was the worst part. I've been to church a lot in my life but rarely seen men move their lips as they pray. You had to physically control yourself to stop yourself fleeing or urinating. I saw a man do the latter. You know civilisation has reached a pretty pass when you witness someone whom you know to be of good standing and decent courage piss himself in public out of plain, cold fear. It doesn't half sober you up. Not that you were drunk in the first place, mind.

I remembered wracking my brain trying to recall who had won Wimbledon in 1914. I remembered seeing blades of grass protruding from a crease between the sandbags in the trench. I'd rather die than be broken utterly, I had thought, like those poor sods I'd watched in their hundreds being stretchered back from the front line the night before.

In my mind I saw a trio of ragged, grubby French children that had been skipping along besides us as we marched out of Béthune. That was the day before. They shrieked: 'Tommee, tommee. Bully beef tommee!' And of course we shared our rations with them.

'CHAMPION–'

Not yet Greenlaw, not yet. Back in the trench the countdown continued. I experienced that comforting rush of delight, as though your brain were sinking into a hot bath after a strenuous walk: Tony Wilding: it was Tony Wilding. The young Aussie. He creamed Norman Brookes in three straight sets, clinching it with a tie-break in the third. And then he went and got himself killed at Aubers Ridge in May. Poor sod was gassed, so he was. I felt the hot warm water running down my leg. Christ, the shame of it. But there's no time for shame. I'm climbing the ladder...

'Champion!'

It's Greenlaw again. I opened my eyes and saw him, staring. He shook me, hissing: 'You're not all there, are you man?' He looked at me, hostile concern knitted across his face. 'I'll not be going up to the line with you if you're going to crack up on me. You can't do that to me, oh no.'

He was right of course. I knew it.

'Come on,' I said, breaking free from his insistent stare. 'We've come this far; let's finish the job.' I stepped down into the trench, leading as the doctors had advised me with my bad left leg; just in case it gave way. My throat was dry – dry as the choking red dust of East Africa, the stuff that the Kikuyu covered themselves in at their *Indaba*. I pressed on along the soft, muddy duckboards of the communication trench towards the supply lines and the front line that would be some hundred and fifty yards beyond. Come on, I thought, I want to see it again. I want to smell it. Greenlaw caught up with me, muttering under his breath.

The trenches got wider here, wider than I remembered and all the better for permitting the inward flow of humanity and goods to further the war. Timber braces reinforced the walls every couple of feet. They were panelled, too, just as I remembered they were. Toiling officials, their heads craned forwards like monks went about their business, (to ensure that they were below the parapet at all times), and barely registered us as we followed the zigzagging trench. Every now and then a blanket or tarpaulin was pulled back to reveal a dimly lit dugout, and men working at desks or completing some military task like cleaning rifles or drinking tea.

We reached a communication trench which led forwards towards the front line and I stopped to ask a sentry the way. 'We're looking for the Staffordshires,' I said.

The lad looked shiftily at me and Greenlaw, before deciding, quite rightly, that we were honest folk. I offered him a cigarette, which he lit with a kneeling stoop. 'I'm looking for a friend,' I explained. 'It's an urgent family matter.' His face was drawn and the rims of his lower eyelids were red, like he was pulling the skin of his face down. A couple of puffs later he gestured for us to continue along the communication trench. 'The Staffs is to the left,' he croaked.

Rapid, breathless machine-gun fire cracked overhead. Stretcher-bearers rushed towards us, wounded men writhing in the litters. 'Make way,' they called, mechanically, 'Make way.' We ducked to one side. Greenlaw glanced at me, his eyes narrowed, 'You're sweating. God damn it, Champion. It's freezing our here and you're dripping like it's the ruddy tropics. You're not right, damn it.'

I shook off his arm. 'I'm fine,' I hissed, but the words struggled to get out. 'I'm fine.' I cleared my throat, 'Let's get on. Come on!'

I pushed past him.

'We've got to get there first,' I said, 'or I'll never forgive myself.'

We proceeded for another hundred yards, another hundred paces. It seemed longer. A huddle of rats scuttled towards us, breaking apart to pass either side, their paws drumming on the planks. The trench deepened again and the ground became moist beneath the waterlogged duckboards, which were slippery. Here sandbags had been placed along the walls, narrowing the passage to about four feet across. Every twelve feet or so men sat or crouched by lamps, reading letters or smoking. Up ahead was a dead end; it was the firing line.

We had arrived at the war and could only now go only left or right. Straight on was not an option – that was no-man's-land. I'd tried that once before and had vowed never to do it again.

We checked our way with a sentry at the end.

My chest was beating fast as we stooped along, the parapet high on our right. The routine business of battle was taking place here: men were standing too, ready and waiting, spread out every few yards, peering through periscopes and occasionally answering the distant machine guns. Mortar shells landed close by and every now and then we got a blast and shower of mud and debris.

The trench was shallow in places, where the men had not been able to dig down further without hitting bedrock, and we had to crouch low to keep our heads out of the firing line. For a moment I glimpsed the little twinkling lights of the German machine guns, firing bursts of lead towards us, before remembering to duck. The tiny, rhythmic yellow flashes were faintly mesmerising, like stars on the horizon.

A heavily built sergeant sprang out of the corner, his voice preceding him, 'What are you doing here?' he hollered. We all ducked as a mortar exploded in front of the trench, shaking the ground and showering us in dirt.

I told him what we were about, my words drowned out by the sound of falling debris, like stormy surf dragging gravel at the beach.

'What?'

'The Staffs,' I bellowed. His face filled with recognition. We were in the right place.

'Who in particular, Sir?'

'Lieutenant McGregor.'

He gave a terse nod and I understood to follow him, which we did low and at the double. My left leg obeyed but not happily, sagging on its turn. I could only pray that it would keep up its side of the bargain. We followed the trench, swerving left, then right, then right, then left, and then straight on, as it sliced its way through the landscape. We passed a machine gunner who was working hard, responding to the German barrage. The muzzle flashes reflecting off the sandbags, the noise deafening. My leg collapsed lower now with each stride, and I was slowing. Greenlaw was at my heels.

The sergeant nimbly ducked into a low doorway, down a trio of steps. We followed through a porch into a brightly interior.

A young captain with watery eyes looked up at me from his desk, where he played Indian Rummy with a grey-haired lieutenant, a dozen cards spread before them. The captain's lip curled, and he addressed the sergeant, 'Who the hell is this, Manners?'

'Civilian detective, Sir. Requesting permission to speak to Lieutenant McGregor urgently, please, Sir.' The older lieutenant looked over, interested. We were a turn up.

'He's making mud pies,' announced the lieutenant, his voice unexpectedly Mancunian. 'He won't be back for hours...' He laid four threes on the table, the captain was piqued by this but hadn't finished with us yet.

His hand wavered into view, like a drunk man confronted by a sobering incident. 'What did you say sergeant?' He scrutinised me, with renewed interest. 'You can't just waltz in here like this, who do you think you are?' Another thought occurred to him, 'And what on earth do you want my lieutenant for? Come on, out with it?'

Minutes later we were following Sergeant Manners, again at the double, along the trench. The machine guns were at it again, brass casings spewing out in an arc from their firing points as we darted along the trench.

'Face forward,' barked the sergeant, as men turned to see us pass. 'Keep your look-out,' he repeated, 'The Hun never sleeps... face forward.'

We reached a low narrow opening, perpendicular to the main axis of the trench. It led towards the enemy, into no-mans-land. A pair of sleepy chaps stood sentry here and acknowledged the sergeant, who stopped and addressed us, 'He's down there.' Manners threw his chin towards the dark outer reaches of the freshly dug trench, which led down to a tunnel. 'You ready?' He unholstered his revolver, gave us one last nod of agreement, and bobbed nimbly down into the tunnel.

I stepped down into darkness and proceeded slowly, bent low, groping my way with my hands, patting at the cold, damp wall of mud, like I was a mole. Clods of earth came away from the raw wall of the tunnel in my hand. It was like travelling along a vast grave. The guns were louder over our heads now, and coming from both directions. A mortar would make short work of us. At last I saw a dim candlelight ahead.

There they were. Half a dozen men; toiling silently, taking measured deliberate spadefuls out of the facing wall and filling sacks of earth with them. Lord, this was miserable work.

I heard a quiet cough and looked over: there was the click of a rifle being cocked and I saw its barrel lift from the shadows and reflect the candlelight. One of the men filling sandbags looked over. He saw us and nudged his officer's elbow. The silhouette turned to us, stepping into the light. His expression was pained, anxious.

He silently exchanged words with Manners; the sergeant moved over to observe the working party and the officer approached. His face had taken on the grey pallor of a corpse.

'Lieutenant McGregor?'

He nodded, frowning. 'What's all this about?'

I explained and as he listened he made no reaction, except perhaps to blink rather more than was usual. Finally I asked, 'Where were you last night?'

'Here, making mud pies – digging this ruddy tunnel.'

'All night?'

'What do you think? The men will vouch for me.'

'And what about March the twelfth and thirteenth, the Sunday night before last?'

He lowered his eyelids; his finger playing on his rough chin.

'We were in the reserve trench that week,' he rolled his eyes, 'taking it easy.'

'What does that mean?'

'Sleeping I expect, that's what I normally do when I get out of here.' I frowned at him, thinking fast, as he complained, 'Look, what makes you think I've got anything to do with this?'

'Is there anyone who can corroborate your story?'

'My story? For God's sake man. We're fighting a war here. It's not a *story*. Ask the captain. And who gives a damn about...' he was struggling to remember the names of the woman, 'who gives a damn about a couple of dead whores? The Germans will shoot the rest of them as quickly as you like, once they've had their fun with them. Now,' he drew himself up, 'I've got a war to fight.'

He strode back over to his men, snatched up a spade, and dismissed the sergeant.

I nodded to Greenlaw, and exhaled.

'Come on – let's leave this man to his war.'

We turned to go and I cursed myself under my breath. What had I been thinking? There was no way that McGregor could have gone to Saint-Omer to get those flowers or the ruddy chocolates. Béthune, perhaps, but not Saint-Omer. Unless he had ordered them, of course. I halted and shook my head. 'Sorry, Greenlaw.' I put my hand out to steady myself for a moment, suddenly feeling a wave of exhaustion overtake me. 'This has all been a dreadful waste of time.'

Greenlaw and I bade each other good night at the back of the hotel where his lodgings were among the stables and garages, courtesy of the British class system. A glance at my watch told me it was nearly five o'clock in the morning. I had been awake for nearly twenty-two hours and was beyond tired, my spent limbs scarcely able to lift me up the creaking staircase to my room. I paused at the landing and massaged my aching left thigh. It had done good work today, that was for sure – more work than at any time since the twenty-fifth of September last year. That was for certain.

Why had I been so impetuous – dashing off into the trenches to investigate something that if I'd only thought about it properly I should have known was impossible or at the very least highly unlikely? I closed the door of my room behind me and reached out for the light.

I never made it.

A sharp blow struck the back of my head, pitching me forward blindly. It didn't hurt. At first. Instead, I experienced the freeing, weightless sensation of falling – then I heard a cry of pain. My own. A knee ploughed into my stomach, breaking my fall. Winded, I hit the floor and struggled to my feet. Then a foot stamped onto my back. I cried out and was wrenched over onto my back – I caught the outline of my assailant – and a powerful fist slammed into my left eye. The darkness became complete and I was sinking fast, like weighted bait vanishing far, far below the surface. It was dark but somehow getting darker...

CUT AND RUN

Chapter Twelve

A brilliant, intense flash of light turned everything bright white, washing away the visual facts of life in a saturated mirror-image of blindness. I was surrounded by the pungent, sweet yet bitter odour of earth.

'Champion!'

Private Cowan kneeled over me, his mouth stretched open as the sound of my name reverberated through in the air. His teeth were caked in mud and he was tearing away at the heap of earth that pressed down heavily on top of me, shovelling it with his hands. He gripped me by my tunic lapels and hauled me towards the grey daylight. I broke free from the earthly coffin.

Then I saw the other members of our platoon – Warren and Cartwright included. Streaked in mud, they looked like they'd been dipped in tar and rolled in the dirt. They lay on their sides, gripping their rifles and cowering as shells exploded all around, raining debris down on us like hailstones. We were in no-man's-land, closer to the enemies' wire than our own. It looked like nightfall, but I checked my wristwatch, noting that the hands glowed. It was only just after five o'clock. The darkness was battle-smoke. The constant staccato of machine gun fire skidded over our heads and drilled in our ears from the German lines. Their muzzles flashed, twinkling with lethal, picturesque charm. The drone was interspersed with the higher pitch of the rifle fire from our side. I'd lost my rifle and was hatless. Our officer, Murray, was dead, I knew. I looked around at our group of survivors and saw from their faces that I was now their leader. I realised I was holding Murray's Webley revolver but I did not know how. And why were they looking to me for leadership? I couldn't lead them.

We had two choices, I told everyone, shouting at the top of my hoarse, shattered voice: stay put till nightfall but risk being blown to smithereens by a Hun shell while we waited or make a dash for it now – and risk being blown to smithereens by a Hun shell, or machinegun. There wasn't much in it, the way I saw it. At least if we ran, we would get it over with sooner.

Our trench, that is the one we left not long before, was a distinct dark line in the mud, probably six hundred yards off. It was on the other side of an undulating, shifting brown landscape of suffering, comprising hundreds of bodies of our comrades in arms, all blended with shrapnel, kit and tonnes and tonnes of earth. The six of us gazed at our trench. At a full tilt it was five minutes hard run across open ground like this. 'If their guns don't get us, our guns probably will,' said Warren with a beastly grin.

We scurried from the crater. Cowan shouted, 'Keep your blinking head down.'

An ear splitting whine tore through the air and we were inundated by earth, like storm waters burying the ploughing bow of ship. I was drowning, spiralling, suffocating under a heavy tide of black soil...

I awoke, gulping for air. My heart thumped against my chest. My face was slicked with sweat.

'Champion –' It was a low voice in the dark, 'It's me.' The voice sounded far away and hollow. I made no reply, I saw no point, but instead became conscious of light – the exterior presence of lightness over darkness. My eyes edged open; I saw Greenlaw's face take shape. My gaze followed the nicotine-coloured tassels of a lamp-shade and explored the outline of my room at the hotel. Somewhere in the infinite space in my head I felt a throb of pain, unreal yet real, like the sound of someone hammering on the other side of the wall. The noise became louder, the sensation more intense and accompanied by the peculiarly vivid feeling I had had before of a glass of cold water being poured into my empty stomach. A white enamel dish and red-stained towel lay on the floor – I felt bile rise to my throat. Greenlaw rested his hand to my shoulder. I buckled forward and was sick into the dish, which he held.

'Take it easy Champ. You've 'ad a right kicking.'

I saw that Greenlaw's cheery optimism had been displaced by concern. I took a deep breath and focused on his face. If I was being sick as a result of a head injury, then I definitely had been given a right kicking. I was sick, again. But it was better than not being sick.

A little later I asked, 'Where's Kennedy?'

'I don't know Champ,' he said uneasily.

There was a knock at the door and Greenlaw went to answer it. That's when I saw the warning. Daubed in large red letters across the far wall in French were the words, 'Go home.'

'The bastards –' I coughed as I tried to raise myself, ignoring the pain in my side – and feeling the returning pressure of Greenlaw's hand. 'They've got a ruddy nerve, haven't they?'

'Aye, they have Champ,' counselled the Yorkshireman. 'I'll give them that.'

He laid me back down and then put a glass at my mouth to help me drink. I winced as it went down but it washed away the metallic aftertaste of blood and the acid of sickness.

When I was next aware of my surroundings, a blanket had been placed over me and my shoes removed. Greenlaw slept in an armchair close by. I felt better – my head was clearer, the pain now reduced to a common or garden headache. The sensation of sickness had been replaced by hunger. I got up cautiously, stretching my aching back and trod gingerly over to the windows where I drew back the curtain. Weak sunlight was visible through its windows. Day had begun.

I reviewed my attackers' crude message, noting that the hand was typically French, and ever so slightly awkward. No one educated on the other side of the Channel formed their letters like that. I steadied myself. I needed medicine.

Downstairs in the bar, an elderly Frenchman, a sprig of silver hair poking out from beneath a work cap, was already at his day, mopping the floor. I took down a bottle of scotch, snatched off the cap and prescribed myself a quadruple measure, a double for the pain and a chaser for shock. I knew my friend Herbert would approve cordially.

My reflection appeared in the mirror that ran on along the wall – between slogans for Ricard and Pernod. My left eye was swollen, closed up – and hideous, like an exhibit in a travelling chamber of horrors. I prized at the turgid lids, wincing at the faintest pressure of my fingertips. A red slit, registering only light, was where the eye should be.

Apart from this my face showed no outward sign of the beating. The initial crack to my head had left a large, erupted egg on the crown of my head, concealed by my hair but tender to touch and still weeping. That would be bad for a day or two and sensitive for a month.

I pumped some water into the basin behind the bar and rinsed my face. The cold water stung my eyes, but refreshed my scalp, reducing the pressure in my skull. On one level I had to be grateful they had spared my life – they might not next time. I took the bottle of scotch with me back upstairs.

At the landing short of my room, I knocked at Kennedy's door. No answer. Was he in there, I wondered? Probably not. I tried again before shuffling back to my room, my left leg tired already and not lifting well. Where was Kennedy? In the room Greenlaw was still asleep. I put on a fresh shirt, then gave his leg a gentle kick.

'Wake up you laggard,' I said. 'There's work to be done.'

Chapter Thirteen

The last time I had seen Fabienne Thomas alive she was striding up the rue de la Délivrance in the rain, dodging puddles, on her way to see the local vicar. Or so she had said. During my conversation with Madam Lefebvre the afternoon before, she had confirmed that this was the man to whom Fabienne made her longstanding Sunday afternoon visits. I was not sure how a sabbath visit by a prostitute to the house of a man of the cloth quite stood in a canonical sense but stand it undoubtedly did. It was time I followed this piece of information to its logical conclusion and I probably ought to have done so already.

The presbytère, or vicarage, was not far away, situated behind the red brick church on the edge of the main square. It was here, despite the early hour, that we presented ourselves.

I pulled the metal, cruciform doorbell above the etched brass plaque that read, 'Fr. André Haillicourt' and a bell tinkled from within. Greenlaw looked over expectantly.

A snowy-haired priest came to door and plucked his breakfast napkin apologetically from his collar. Beaming as best he could at the strangers before him, he welcomed us in and led us into a small book-lined study, where Molière and Rabelais jostled with volumes on liturgy and theology under the scrutiny of crucifixes and the gilded visages of a dozen saints. The room reminded me a little of my own father's study, not just for obvious reasons, though his selection of decorations was rather more austere, so much as for the dusty smell of books. I started by confirming with Father Haillicourt that Fabienne had visited him the Sunday just past.

'As normal,' he said, adding a congenial bob of the chin.

'Did she say where she was going after visiting you?'

He shook his head, 'I'm afraid she did not, my son.' He smiled again at Greenlaw and offered him a biscuit from the tray.

'And what did your weekly sessions entail, Father?'

The priest smiled, causing his chins to swell. 'A passion for learning, Monsieur.'

'And that was the only passion, Father?'

He inclined his head towards me, and chuckled, 'I am a priest, my son. I was teaching her to read and write.' He gave a long, despondent sigh. 'She was doing so well. She was on the cusp of Voltaire.'

'I found a copy *Dangerous Liaisons* by her bed. That wasn't one of your set texts, was it?'

He beamed, 'God gave us the gift of language for a reason, Monsieur. We should cherish it, nurture it, explore it. Words and faith are all we ever really have, are they not?'

I wasn't quite in the mood for philosophy. On the shelf above his head I noticed a book on the Cathar heresy alongside several titles on the Occult.

'Did she confide in you at all, Father?'

'Oh no, not as such. Nor did she confess to me.' He raised his white eyebrows. 'Although, I'm sure if she had, it would be an education.' He let out a chuckle, 'You know, regardless of her sinful occupation, she had faith, of sorts, at least.'

'Did her occupation not bother you, Father?'

'Bother me? There are worse things than sin, Monsieur. Evil, for example. But sin? Sin is normal.'

'To err is human, is it not?' I agreed.

'Precisely.'

'Did she ever mention an appointment that she may have kept after coming here, last Sunday or on any other Sunday for that matter?'

The priest turned the delicate cup and saucer on his knee.

'I don't think she ever mentioned it and I never thought to ask.'

'If you happen to remember anything, however trivial-seeming, do let me know.' I nodded forcefully. 'There's a chance that whoever she was meeting was responsible for her death.'

He stood his cup and saucer on a lace-covered side-table and pressed his hand into his voluminous chin. His fingernails were bitten short. 'I really wish I could be more help,' he offered a smile of condolence. Then he blinked, and his expression changed. 'Well now, something odd *did* happen on Sunday. Before she left, she said she wanted us to pray together. She had never done that before. I remembered thinking – hoping – that literature was working. She's turning to God, I thought.'

Greenlaw cleared his throat discreetly, 'What did she want to pray for, Father?'

The priest's hand went to the wooden crucifix that hung at his breast and he frowned as if pained, 'Her soul.'

I left the presbytère with a sense of disappointment, and I decided it was time to go in search of a friend. So we got in the Crossley and drove east of Béthune into the countryside. I knew the way. We passed through a small village, Les Chopettes – it was no more than a handful of dull grey and dirty-looking houses and barely qualified as a village by English standards where greens and pubs are generally required for the classification. Then we took a right-hand turn along the side of a vast ten-acre field. It was ploughed dark brown, but when I'd first seen it last September was a whispering sea of high swaying corn. We followed this lane for several hundred yards before arriving at an imposing stone and red brick rococo archway: the magnificent and somewhat out of place entrance to Choques Field Hospital. I forget the military numeric designation, but I knew it well enough. It was here that I came on the morning of twenty-sixth of September last, and where I then spent eight weeks recovering after the battle of Loos.

I left Greenlaw at the car, having primed him on where he could get a mug of tea. Inside I followed the green and white tiles and smell of disinfectant along the corridors past the red-capped nurses, busy orderlies and an assortment of crippled soldiers. They reclined in chairs or hobbled along on crutches, smoking, chatting, playing cards or reading dusty old paperbacks.

I found the door that I remembered and was delighted to see the same yellowing typed card with the dropped 'a' in the brass slot. It read: Cpt. H. A. Macmillan. I knocked, waited for the kind-sounding summons and entered.

Captain Herbert Macmillan looked over from the basin, where he was scrubbing his hands. 'Frank!' His face lit up and he hurried over, drying his hands. 'What the dickens are you doing here?'

Herbert was a small alert-looking man of forty with ginger hair parted along the left side. His close-cut beard was redder still, though now flecked white at the chin. He was a first-rate surgeon and popular with the theatre staff and nurses, but not in a way that would worry his wife.

We shook hands enthusiastically and then he gripped me by my shoulders, quickly looking me up and down. His restless light eyes roamed over me, appraising me as was his wont. 'Well,' he pronounced at last. 'I'm pleased to see there's been no substantive disimprovement since I last stitched you up, except for that eye –' He peered at the shiner and then folded back my hair to look at the bump on my scalp, in a way that was apt to remind you of a vet inspecting cattle at an agricultural show. 'You've had at least two proper knocks on the head in the last day or so. In the wars again eh, Frank?'

We sat down and Herbert poured a pair of highly diluted whiskies, something I knew that he lived on, more or less, along with tea. I counted eight different pipes in various stands and brackets, lined up along the front of his desk and the shelves, which were otherwise loaded with medical volumes. I took out my pipe and filled it. He smiled.

'You've still got Achilles.'

'I'll never part with it,' I said as plumes of smoke emerged from the bowl. Herbert had given me the Hornbeam pipe while I was recovering in the hospital – because of my strength, so he said, and had named it Achilles, after the Greek hero of the Trojan war. This was after I had lost my pipe, along with so much else, on the battlefield. He picked up his pipe of choice: an ornate white pottery meerschaum cast in the head of Neptune, with curling beard and wild eyes.

'How's the leg?' he asked, as he lit his pipe and flicked the match into the bin.

'I get occasional pain – but it's about eighty per cent strength, maybe more. Pretty good, thank you.'

He grinned, 'We must have done a better job than I thought.'

He puffed on his pipe and watched me a moment longer.

'All right, Frank. So what brings you to France and how on earth did you get the ruddy great shiner? I dare say they're not unrelated…'

I explained what I was about and told him everything he needed to know about the case to serve my needs. 'I have some photographs,' I said, taking out the prints I wanted him to see. 'I was hoping you would look at the wounds for me and tell me what you think… if there is any commonality, for instance?'

He examined the photographs of Marie-Louise first, head bowed close, magnifying glass held an inch or two from the image. Over his right shoulder, through the window, I could see into a large quad in which injured soldiers relaxed in deck chairs smoking and socialising. Others hobbled about, as one group was trying to play French cricket with only limited success. Herbert's breathing changed.

'It's hard to say from the image,' he announced. 'As you probably know the laceration severed the common carotid artery and her jugular, so your killer was exceptionally thorough or just lucky.' He looked up at me, 'Cutting either blood vessel would do the job more than adequately. It's very hard to stem the bleeding in either case and she would certainly be dead within minutes. It was crudely done but highly effective.' He took another look and shook his head. 'More than that I couldn't tell you, I'm afraid, but there will have been a lot of blood. Buckets of the stuff. A right mess.'

He turned his attention to the shots of Fabienne Thomas from the Hotel du Nord. After several minutes, Herbert presented his conclusions.

'You see this –' He pointed with his little finger to the starting point of the cut on the neck. The photographer had placed a ruler by the incision to show scale. 'This is where the cut starts where the line is faint, where the tip of the knife takes the flesh and then bites properly, deepening and darkening in colour. You see? This is telling: the cut isn't quite straight – it doesn't cross the neck at ninety degrees, as one might expect. Instead it starts up high and then it continues down to the left, before turning sharply and rising up with the depth of the incision shallowing. So in other words the cut describes an arc, one that ends on the left as you look her. It means that this injury was made from right to left.'

'So the killer is left-handed?'

'Exactly. Moreover, if he's tried it the other way he'll have ended up in a buggers' muddle because he would have had his other hand over her mouth. You can see the bruising starting to show, there.'

'That's assuming she was murdered where we found her, but there was no blood anywhere else in the room.'

'Which means you can assume you've got a left-handed killer, or a killer capable of using his left hand. It's also worth considering that it actually takes rather a lot of pressure to inflict this wound. I can't tell from the pictures but given the swelling at her neck it's certainly very deep, something both wounds have in common.' His expression changed as another thought struck him. It took a moment to form in his mind.

'Speaking from a surgical point of view, I ought to say – and forgive me if I'm stating the blindingly obvious Frank, but you don't inflict this precise type of wound by accident. This was very deliberate.' He looked over. 'You don't just make this cut, Frank. You *know* it. You feel every ridge and pinnacle of the cartilage and bone and the tissue as the blade does its work. It's a hideously intimate way to kill someone.'

'Do you think it would require surgical skill?'

He dismissed the idea with a shake of the head.

'I've seen worse incisions in theatre. No, I wouldn't say this was a cause to suspect a medical man, not that I'd rule them out, of course.'

'What about the knife?'

'H'm.' This question prompted him to gather up the magnifying glass and peer down at the pictures again. 'Well, at a push I'd say it was a knife with a curved tip, like a common or garden carving knife. You can tell by the way that cut starts in such a faint ... it takes an inch to bite, as the blade takes hold. You see?'

'And what of Marie-Louise? Does that look like the same, potentially, left-handed, killer?'

Herbert shrugged. 'Hard to say from the photographs. There's certainly a strong similarity of course in the choice and location of the injuries so I think it's a high certainty. And let's hope so, eh? Otherwise you've got two maniacs on your hands.'

In the quad behind Herbert's head, I noticed the soldiers start rising obediently from their deckchairs. A visitor had arrived. Even at this distance I could see from the gold braid on the peak of his cap and the red collar flashes that it was a senior officer. There was a taller, broader younger officer with him. Herbert saw me look and glanced over.

He swore quietly. 'It's the infernal General Risborough and his odious underling, Major Webster. Back to terrorise the men with a morale-raising visit. It really doesn't do them good – after all most of them are in here precisely because of men like him.' Herbert frowned down at his desk calendar and sighed, 'he usually comes on Monday.' He slotted his pipe in the rack and got to his feet. 'Apologies, Frank, you'll have to excuse me.' He reached for his service cap and stethoscope. 'I'd better do the traditional obsequies. Generals do love being grovelled to.'

I took my leave and returned to the Crossley. We drove east, in the direction of Calonne-sur-la-Lys. The route took us along the Canal d'Aire, which ran due east through empty fields to La Bassée and once again right bang in the direction of German territory. The sun had come out and offered a small compensation against the biting wind. There was little traffic: once a motorcycle passed us but that was it apart from the occasional farm cart. A little later we overtook one of these, laden with straw, and took the opportunity to confirm our precise location with the driver.

At the crossroads approximately two miles beyond the village, we took a left turn and drove through the hamlet of Riez du Vinage. Here, through the trees on the right, I got my first glimpse of the substantial farmstead that I supposed, from Catouillart's description, belonged to the Robecq family. The broad-fronted stone house was shielded from the road by an arrangement of tall Douglas firs. A little distance off, a string of scruffy out-buildings corroborated what the Frenchman had told me about the setting and sure enough these led to several barns and a larger factory-like structure, from which iron girders with hooks and pulleys protruded, as well as several chimneys, each releasing twists of smoke. Based on the stern warnings I had received from the Eagle and Catouillart, I thought it wise to do some research before coming face-to-face with Robecq.

We stopped a distance off and I instructed Greenlaw to return for me in two hours.

'What happens if you don't come back?' he asked as I headed through the shrubbery at a discreet, limping jog.

Good question; one I knew there was no decent answer to. I followed the hedgerow along a rutted earthen lane that spurred off the main road towards the farm buildings. After several hundred yards, with no one in sight, I crossed the yard towards the side of the largest of the structures, the one billowing smoke from its chimney stacks.

Suddenly there was the rush and snap of chains – and an eruption of growls and savage barking. Beyond wire mesh, a pack of muscular white dogs thrashed ferociously at me, their powerful bodies snatching at their chains and their paws throwing up dirt. I exhaled with relief and headed for the side entrance.

The metal door scraped open against the concrete floor, leading in to a large industrial space, dominated by a broad circular installation, which was encompassed within a raised wall, like a large public fountain. From its centre was a long arm which would clearly be tethered to a horse or donkey and would be used to roll a circular stone that it was connected to. It was a press, presumably for cider, which was consistent with the fragrant fug of fermentation in the air. Outside the dogs had fallen silent and I wondered if anyone had heard them. At the far end of the room tall presses and racks containing crates of bottles lined the wall. The labels showed the Madonna and Christ child with the legend, 'The Lord's Comforter'.

Chambord was a cider man, I recalled. In the next room, there were packing cases printed with the same religious motif. I lifted off the case and parted the straw; this time instead of bottles there were slender bricks in thick foil, like army rations. I tore one of these open and saw its contents, a dark brown, almost black, sticky substance. I gave it a sniff, and that mild acidic, vinegary odour confirmed it was opium, which it undoubtedly resembled. I slid this back in the box and closed the lid. I'd seen enough of the stuff in East Africa to last a lifetime. So that was Robecq's game.

My thoughts were interrupted by the grinding sound of metal on concrete. I turned. It was the door I had come in by. Next there was an exited yelp and scuttle of paws. I stepped nimbly to the door nearest to me and tried it. Locked. The sound of scurrying paws grew louder. There was no other way out. I seized a broom handle, holding it ready like a bat.

Scanning the floors around me – my back to the wall – I weight up an escape route. I had but seconds before they'd find me. There had to be a way out. The scrape and skid of the dogs' paws grew louder...

Then I saw it. *There*, a slim doorway, concealed behind a cabinet – I broke into a run, not caring how much noise my footsteps made. Behind me I heard the rush of paws and the squeal of canine delight. They'd seen me.

I heard a deep growl and looked back, just as a dog hurled itself at me – a white blur against the grey concrete floor. I lashed out – the broom connecting like a blunt lance – and the dog rolled to one side, whining. A second dog sprang forward, its jaws snatching the broom from my hands. A third flew at me, clamping itself to my right shin. I went down, a searing pain shooting through the leg. Another dog – its jaws agape – was charging, its crazed eyes fixed on me...

A loud guttural shout called the dogs off me. I was then hoisted up by a pair of burly farm hands. The taller and broader of the two braced my arms while the second tied my wrists with a coarse rope. He then searched my clothes methodically and along with my matches, anything that could be improvised into a weapon, such as my fountain pen, was turned out and tossed on the floor. The five dogs, meanwhile, sat in an obedient row, looking pleased and licking their gums. Neither man spoke as I was led out of the factory, limping and leaving bloody marks, into the muddy yard. Here there was a covered van, its engine running. The doors were yanked open and I was bundled in head first, landing in hay and manure. My feet were pushed in after me and the doors slammed shut and bolted on the outside.

We set off, the van bumping along what I imagined to be a pothole littered lane. I was bounced around the back with the straw and excrement as my mind contemplated what was to become of me. After a mercifully short drive we stopped, and I heard the Frenchmen get out, slamming the doors after them. I waited in silence but nothing happened; then I heard footsteps and the doors of cab opened and shut and the engine started up. We bounced along some more, then the noise of the tyres changed as, I guessed, gravel gave way to grass. The little van began to undulate and I imagined that we were crossing a field.

When we stopped again the men got out and then held a conference in low voices outside. The rear door then swept open and I was dragged out – and dropped on my feet. Squinting at the daylight, I saw a wooden hut, rather like you might find in a large suburban garden, but this was in a grassy opening surrounded by nothing but trees. Immediately behind the hut rose a tree-coated hillside, making it all the more isolated. In the other direction I could see no other buildings, just the terrain falling away, with trees on the far side of the small clearing in which we were parked and the tracks formed by the wheels of the van in the grass. If nowhere had a middle, this was it. My captors, watching me take all this in, broke into an unappealing chuckle.

The bigger of the two shoved me towards the wooden shed and I was led inside. It was immediately dark, almost pitch black, saving for narrow beams of daylight that sprang like leaks in a boat's hull through the small gaps between the stout timbers. There was movement within the thick layer of straw covering the ground: then in the corner, I saw the brooding mass of a large sow. Her piglets darted about the hut, squealing in the gloom and occasionally visible in the shafts of light from the spaces between the timbers. A heavy brace was levered out of place on the far wall and an interior door opened. We halted as a torch was lit. I was shoved towards the inner doorway. This was going to get worse before it got better.

CUT AND RUN

We entered a cold tunnel that clearly ran straight into the hillside. The soil hardened underfoot becoming rock and a cool, fresh wet sweetness scented the air, as damp timbers were replaced by granite and trickling water. Behind me the door to the hut was closed. I swallowed. The man next to me, the smaller of the two, was strongly built with a neck like a bull elephant's trunk and eyes too small for his head. He grinned at me.

A vindictive slap over the back of the head prompted me to bend down, following the torch-bearer in front, as the ceiling lowered. In the flickering patches of light, I glimpsed rotted pit props lying against the walls, and here and there piles of stone spoil showed where the sides or ceiling had given way. It was an old miners' path. After some thirty feet, we went through a doorway and the ceiling suddenly rose up, so that we were now in what was essentially a cave with a low ceiling. The bull elephant kept hold of me while the other lit more torches, these set in mounts on the walls. The light showed a bolted wooden chest, like a sea chest or blanket box, in the middle of the cave and a stout chair which I saw was fitted with leather restraining straps on its arms and legs. And that's where I was headed, plainly. Within a minute they had pressed me into the chair and strapped my ankles and wrists tightly to it. Blood was seeping through the shredded fabric of my right trouser leg where the dog had bitten me, but that might be the least of my problems. Over the men's thickset shoulders I saw words and images scrawled along the walls. In the flickering light, the words appeared in fragments. 'Death awaits you,' declared one. The men, noticing me see the words, exchanged a grin.

The door opened and I after a second I realised that the newcomer was Bernard Robecq – that's if Catouillart's description was correct. Two scars ran down his otherwise handsome face, almost parallel, beginning at his hairline before petering out either side of his chin. His complexion was darker than what was typical among the pale northern French farming stock I had seen. It was almost reddish, like the sun-bleached mountains of Province. He might have been fifty; his wiry hair was short, dark and thick. He stopped in front of me, took in the bloodied shin with evident satisfaction, and introduced himself.

'I take it you know who I am?'

I nodded.

'Good. Well I know who you are. What I don't know is why you trespassing on my property. Explain yourself.'

'I was trying to find you.'

'Were you know? When there's a perfectly good front door you could have knocked at.'

'I didn't think you were in.'

A kind of smile spread across Robecq's lips, one that betrayed a sense of pleasure at my response, though I did not know why. Or not yet, anyway. Then I saw his mouth tense – and he grunted with effort. Immediately, his fist flew at me, catching my jaw hard. A tooth splintered towards the back of my mouth and the impact threw me sideways, yanking at the straps that held me fast to the chair. I spat blood and rolled my jaw. My mouth was full of a mulch of grainy shards of tooth, gum and blood. I saw now that the Frenchman's fingers were closed around a knuckle-duster; he wiped it on his trouser leg. 'I won't have the British Army spying on my affairs, Champion,' he hissed.

I raised myself up and looked back towards him, my tongue playing on the sharp stump of my molar. He leaned in, 'I'm surprised you didn't take the hint last night.'

His voice rose with effort and his fist blurred towards me, stinging against my face and catching my cheekbone. I was thrown back, but then slumped forward, breathing hard, a tendril of phlegm hanging from my gaping mouth. I saw rapid droplets of blood pepper the floor between my feet and start to form a small puddle. My cheek was livid. I saw Robecq shift his weight on his feet.

'Now tell me Champion, why were you snooping around the farm? Who sent you?'

I swallowed down some blood, 'I came to speak to you about the Blue Lamp, Robecq, about the dead women. I need your help to find their killer.'

'And what help were you hoping to find in my cider factory?'

'I was looking for *you*,' I repeated. 'I'm also searching for another woman from the Blue Lamp – Suzette Emmolet. You must know her.'

Robecq's face stiffened and I saw him swallow. That had taken him off-guard somehow. He licked his lips.

'I know you've been to visit the Eagle,' he said. 'I know you've been stirring up half of Béthune to get the Blue Lamp closed. So tell me who told you to come here? Was it the Eagle?'

I shook my head...

The knuckle-duster slashed across my face, tearing at the cut on my cheek. For several seconds he waited as he recovered, my head bowed, more droplets of blood gathering on the stony floor.

'Who was it Champion? If it wasn't the Eagle, perhaps it was one of the bitches at the Blue Lamp? No?'

I looked up at the hard face and realised that this was not going to end unless I gave him something.

Robecq's eyes narrowed.

'Who sent you?'

'Damn you –' my voice cracked with anger. I coughed on some of my own blood and spat it out, 'I came here to ask you about the murdered women and the missing girl, Robecq – and that's the truth!'

'Don't lie to me!'

He was glaring with fury and that knuckle-duster twitched restlessly. Unfortunately, in the absence of the truth, I could think of nothing else to say. 'I came here to see if you could help me. I'm trying to find Suzette Emmolet. You must know of her. She's one of your girls ... for God's sake!'

The fist holding the knuckle duster tightened and I saw his eyes widen – and that same, joyless flat smile that I had seen before his first blow returned to his face. He took a step back and signalled to his men. They quickly doused the torches, until just one remained, which was passed to Robecq who waited for them at the door.

'Very well, Champion. We shall leave you to your secrets. When I come back I expect you to tell me everything.'

The door slammed shut, plunging the cave into darkness...

Chapter Fourteen

The only thing visible at first was a thin strip of light from under door. I heard the distinctive sound of a heavy beam being secured across it on the outside, then this invaluable luminous strip began to dim until the light had faded so much that I realised it was no longer there at all. In fact, it was simply an image in my mind, a memory. Then the sounds of the footsteps and voices of my captors faded, ending with the metallic 'clunk' of a distant lock being turned. I realised that the only sound I could hear was my own rapid, light breathing. I held my breath for a moment, proving the point to myself. There was absolutely nothing.

I pulled my wrists at the leather bonds – they were fast to the arms of the solid wooden chair and even they made no sound. My breathing was anything but. It was fast and vocal like an animal on the run. My chest was stretching with every breath I took.

I had to stay calm, I told myself. I swallowed, and realised my chest was heaving. *I needed to be completely calm.* A surge of electricity tensed my muscles, sending a shudder through me, like the urgent pitter-patter of rain. I caught my breath. I was panicking. Another spasm of tension convulsed me. I gritted my teeth and exhaled as the surge abated.

I took a very deep breath and tried to focus on my eyes. Surely I could see something out there – that wooden chest for instance? I knew where it was. I had seen it. Perhaps I could imagine it if I tried hard enough. This cave, after all, was not an infinite void; it was barely fifteen feet across. But where was the wall? Where was the chest? Where was the floor? Where, in point of fact, were my hands?

My tongue gingerly probed the sharp, broken side of the tooth inside my mouth, which somehow had not exposed a nerve. That was something to be grateful for. After all, if my last hours were to be spent in this cave, then passing them without a painfully exposed nerve in a tooth would make it all the more bearable. I laughed at the inane crassness of that thought. Was I becoming hysterical?

I focused on taking long deep breaths, and then my mind turned to Elizabeth.

It shouldn't do this. It should focus on the matter in hand, but I wondered where she was and what she was doing. Right now at this very instant? I felt the sunshine on my face and saw her riding through her father's fields of wheat on that elegant mare of hers. Was she inspecting crops or going to see to the cattle? In the distance was the low blue plateau of Nairobi to the north and in the far south the distant snow-capped peak of Kilimanjaro. Closer, beyond Elizabeth in mid-gallop, there is a party of tall, noble-looking Masai going about their business framed by the lush green woodlands beyond. And below, is the benign chirrup of cicadas, Africa's heartbeat. And then of course, there were the hooves of her horse ploughing through the dusty red soil, followed by its snort, and finally, her voice, hailing me, in that charmed sing-song voice of hers, 'Why Francis, what the dickens are you doing here?'

Had we world enough and time. I sighed. She was married now, or ought to be, and probably had a family. At least I hoped so. It's what she wanted, just not with me. I took a deep breath and then felt the air leaving me... Perhaps I didn't need to get out of this cave, after all? Perhaps I should stay here and let nature take its course. I emitted a deep sigh and felt myself start to give in to self-pity.

It matched the darkness in its way. I shut my eyes and steadied my breathing, just aware of the blood pumping in my temples and nothing else.

Presently, a sense of resolution returned. Don't ask me how, but despair can be boring.

I opened my eyes to confront the inky blackness surrounding me. Could I see anything? No, the world around was a black depthless fog. What about my feet? Surely I could see them? I wiggled my toes optimistically, shifting them, hoping that the movement of my shoes might disturb the black void. But it didn't. Truth was I couldn't even see my own hands – or even my lap. I was blind. I felt the droplets start to fall again, the pitter-patter of rain on my heart. Logically, my situation was almost certainly beyond hope.

I jammed my feet to the ground and braced my body against the bonds, straining hard. I imagined myself trying to lift one of the bronze lions on Trafalgar Square and heaved with all my might. The chair was strongly built, but I had seen it was secured only by a pair of bolts at the front legs, albeit they were substantial looking. I pressed forward – lifting the lion with everything I had – and the rear two feet of the chair lifted. Next I pushed backwards with my shoulders and stamped down with the balls of my feet, groaning with effort. I then went forwards again, straining everything. I would get the damned lion off the ground if it was the last thing I did. I counted to ten.

I kept going back and forth until my neck ached and my shoulders cried out with each heave. I kept at it until my feet were sore against the floor, and then some. I just kept going, straining my whole carcass, till my face burned with the blood pounding around my head...

Suddenly the bolt by my right foot yielded and I pitched forward – I threw my weight to my right just in time to stop myself head-butting the stone floor. I rolled with the chair onto its side and lay there in the dark, panting hard. Gradually, I controlled my breathing as the question of what to do now framed itself in my mind. I was still attached to the chair, in the pitch black and locked cave deep in a mountain in the middle of nowhere ... with a psychotic Frenchman due to return at any moment.

But the first step had been made.

I craned my head forward as far as it would go, then pushed it some more. From here I could just smell the leather of the strap that trapped my right wrist. I groaned in pain as I strained my mouth, pushing my jaws towards it as far as it could go without snapping the tendons. I spat on it and pecked at it with painful lunges to get my teeth into it. It was no good. After several minutes I sat back up, straightened my aching neck and cursed. The strap was just too far away. Damn that Robecq. He had clearly given some thought with the design. I shrank back and took several breaths. There had to be a way...

The wooden chest. It was padlocked, but the lock was not a substantial affair. Rather, it was the sort of lock one might purchase only to regret later when the contents one valued had been stolen. I needed to find the box. If it could be opened it might contain something to assist me.

I advanced blindly on my hands and knees in a slow syncopated shuffle. I could only hope that I was going in the right direction and that part of me or the heavy chair I was attached to would collide with it. After about a dozen short paces, beetling forwards over the cold, hard ground, the crown of my head connected firmly with the wooden chest.

With some effort, I positioned myself sideways to the front of the box, parallel to the lock. I then insinuated the tip of the end of its metal latch between the leather strap of the binding and my right wrist. It went in on the second try. Then I twisted my wrist against the metal. As I did so, I attempted to get to my feet, thereby taking the weight of the chest on the binding – and my wrist, of course. The strap cut sharply into my arm but I held it as long as I could. Gritting my teeth and heaved, feeling the leather slice into my skin as the wooden chest lifted off the ground. The pain was severe, but I kept going and levering my arm as much as I could. My growl became a roar and then the strap gave way.

I tore my hand free, panting in pain.

For a moment I lay there, mouth clamped shut, gripping my raw right wrist in my tied left hand, tightly yet soothingly. The pulse charged through my arm like my blood vessels were going to burst. The grip numbed the agony and, with luck, would stem the bleeding that was leaving my wrist tacky to touch. After a minute the agony began to abate and I pressed on, reminding myself that Robecq could return at any moment.

I quickly unbuckled the remaining restraints and then smashed the lock with the chair. The padlock itself did not give in, instead the metal latch it was connected to sheared off, and scattered across the floor. Victorious, I threw back the hinged lid of the chest and dived inside, feeling the grain of the wood under my fingertips and the damp smell of the timber. Moving methodically from left to right, my hand bumped into something solid, wrapped in a thick cotton cloth. It was hard, dense and cold feeling to touch. It might be a tool of some sort... I unwrapped the parcel eagerly feeling along the narrow span of whatever was inside. Just then a sickening, putrid smell caught the back of my throat and I realised what it was. It was a hand and those narrowings were fingers. I dropped it, retching.

It was a hand. Yes. I exhaled and willed myself to return to it. There was the hard, swollen joint – knuckles; the first lower quarters of a thumb, then I found the nail. I felt each finger in turn. By the proportions, the softness of the fingertips and condition of the nails, it was likely the hand of a woman or perhaps a boy. There was a ring – a simple band – on the middle finger, and then there was something unexpected. The third finger was much shorter than the others, terminating, just after the middle joint, with smooth ending, indicating perhaps that its severing was long past and nothing to do with however this body part had ended up in this box.

Which was right and I suddenly remembered what the Eagle had told me. Suzette Emmolet was missing half of her third finger. So if that answered the first question: whose hand and forearm did this belong to, the next question was, where was the rest of her?

I must have laid there contemplating all this for some minutes, not quite sure what to do. The box had yielded nothing that would help me escape, but it had given me a significant clue. My captors had not been gone long, perhaps half an hour or more, I could not be certain. I checked my watch: the large fluorescent numerals told me it was midday, or rather had been before it stopped. I could not know how much longer that I would be left in here undisturbed. All I had in my favour for when they did return was the element of surprise but I would still be out-numbered.

I wrapped the hand back up and put it in my overcoat pocket.

Next, arms outstretched, I approached the wall and began to search for one of the iron torch brackets I had seen earlier. One of these might make a useful weapon and help me escape. I located one quickly but it was well-attached to the wall and would not come off. Only after hanging from it and using my bodyweight and what strength that remained to lever it, did I manage to prise it off.

I found my way back the chest and then dragged it to the wall, which I then followed until I reached the door. It was stoutly made of timber planks and I remembered that it opened inwards. But at this stage I could think of nothing more clever than brute force...

I took the iron torch mount and stabbed the spiked end of it into the wooden door. It bounced off. I cursed and drove it against it again. Still it wouldn't take, but desperation is a wonderful motivator, and eventually I fixed it with the help of the heel of my boot. I then got the wooden chest and manhandled the beastly thing so that it was sandwiched between the end of the iron mount and my sternum. It was not a complex system that I had devised and I knew that it would take another timely application of force – and good fortune – to come off. What's more, whether or not it worked, I knew it would hurt.

I took a few preparatory steps back, drew a deep breath – and charged. The box struck the spike hard. I dropped the box and staggered backwards, clutching my chest, asphyxiated by the agonising pain. Christ alive... I wasn't doing that again.

What's more, the door remained remarkably unscathed and rock solid. All I had succeeded though in burying the torch mount more fully and almost shattering my sternum. Now it was entirely wedged in so I couldn't even use it as weapon if Robecq and his men returned. I swallowed hard. I had no alternatives but to keep trying.

I took off my overcoat, folded it up and bunched between my body and the wooden chest to act as a crude cushion. Then I got the box in position, took a several steps – more than before – and, with a roar, sprang forwards, giving it everything. I heard the sound of splintering timber and the box and I burst through the cleaving door panels, tumbling into the passageway.

Lying among the shattered timbers, I permitted myself a moment of delicious triumph, crying though I was in agony as the pain seared through my sternum. It felt like my heart was being sick. Crouching down on all fours, the blood pumping hard through me,

I caught my breath back at last and then scampered along the tunnel, ducking down, hands outstretched blindly, until I reached the next door. This was locked like the first and also strong. Then I remembered the loose pit props that I had seen on my way in. After a few swift blows with one of these at the hinges of the door, it gave way, and I took great pleasure in kicking it out into the damp, timbered shed and praying that none of Robecq's men were close enough to hear.

Now the dim shards of light I had seen earlier were dazzling beams.

I heard a snarl. It was the sow, and then the piglets squealed and started to scramble around me, rustling the straw and sending clumps of it into the air. The great pig grunted – a challenge – and she stamped her hooves against the ground beneath. I have never heard a pig scrape the ground with its hoof but that was what it was. Plainly it was the prelude to attack.

Snatching up my pit prop, I brandished it half-blindly in a low fierce arc around me. The sow growled from the shadows. 'Get back you bitch,' I hissed, remembering her large teeth.

There came a shout from outside, and the metallic sound of a bolt action rifle being cocked. I hopped backwards, beside the door, and lifted the prop high above my head, ready to strike. A second voice joined in, which I recognised as belonging to the bull elephant. The two of them were now on the other side of door, talking in low voices. The sow, meanwhile, snarled at me from the corner. One solid bite from those teeth in the leg and I would lame for life. I braced myself.

The lock snapped and the door flung open on the end of a boot. A blinding shaft of light strobed through the interior.

'Come out!' cried the first French voice, belonging to the bigger man.

I stayed perfectly still.

There was a pause – and then the men conferred. It appeared they weren't now positive that anyone was there after all. Was it just the damned pigs? They were always crashing about, weren't they? I bent down on my haunches – aware of the orthopaedic creak of my knees – and bowed my head to the floor, allowing myself to exhale.

Just then, the sow snorted angrily – and the straw began to fly apart before me. She was coming. Her massive bulk flashed ghostly white ... and she bowled straight by me, out through the open door to freedom.

There was a cry from the Frenchmen and a gunshot boomed out – followed by a thud as the bullet made contact with something weighty. Through a crack in the timbers I saw the sow halt, mid-sprint and collapse all at once to the ground. There was a moment of silence.

'Ah... shit.' The bigger of the two men lowered his rifle.

'What the fuck did you do that for?' cried the bull elephant. 'It's the chief's prize pig.'

'I know that, moron –'

'Moron? You're the fucking moron, you just shot the chief's prize pig. You know what he'll do to us…'

The shooter silenced him with a raised hand. Then I heard it, the pained breathing of the sow, low and hoarse like someone unevenly pushing grain through a cheese-grater.

'She's not dead,' said the second man, hope coming to his voice.

'I know that,' the shooter cursed, shouldering his rifle.

I heard the bolt go back – there was the metallic tinkle of the spent cartridge being spilled – and then he snapped a fresh round back into the chamber. There was a brief, efficient pause, filled by the uneven wheezing of the great sow.

'Wa-wa-what are you doing?' panicked the bull elephant. 'She's not–'

A second shot rang out.

And now the straw in the shed began to jump around me as the piglets started to panic. With shrill cries the army of porcine young sprinted past, their shrill notes drowned out by the agonised wailing of the sow that was still not dead yet.

I peeked through the slats just in time to see the smaller guard scurrying in the distance after the piglets. The other stood over the stricken sow, its vast belly pumping back and forth. He reloaded and took aim.

As the third shot rang out I slipped into the cover of the trees and scrambled up the hill away from the cave. I stopped just once to look back. The unfortunate sentries were still charging after the renegade piglets.

It was getting dark by the time I reached the road that led directly into Les Chopettes and the rendezvous point that I had arranged with Greenlaw. I was far later, but I also knew that I could trust Greenlaw.

Alas, neither he nor the Crossley were anywhere to be seen, but then, I told myself, nor should they be. But then in the gloomy shadows of the trees I saw the burning end of a skinny hand-rolled cigarette and the ghost of smile appeared in the shadows.

'Greenlaw,' I sighed, taking his hand. 'Are you a sight for sore eyes.'

Chapter Fifteen

My friend, Captain Herbert Macmillan, was talking to one of the senior sisters when we arrived at his office. The sight of me concluded their conference, to the evident displeasure of the nurse, who viewed me coldly and flicked her crimson cape at me as she walked out.

Macmillan sighed, but whether at the sight of me or the sister, I couldn't be sure. 'What have you done with yourself now, Champion?' he demanded. He appealed to Greenlaw. 'Look at this. I've not laid eyes on this man in eight months and then I see him twice within the space of hours and on his return he looks like he's gone six rounds with a prize fighter.' He addressed me, 'You – sit.' He took out a plain oak pipe and pressed it into my mouth. 'Have a puff of that and tell me what you've been up to, while I'll get a needle and thread to sew up your face.' He glanced sourly over at Greenlaw. 'Ruddy socialists.'

I gave a brief outline as Herbert cleaned by cuts and dabbed iodine on them in preparation for stitching. 'Hold steady if you don't mind Frank –' I felt the needle prick and saw him wink at Greenlaw. 'You'll look even more like a pirate after this.'

After his medical attentions, we both smoked a pipe and then I showed him the limb I had found in the cave. It was the first time I had seen it and I shouldn't have been surprised by its grey, pasty colour, not unlike a severely over the hill piece of beef.

Herbert removed his pipe, stood it in the rack and took out his magnifying glass.

He turned the grisly artefact over carefully, handling it with a pair of stainless steel tongs, before examining the palm of the hand closely with the magnifying glass. I looked over, Greenlaw watched closely, a rolled up cigarette burning close to his fingers. He was doing very well. Herbert set down the glass and his eyes went to mine, and then back to the hand. He cleared his throat in a businesslike manner.

'A woman's hand,' he pronounced. 'Nearer twenty than thirty, I'd say. Certainly not a manual worker, that's clear as daylight.

That said, she's plainly been the victim of an accident,' he indicated the shortened third finger, 'but that was a long time ago and there is actually very little scarring to do with that, except for that small cartilaginous protrusion here, so I suspect it was in childhood. My guess would be something extremely sharp and powerful, like a cutting machine of some sort, from which one can deduce that perhaps she grew up in a setting where machines were commonplace, which around here would make her farming or peasant stock or perhaps the offspring of a factory worker.' He gave an audible intake of breath. 'Similarly I would say that the hand had been severed well above the wrist by an extremely sharp implement – that much is fairly obvious from the crisp split of the bones. If I had to guess I'd say it was, well,' he hesitated, 'I would say that it was something like an axe or a sword. But all of that I'm sure you know.' He looked up at me. 'How did I do?'

'*Valedore*,' I said. He smiled back. 'I understand she lost her finger in a threshing device of some sort.'

'Good,' he said, smiling.

'When do you think it was cut off?'

Herbert pressed the tip of the metal spatula to the fleshy parts of the hand – against the bump of the palm, and the swellings of the insides of the fingers between the joints. He exhaled thoughtfully.

'It's not really my territory –' His mouth formed a thoughtful semi-circle. 'I'd be guessing. I'm sure you know they dig bodies up on the sides of mountains that have been there for twenty years and look as fresh as someone dozing on the number twenty-eight bus. It all depends.'

He cleared his throat, scooped up the spatula and tongs and went to the basin, where he proceeded to scrub the implements vigorously under the hot tap before submerging them in surgical spirits.

'The best I can say, Frank, is that this hand was severed within the last month.' He looked over. 'It's really a case of common sense. I would say it's been in that box of yours for at least a week, so,' he was now scrubbing his hands with a brush, making sure to clean every surface of his fingers and between the knuckles. 'So as it's the twenty-first today, that means – it was snipped off between around the fifteenth or twenty-seventh of February.'

'And what about her?'

'What about her indeed? Well there's a high probability that she will have died either during or because of its removal due to blood loss or indeed afterwards due to infection, assuming as we can that proper medical attention was denied her.'

My mind went to the cave and wondered if it had all happened in there.

'Are you certain that she was alive when it was removed?'

'No idea, I'm afraid. I assumed so, but –' He looked down at the hand with fresh distaste. 'You know, I really don't know. A pathologist would know, probably.' He finished drying his hands and picked up his meerschaum pipe. 'But I'll tell you this, if she was dead before this was cut off, it will have spared her a great deal of pain.'

We drove straight to the Blue Lamp where I found Celine mopping the floor of the main salon and no sign of Lefebvre. Taking her to the small study, I asked her to identify the hand, which she recognised as being that of Suzette Emmolet, even confirming the simple silver ring, too. Celine also confirmed that Suzette's last day at the Blue Lamp was the twenty-ninth of February, which fitted nicely with Herbert's estimation. I then left, but told her that I would be returning to question the other women over Suzette's departure later on.

First I was mindful of a certain task required of me in respect of Suzette Emmolet and a promise made. We headed across town and rapped at the door of the Red Lamp, which at this time of day was closed up. The murderous monk admitted us and led us through the enclosure which now resembled a women's campsite populated by females in various stages of undress. It smelled somewhat better than when I had visited on Monday night.

As we approached the Eagle's chamber we heard music.

The monk knocked and opened the door, but rather too quickly. Across the darkened room a woman faced us, bent over the long table, her generous breasts on show and around her gathered skirts. The Eagle – grim-faced and bare-chested – stood behind her, exerting himself and with each thrust, she cried in apparent pleasure and her commodious bosoms surged towards us with surprising elasticity. From somewhere a gramophone was playing Handel's *Messiah*, the choir building to the Alleluia chorus. The Eagle noted our arrival and didn't stop. Instead he shouted over the top of the music and beckoned us into the room.

Even Brother Christian appeared to view this with disquiet and he stood back, leaving me to enter. His nod told me I didn't have much choice.

'You got news?' barked the Eagle.

'Suzette Emmolet –'

His eyes locked on mine – and he halted. The woman's face relaxed...

'What about her?'

Another thrust. The woman gasped.

'I've found her hand.'

'Her hand? You sure, Hornbeam?'

As I nodded the choir reached full pitch. The Eagle pinioned the woman once more, she panted expansively and the Eagle's muscular arms swelled as he gripped her. She cried out again as he resumed, his pace quickening.

'Where?' he cried.

'Robecq.'

'What did I tell you? And the rest of her?'

I looked away...

'Hornbeam?'

I shouted out, 'No idea.'

He glared across the room at me – and clouted the back of the woman's head angrily.

'A one-handed whore's no good to man nor beast –' His face reddened. 'You'd better go and find the rest of her. Hadn't you?'

The Eagle abruptly bowed his head, showing us the sweat glistening on its crown and growled, like a strongman using all his might to lift a considerable weight. The muscles in his arms braced rigid. He froze. *The Messiah* continued.

CUT AND RUN

A split second later the owner of the breasts looked up as though peeking out of a doorway after some natural disaster and expertly extricated herself. She scampered from the chamber, holding her clothes together.

The Eagle did up his flies and pulled on a singlet vest. He strode over to the gramophone and lifted the stylus.

'So where was it, this hand?'

As I explained he put on a long brown leather waistcoat, fastened with a leather strap, which gave him the appearance of a medieval ploughman. Albeit one with a hideous tattoo of a bird of prey eating its young and a heretical tattoo of the Passion of Christ.

'They used to mine barium out there,' he explained when I'd finished. He poured himself a tumbler full of red wine and approached us, acknowledging Greenlaw with a terse nod. 'I heard that Robecq had some cabin up there, where he scares people.' The Eagle noticed my fresh injuries and smiled with satisfaction, 'I see the two of you have become acquainted.' He spotted my tattered trouser leg. 'I was right about Robecq, wasn't I?' He had another look at Greenlaw, giving him an up and down, and said, 'Come on, show me.'

I went to the table, and he stood there, mug of wine in hand, watching wordlessly as I unwrapped it. 'That's Suzette's,' he stated, without emotion.

He leaned in close and sniffed at it. Then he pressed it several times, like a chef judging a piece a sirloin on the griddle. Rare, dab, medium rare, dab, well done... 'Two weeks, I'd say, give or take.' The Eagle's large foxhound eyes sought mine out. 'It would be an axe, wood-splitter or machete of some sort that did that. A machete will get through most things. You'd be surprised.' He looked back down at the hand and shook his head. 'That's a fucking waste. The things she could do with that.'

Jesus twitched on the cross as his hand balled into a fist. Was he imagining what he would do to whoever had done this – presumably Robecq and presumably with a machete? The Eagle met my gaze.

'This girl was a fucking gold mine,' he stated.

I left that distasteful comment alone but I had questions of my own, which was the real reason I was here.

'Did Robecq do this because she wanted to come to the Red Lamp?'

'Who knows, Hornbeam? Perhaps he was protecting his business interests. Perhaps he took offence at what he considered to be her lack of loyalty. You'll have to ask him, if you've the guts.' He took in the injuries to my face, 'Or maybe you have already?'

'What can you tell me about Robecq's business interests?'

He exhaled.

'Varied. He flogs bootleg cider to whoever will buy it – the Germans included, I'm told – and legitimate cider to everyone else. He's got a couple of pawn brokers and an underground gambling establishment. He also does a bit of protection, but nothing worse than anyone else.' He sighed, 'As you know he's got the Blue Lamp, but that's really to stop someone else having it, I'd say. He's not really interested in pimping. More's the pity, that place could be a mint if it was run just so. But that's not the point because he can turn the Blue Lamp to his advantage when he needs to – you know, with special favours to the powerful. A beautiful and willing young woman like Suzette Emmolet or Marie-Louise Troyon can make you a very satisfactory return, but also give you a great deal of purchase. Yes,' he smiled unpleasantly, 'She opens her legs as well as doors for you.' He reviewed me, seeing my disapproval, his heavy eyelids closing and opening like the shutter of a camera on a long exposure. 'I sense there's something you haven't told me, Hornbeam?'

'There's opium in Robecq's cider factory.'

The Eagle nodded, hesitating. This was new information to him. 'That's interesting. I'm not surprised. He'll be broadening his horizons.' He tilted his head to one side and added placidly, 'Diversification is always very prudent in uncertain times.'

So it was. 'What about Chambord,' I asked. 'Do you know if he and Robecq have any business together?'

The Eagle arched an eyebrow at me. 'Are you in earnest, Hornbeam?' He shook his head at me. 'Course they do – not just apples, neither. Robecq is Chambord's uncle, by marriage. Oh yes, they're thick as thieves, which is precisely what both of them are in their separate ways.' The Eagle plucked up a book from the table and sat in the armchair. 'Now,' he said. 'Piss off, and take that thing with you. I've got work to do…'

Chapter Sixteen

I felt dirty, sullied, as I made my way from the Eagle's premises and into the last of the daylight. We strolled back to the centre of town under a dusty, speckled, tortoise-shell sky and entered the lodgings the back way, to reduce our chances of being observed. Plainly, Robecq would not be satisfied to have me running around after what had happened and it was anyone's guess to know how long it would be before he returned to the cave and discovered I was gone. If indeed he hadn't already.

For what little good it would do we went through the motions. I changed my room, aware that that would merely just slow down Robecq's efforts to get to me, the next time he tried. Kennedy, I discovered, was once again absent. Greenlaw fetched me some supper from the kitchen and I ate alone in my new room, overlooking the dark square, where a lamplighter was at work. I had a headache now and my body was bruised and tired. Greenlaw had fetched me a bottle of whisky from the bar and I sat Murray's Webley revolver within reach. I sipped diluted whisky and mulled the incidents of the day as well as the seemingly multitudinous threads of the case.

Where was Kennedy? What should I do next? I quietly self-medicated with another serving of whisky, this time not quite so diluted, and then there was a soft knock at the door. It did not sound like one of Robecq's men, arriving to finish their work off, but you could never tell. I gathered up the Webley, went to the door and unbolted it silently. Pulling it ajar, Celine peered in through the gap.

I slid the gun into my pocket and welcomed her in.

Even as I locked the door behind her, she made an announcement.

'I've come to tell you something,' she said, 'something I probably should have told you on Sunday.'

I poured her a mug of whisky, sat her in my armchair and drew over a chair for myself. There is often, I told myself, a moment in a case when something of the hidden truth begins to emerge, and I knew that this was it. She took a taste of her whisky, winced at it, and began.

'If you look at the Blue Lamp's ledger for Friday twenty-fifth of February, you'll notice that it is blank for Marie-Louise and Fabienne. It is blank also for Suzette.' Her eyes scanned my face with a guileless intensity, weighing me up, one last time. Her mouth bobbed to her whisky, drinking up some more courage, and then she came out with it.

'There was a party.'

'It wasn't logged...'

'Because they weren't paid for it. We only log *paid* work in the ledger.'

There was a clear emphasis in her statement, one reinforced by the uneasy shift of her eyes behind the thick lenses of her spectacles.

'But they *were* working, right?'

She nodded and bowed her forehead to her hands. I saw the silhouettes of her eyelashes flicking with each blink. 'All I know, Monsieur Champion, is that they went to a party...'

But it's never all anyone knows and over the course of the next half an hour, Celine told me more than I could have imagined. It was a small, exclusive party held at Monsieur Chambord's large yellow house on the park, she said. 'What I am going to tell you, Fabienne told me,' Celine added. 'She swore me to secrecy. The guests were British Army officers, some of them very important and older. One of them had a hand missing, she said, and instead he had a metal pincer. He was called 'Hooky', and he was a general. They were much older than the customers we get at the Blue Lamp. Chambord served champagne – and the girls and men mingled. Then as the night wore on, Fabienne said the atmosphere changed, "soured" was her word. She had been to parties at Chambord's house before, of course, but this time, when the moment came, the girls were not taken upstairs but, instead, led downstairs to the cellars. There they were put into two rooms –

one with Marie-Louise and Fabienne together. They were told to take off their outer clothing. They were then tied to either end of a long bench by a servant. Fabienne did not say more, other than that she was gagged and facing Marie-Louise, while Marie-Louise was blindfolded. It was dark and cold, she said, and the gentlemen soon arrived – in twos and threes. She heard loud male voices coming from the next room where Suzette was. They were enjoying themselves, she said.' Celine shook her head despairingly. 'Then after the first set of guests had finished with Fabienne and Marie-Louise, two more arrived and it began again. That's when Fabienne saw him.'

'Who?'

'Marie-Louise's father – General Troyon.'

'Are you sure?' I removed my pipe, 'How did she know he was her father?'

'Because she recognised him. She had seen Marie-Louise's family photograph beside her bed. But the general could not see Marie-Louise's face because she was turned away from him and because she was heavily blindfolded.'

My stomach turned.

'He had aged little since the photograph was taken, but he had the same eyes, the same piercing eyes as Marie-Louise. Fabienne tried to shout, to tell him but she was gagged. And when she tried to raise the alarm the men thought it was part of the fun so held onto her all the tighter. Poor Marie-Louise knew nothing, of course – until afterwards.'

A feeling of sickness rose up from deep inside me. Celine shook her head for the shame of it. I watched her take a drink and asked, 'What happened next?'

'The general finally registered Fabienne's protest. That's what made him stop, she said. He stepped back, she said, stared at Marie's naked body, and then went white as a sheet. Fabienne said he tore the blindfold from her, his hands shaking violently, from horror. Then he was in a rage. Poor Marie-Louise was beside herself. Chambord arrived and there was a mighty row, as you would expect.' Celine took a drink. 'Fabienne was sent away back upstairs and was sworn to secrecy. Marie-Louise was sent home immediately. I heard her being sick in her room and assumed she was drunk.'

I topped up Celine's mug and she continued.

'But the moment I saw Fabienne arrive I knew something was wrong – she was back earlier than she should have been and she had been crying. I didn't try to comfort her because she had never confided in me. Madame Lefebvre was furious at them for leaving early and demanded to know why. There was an argument. After that they did not talk for several days.'

And just over a fortnight later Marie-Louise was dead, and a little over three weeks to the day Fabienne was dead also. Along the way Suzette Emmolet would also go missing and was likely dead also.

'Who else knows about this?'

'No one, as far as I know. Marie-Louise would have told no one, not even Fabienne I would think, if she hadn't been there. Fabienne made me swear I would tell no one.'

'And Suzette?'

'I couldn't say. But if she'd ever seen the photograph and remembered it, then she may well have remembered him and put two and two together. But the girls seldom go into each other's rooms and she was not particularly friendly with Marie-Louise.' Celine shrugged despairingly. 'No one was. I had only had seen it myself because I do the cleaning.'

'And Lefebvre?'

Celine drained her whisky and shook her head.

So, Fabienne knew Marie-Louise's secret, and so did Chambord and Celine, and possibly Suzette if Fabienne had told her. Was General Troyon's unintended act a secret worth killing for? Quite possibly – if you had a public profile, a reputation to protect, or political ambitions. And he had all three. And what if someone had tried to blackmail him?

Chambord, possibly, could probably be trusted to remain silent, since he was implicated in it all, which helped provoke a notion of *esprit de corps*. He would be harder to eliminate in any case because he had a public position, but he also had that to protect so his silence could be counted upon. But people wouldn't ask questions – or were less inclined to – about a girl like Marie-Louise, Fabienne or indeed, Celine, if they went missing or turned up in park bandstands.

I refilled our drinks and asked, 'Was Fabienne good at keeping secrets?'

She looked down at her hands.

'Would she have told anyone? Who knows?'

'Well, she told you the whole story…'

Celine nodded sombrely.

'And what about Suzette? Was she a talker?'

Celine dismissed this with a shake of the head, 'Normally, yes. But in point of fact she never said anything about the party at all. If she did I never heard it. There's been no gossip about it at the Blue Lamp.'

That was something at least, for her sake.

'Does anyone else – apart from me – know that you know all this? You haven't told anyone, have you?'

Hesitantly, she shook her head.

'Good. Is there somewhere you can go? Could you go back to your family?'

Her small eyes looked at up me, fear in there. I could see she didn't want that.

'Whatever's happened in the past, they'll forgive you. That's what families do.' But, on the other hand, could she forgive them?

Either way Celine did not look convinced.

I told her about Fabienne's store of gold sovereigns.

'It's English gold,' I said. 'More than enough for you to get by on until you get yourself set up somewhere far away from here.' She looked undecided, her lip pursed doubtfully. 'Take my advice, Celine, disappear. Fill a small, inconspicuous bag with only essential items and go immediately to the railway station. Don't look like you're going anywhere and for heaven's sake don't tell a soul that you're leaving. *Just vanish*. You can see for yourself what's happened here – these are brutal people and you need to protect yourself because there's no earthly reason why it should stop now. You might be next.'

Slowly she lifted her face and her eyes took me in.

'Or you,' she said. From across the expanse of the medieval square we heard the bell from the tower begin to sound the hour.

She set her mug down, rose to her feet and moved to the door.

'Will you at least consider what I said?'

'I will,' she pronounced.

'Good luck then –'

I extended my hand and she shook it, like someone unaccustomed to the act. She started to open the door but then pushed it shut.

'Champion, there's something else you should know – 'something about Captain Kennedy.'

Kennedy? She registered the change in my expression with a small, confirmatory nod. My mind was already so full I had forgotten about the man who had got me involved in this mess in the first place.

'What about him?'

'You do know he used to come to the Blue Lamp, don't you?'

A penetrating sense of sickness overtook me, one ripened by a tang of betrayal.

'When?'

'Last year. He liked both Fabienne and Marie-Louise,' she added a determined nod. 'I know he also saw Suzette at least once or twice. But I am sure Marie-Louise was his favourite. Then one day he stopped – I cannot remember exactly but it would have been late last year. He just never came back…'

Chapter Seventeen

In the moments after Celine left, my mind started to hurry as it filled with unsettling possibilities: Kennedy's location was unknown, to me at least, on the night of Fabienne's murder. He could have dispatched Captain Bradbury and Madame Fortier. He had ready access to transport and to Saint-Omer. Was he also at Chambord's party? With the circles he moved in it was not impossible.

Regardless, Celine's revelations explained a great deal, not least Kennedy's deliberate absence from the case. It might even explain his decision to go all the way to Wivenhoe to track me down – and commission me to take on the investigation in the first place.

If he was involved what could be his possible motive?

I poured myself another whisky returned to my chair, drawing my thoughts to order.

First, assuming that Chambord's party and what had transpired were true, it meant that Troyon had a strong motive for the murder of Marie-Louise and Fabienne. As unlikely as it seemed, when you considered his political ambitions, it was an inescapable conclusion. There was also more to it than just politics: she reminded him of what he had done at the party – she was a standing reminder of his own guilt and shame. What's more he also had means to do the deed or to engage an agent to act on his behalf. Don't forget also that he also was in Saint-Omer on the evening that Fabienne was killed in Béthune, close enough, in other words to make the journey. It was almost credible. Or rather, in the light of Celine's information, it was now significantly less than incredible.

Was it enough? Was something missing? Because, surely, notwithstanding the horror of the party, this all required an additional push – perhaps a psychological complaint or shortcoming of some sort, alcoholism, drugs use, one of which might push an inert impulse into barbaric, flagrant action. If it had just been his career that he was worrying about, then surely money could have secured her silence, facilitated her move from the Blue Lamp and, perhaps, placated his conscience? But what if she'd not wanted his money? What if she was so angry and full of hatred that wanted to destroy him – all of which might have been a perfectly natural reaction on her part?

What if she wanted to ruin him and saw this as her opportunity? That could give him the push he needed, perhaps. But where was the evidence? There wasn't any and, besides, he was apparently in Verdun on the night of her death.

I lit a pipe and stood by the window in the darkened room looking out over the square. The tobacco was soothing and warming. But then why would he kill his daughter in such a fashion, leaving her body in a public place as he did? If he wanted to rid the world of his troublesome daughter there were countless ways to do so with less fuss. I sighed. It didn't really make sense...

What a ruddy tangle. The secret with any tangle, whether it was ropes or facts, was to approach it methodically. First, I needed to find out who else was at the party and confirm what transpired. According to what Celine had told me we only knew of three people who could now confirm it: General Troyon himself, Monsieur Chambord and possibly Suzette Emmolet. There was a fourth – a British general, apparently, one identifiable by having a metal prosthesis instead of a hand – but that was not a likely looking or immediately available option. No, the path before me was clear. I drained my glass and snatched up my coat.

Downstairs I found Greenlaw sitting by a burning brazier playing twenty-one with the cook and a couple of his mates in the yard behind the hotel. The Yorkshireman looked surprised to see me but grinned gamely all the same as I explained my plan.

Minutes later we stood before the glittering glazed rectangles in Chambord's front door watching the distinctive outline of the uniformed servant approach. The hands on my watch told me it was nearly nine o'clock so not a customary hour for unexpected house calls. But this time I had Chambord on the back foot, not that he knew it yet. The servant led Greenlaw and me into the mayor's presence in his study at the rear of the property, a room remarkable for the quantity of horned trophies – from stags to roe deer and so on – arranged around its walls. A glance at the plates of this decorative multi-species massacre told me that Chambord had personally accounted for them. A rifle leaned into a corner.

The mayor didn't remark on the marked deterioration of my physical appearance or even register surprise at it. My tattered, stained clothing, my bruised, swollen, scuffed, stitched face did not move him to comment. Which was interesting. He merely looked up from his desk and lifted his eyebrows. What do you want, he was saying?

So I told him.

'On the twenty-fifth of February you hosted a party here. Among the guests was General Maximilian Troyon. In addition to the guests, three women from the Blue Lamp attended with the purpose of providing sexual entertainment. They included Marie-Louise Toulon. I want to give me the names of the other guests.'

If I had hoped my revelation might shake his equanimity I was deluding myself. His eyes narrowed but he looked at me with something approaching a playful sense of implied injury. His voice remained cordial, 'Why don't you have a seat, Monsieur –' He gestured towards one of the tightly stuff armchairs. 'Tell me, what's this is about?'

I stood my ground, my heart beating fast. My voice fell to an accusatory whisper, 'I have information that the general attended a party here hosted by you – a sex party with at least three prostitutes from the Blue Lamp held in the cellars below us.' I stepped towards him. 'I have information that the other guests were high-ranking British Army officers. As you know, soon after that party took place, two of these women were murdered. The third is missing, feared dead. You will know also that some of the evidence from the murder scenes points to a British Army suspect. Therefore, I need you to tell me who attended your party.'

Chambord's frown relaxed and he broke into a confected chuckle.

'Goodness me, Monsieur. Who on earth have you been speaking to?' He managed a convincing laugh. 'This is a fantastic story, no?'

CUT AND RUN

I removed the bundle containing Suzette Emmolet's hand from my overcoat pocket and laid it on the desk in front of him.

'Unwrap it –'

A distasteful twist came to Chambord mouth and he peeled back the layers of the brown cotton cloth. As the hand emerged, he froze and his fingers hovered in mid-air above it, unwilling to touch it.

'What is the meaning of this?'

My voice broke, 'You recognise it, Chambord. It's Suzette Emmolet's left hand.'

The mayor's eyes registered nothing more than disgust.

'That's right,' I said, thrusting a fountain pen and piece of paper on the table before him. 'Now, take up the pen. Give me the names. Who else was at the party? Everything you tell me will be treated in confidence. But I will have those names, Chambord and if you refuse, I'll tell the police about your deviant parties. I'll go to the newspapers. They'll have a field day with you. You'll be finished –'

Chambord leaned back in his chair in sullen defiance. The skin tightened at the corners of his mouth and the faintest blush of indignation arrived at his cheeks. He started turning the gold signet ring on his little finger.

'I know nothing of the parties or prostitutes you refer to. And as for that,' he curled his lip at the severed hand. 'You can dispose of that item as you will.' He cleared his throat. 'I never met anyone called Suzette Emmolet. Kindly remove this artefact.'

I picked the hand up and held it close to his face him, 'Perhaps you should take a closer look, Chambord? It might jerk a memory.'

His temper flared – he pushed my arm away and was on his feet, 'Get out, Monsieur! Are you demented? I have no idea what you are talking about. I wonder if you have had a bump to the head.' He laughed at that. 'Several, no doubt!'

He looked over to Greenlaw and gave an ostentatious sniff, like a singer in an operetta or mime artist in Covent Garden. 'And what's that? Is it whisky I can smell? No wonder your imagination is running away with you, Monsieur. You are a drunkard!'

I snatched up the pen and held out to him, 'Give me the names, Chambord!'

The mayor's chin went up and he squared his shoulders, his hands on his hips.

'There are no names,' he roared, 'because there was no party – now get out, before I have you thrown out.'

His staring eyes pricked with newfound resolve and I could see I had failed. I put the bundle containing Suzette's hand in my pocket.

'As you wish. But before I leave, you'll have no objections to my searching your basement to confirm this?'

'Whatever you wish, Monsieur –' He grinned and yanked a red cord hanging at the wall to summon a servant. 'Be my guest.'

I bowled past a young maid answering the bell and followed the staircase down into a brightly lit basement. Here domestic staff bustled back and forth in the heat and steam, folding sheets, pressing shirts. In a second room, a cook was preparing dough for the morning's bread. At the far rear was a kitchen, where onions and garlic hung from hooks by a broad iron range, and another person was washing pots. A dungeon this was not, nor could it possibly be converted into such to fit with Celine's story.

I halted an older woman, a servant of authority judging by the imperious look she gave me, to ask if there was a lower floor beneath this? Absolutely not, she said, and meant it. She stamped the brick floor with her foot to drive home the point, and her expression rather implied that I was a half-wit for suggesting it.

My resolution started to crumble.

This wasn't it. I was sure that Celine hadn't lied, but this wasn't it. Something was wrong. I reached out my arm and steadied myself, my head suddenly spinning as I looked up the long staircase towards the ground floor.

Chambord was waiting for me in the hall. Behind him stood half a dozen members of his household, including several unshaven, strongly built outdoor workers. Greenlaw stood outside the front door, cradling a bloody nose. The ginger-haired butler held his fist in his hand.

'Damn you, Chambord,' I said. 'I'll find your grubby dungeon, before I'm finished.'

As I said this my food slipped on the wet step outside the front door and I went down, cracking onto my knee.

Chambord grinned and swaggered towards me.

'Go home, Monsieur. You are an embarrassment. You stink, and your absurd allegations are baseless… Go back to England or I'll have you deported!'

He flicked his meaty face towards the gate, 'And make no mistake, I shall be lodging an official complaint with the British authorities in the morning. If I were you, I would not expect to be in Béthune – or France for – for much longer.'

Chapter Eighteen

Greenlaw and I walked back to the hotel in silence and parted company at the rear of the property without a word being said. He didn't need to say anything. The look on his face was of marked disapproval, one verging on anger. Worse than that, ascending the stairs, I realised that he had lost his faith in me.

Upstairs in my room, I wedged the armchair against the door – no one would get in without waking the dead – and finished the bottle of whisky before putting myself to bed. I slept badly and awoke for the last time at five-and-twenty to seven. I knew this because in the darkness I immediately confronted the insistent, penetrating glow of the fluorescent hands on my wristwatch. Then I heard the *tick, tick, tick* – more like a hammer blow than a soft metronome. My gaze shrank from the brightness and I rolled over, groaning. After a few minutes I heaved myself out of bed.

I stepped wearily to the window and drew back the curtains; the dusky dawn glimmer was sharp in my eyes. My focus shot to the bottle of whisky, killed. Then I saw a stain on the floorboards where I'd been sick. I cursed as loudly as I could manage – a hoarse whisper, really – and gripped my bird's-nest beard, clutching a great thatch of it, like Lord Salisbury gone to seed.

I took a pair of scissors from the drawer, went to the mirror and started to cut. My hands trembled but there was enough beard to go at without endangering my face or throat, and they just moved in concert, guiding, pulling and snipping through the hedge, as my bloodshot eyes looked on. The thick, entwined tresses yielded to the blades and tumbled to the floor, but not without resistance. It felt like curbing an impenetrable, ancient ivy with countless branches being torn free against the effort of their locking, asphyxiating vegetable teeth. And then I confronted myself in the mirror again; the thatch all but gone. Next, I took a razor blade and a bar of soap, and shaved away the remnants, taking care around the angry cut that for months had been lurking beneath the hairline. Sliding the razor towards the scar, the bristles came away easily. I took it as far as I could, and repeated the process from the other side. I then rinsed my face and dabbed it dry before looking closely at it once again in the mirror.

Perhaps the scar was not as bad as I had thought. On course, it was still very ugly, but that was the worst that could be said of it. I had imagined it to be much larger and somehow fundamentally grotesque, horrifying even. In reality, it was merely four or five inches long, running from my left cheekbone, down to the curve of my jaw. The stitches had left their mark but Herbert's handiwork had been masterful and the puncture marks were now little more than smooth ridges, like the imprint of a toothbrush on soft butter. I touched it with my finger, feeling the raised lump of the scar tissue. It was sensitive, raw-almost, particularly if pinioned against the pressure of my tongue from within. But it wasn't so bad.

Taking hold of my hair in bunches, I next started to prune, cutting the next bank of ivy, until what stood before the glass was something more closely resembling the Francis Richard Champion that I had known in August 1915, before the fall. I nodded a silent greeting to myself. The old face was there, alright; the nodules and the bumps of long acquaintance, the bags under the eyes. The innocent, clumsy scars of childhood. But the skin, once youthful, was drier and greyer somehow and seemed less elastic. And that scar was bloody hideous, when you thought about it.

I dried my face, the sensation of the towel unfamiliar against my skin, combed my hair neatly, and nodded. That would do for now.

In the same moment, I started to think.

The twenty-fifth of February, the day of Chambord's party, was four days before Suzette left the Blue Lamp. It was seventeen days before the body of Marie-Louise Troyon was found in the park in Béthune. And it was precisely twenty-four days before Fabienne Thomas turned up dead at the Hotel du Nord. Three women at one party, now all dead or very likely dead. Therefore, Chambord's party was critical to everything that followed. As surely as night followed day, so it was. But if Chambord refused to provide the key to unlock the mystery then someone else might. General Troyon, for instance.

I put on my only clean shirt and brushed my tweed suit with military punctiliousness. I had a needle and thread and I used it to close up a prominent tear in the sleeve of my jacket, and the tears in the left trouser leg. All this done, I did up my bow tie, which was burgundy with small golden swallows. I checked my reflection in the mirror and for the first time in a very long while allowed myself a smile. Well. I still looked like someone pretending to be me, but it would do for now.

Hauling the heavy armchair away from the door, I went to call on Greenlaw. At first there was no answer from his door, but after a while I heard a groan from within, louder, closer than I had expected.

The door cracked open. The young Yorkshireman stood in the gap, his sandy hair askew, sleepily pulling braces over his bare shoulders. The bruising on his nose had come up nicely.

'You all right?'

'Been better.' He scratched his head and gradually, I think, my face came into focus.

'Fuck me, Champion –' A smile come to his face. 'Is that really you?'

'It most certainly is, Comrade Greenlaw.'

'Aye?' He chuckled and we shook hands. Then he spotted my Gladstone bag. 'We off somewhere?'

'Verdun,' I said.

'Verdun? Christ, I'd better fetch my toothbrush...'

But before we left Béthune, I called in at the gendarmerie to see Inspector Catouillart. He was at his desk, unshaven as normal and drinking a cup of strong black tea. He regarded me across the room, unsure in the half-light if he had seen me correctly, then lowered his spectacles.

'Monsieur Champion!' he exclaimed, his eyes scanning my face. 'You appear to have won a fight with a barber?' He peered at me, 'Or perhaps lost it, looking at all these bruises!'

'The bruises are Robecq's –' I poured myself a cup of tea. 'I can't say you didn't warn me.'

'Robecq!' he hissed.

'The Eagle also warned me.' I blew across the top of the steaming cup, forcing myself to wait rather than burn myself, and told him what had happened at Robecq's farm – the dogs, the cider, the opium and then the cave. Finally, I placed the bundle containing Suzette Emmolet's hand on his desk – and told him to take a look.

He shrank back from it and a black cotton handkerchief went to his mouth.

'Mon Dieu!'

'It's been identified by at least two people,' I said, before explaining.

The points of his moustache fell and he looked at me quizzically; he was placing her.

'Ah, yes, the missing woman from the Blue Lamp...' He shook his head, 'Mon Dieu.' He leaned back in his chair and gestured towards the hand. 'Put it away. Please. This is too early for me.'

As I did as he asked, Catouillart emitted a sigh and reached for one of his turmeric coloured Turkish cigarettes. As the smoke filled the space between us, I saw him swallow and his eyes flit from the ceiling to the window and to my bow tie.

'Alors, so we need to speak to Monsieur Robecq.'

'We do, and when it happens, I'd dearly like to be the one asking the questions.'

Catouillart nodded, a sour expression on his dry, pale face. 'It won't be easy, you know.' He added, moisture on his lips making them look red. 'Robecq is connected to all the powerful people in the area; the mayor and other politicians, the magistrates, the newspaper editor. He wields considerable influence through brown paper envelopes. You understand?'

'I'm familiar with the methodology.'

Catouillart sucked his teeth, 'But even in a backwater like this you can't just kill people and expect to get away with it.'

You could have fooled me, I thought. Catouillart met my eye and nodded firmly. 'Trust me, Monsieur. If Robecq is responsible for any of the deaths at the Blue Lamp, he will answer for them.'

'We'll need to find Suzette's body first,' I said. 'Mind you, before we do that there are plenty of other bodies we already have to account for.'

The Frenchman conceded the point with a nod.

'On a different subject,' I found myself sighing, almost by way of apology. 'Do you happen to know where Captain Kennedy is?'

'Capitaine Kennedy?' The Frenchman stifled a smile, the points of his moustache rising smartly to forty-five degrees. 'What is this? Have you lost him?'

He read my flat expression and continued, 'I see. But how do you imagine that I can assist in this matter?' I made no reply, but cocked an eyebrow disbelievingly at him. At length his cheeks puffed with indignation – then he exhaled and the jaunty waxed tips of his moustache lowered. He cleared his throat.

'By happy coincidence, Monsieur –' He reached for a scrap of paper and began to scribble. 'I *do* happen to have an address for your Capitaine Kennedy. He keeps a cottage on the road to Choques...' Catouillart had a look of mild distaste on his face, 'It's not far from the British hospital.'

'I know it,' I said, taking the note from him.

'I know you know it,' he smiled. 'Just so we all know where we stand.'

Rather than drive straight for Verdun we took the Calais road for Saint-Omer, Greenlaw at the wheel. It was an eighty-mile round-trip out of our way but, unfortunately, there was no way of avoiding it. To go to Verdun without official permission and paperwork to prove it was quite impossible.

We arrived at the centre of Saint-Omer shortly after ten o'clock and went straight to British Army headquarters. As Catouillart had said during our visit on Monday night, it occupied what was once a very grand hotel in the middle of the city, just a stone's throw from where Troyon had addressed the eager masses two nights before. A sand bag wall some eight feet high and topped with curls of barbed wire had been erected along the pavement out front, and white tape criss-crossed the myriad panes of glass in its high windows. It was, as I had reflected before, just like home.

At the door I asked to see General Risborough and was admitted. Passing through the outer courtyard, I learned immediately that

CUT AND RUN

rumours that headquarters was on the move were true: soldiers were taking down a large Union flag from above the front door and several green military lorries were being loaded with desks, filing cabinets and typewriter boxes. The move was well advanced.

Inside, I obtained directions and eventually found the appropriate entrance; the typed print on the cream card announced the occupant as Major R. Webster, *aide-de-camp* to General Risborough. I knocked and entered after receiving a curt summons.

On the far side of an expanse of golden parquet, adequate for a squash court, a smug-looking major – the man I had seen briefly in the quad at Herbert's field hospital – reclined in his chair, perusing the *Daily Telegraph*. His dirty brown soles were propped up on the corner of the desk, which was similar in proportion to a full-sized snooker table. The officer possessed a muscular ramrod jaw and a broad, black handlebar moustache that you could have hung your washing on. However, any notion of absurdity was obviated by prevailing British military tradition which dictated that in the Army at least, the larger your moustache the higher your star would rise. With a frontispiece like that Major Webster would easily make general.

'So you're Kennedy's fisherman,' he drawled, as he viewed me up and down. He had supercilious smirk on his face and was evidently one of those people who considered themselves amusing. 'I see you've dressed up for the occasion,' he added, lifting a doubtful eyebrow. He should have seen me before. Webster flipped open a dossier, which he now referred to from time to time.

'Captain Kennedy has given me a full briefing on you: Haileybury, Teddy Hall, Colonial Service and then the Essex Regiment. So far, so conventional…' There was a hint of Scots in his voice. At first I thought it genteel Glasgow, then I realised it was softer, Ayrshire perhaps. 'But what I don't understand is why you enlisted? With your background, you could have been an officer.' He lowered the piece of paper to reveal a mischievous expression. 'There's no telling that you'd have been up to it, of course –' He turned the corners of his mouth upwards to a smile. 'But they'd have let you given it a go.'

I wasn't sure that this merited an answer but I knew he would expect one.

'I didn't become an officer, Major, because I realised that I'd made enough mistakes in peacetime. I decided it was time to give someone else the chance.'

He gave a staccato laugh. Just one, like a cap gun going off, and nodded. In that moment he decided what I was, but he wasn't going to share it. He tossed the sheaf of buff-coloured foolscap onto the desk and swept his leather boots to the floor, the heels landing with percussion of spurs. He was tall, broad shouldered, and would have been a quite an athlete in his youth. 'Come on, then,' he slapped his hands together. 'Let's go in.'

We entered the adjacent apartment through a grand pair of double doors and arrived at the office of General Sir Charles Risborough, the man who had authorised Kennedy to engage me in this project in the first place. Kennedy had told me that he was on the general staff at General Headquarters in an Allied Liaison role, meaning he talked to the generals from the French and Belgian forces and kept them as happy as possible – or at least tried to. One could only assume that it was a thankless task. It also explained how the paper trail concerning Marie-Louise Toulon and the others had arrived at his desk, the one that right now he stood behind. Risborough looked up and pulled off his tortoiseshell glasses.

He was wiry beneath his field green uniform. A mass of decorations on his breast held my attention, along with the brilliant red collar flashes and gold braid. There was more gold braid on the shoulder straps and beneath the tightly knotted tie, three tunic brass buttons shone above the belt, with another peeping out just below, before the ostentatious flair of his riding breaches. A British Army general is an impressive sight and this one was no different. Webster introduced us.

Risborough's slightly oversized, domed head frowned down at me. He was tanned, too, in a way that had aged him prematurely, like some of the white settlers I'd seen trying to rehydrate their baked bodies with gin in the Muthaiga Club in Nairobi. 'Have a seat,' Risborough said genially. His voice had a worn-out dryness to it. His eyes creased, 'You look like you've been in the wars, what?'

I explained that I had, on several different fronts. He liked that and, then pressing down his grey moustache, asked, 'So what can I do for you?'

I briefed him on everything that I had learned since I arriving in Béthune, with exception of the party at Chambord's and what happened there. That level of salacious detail and whiff of scandal would put an instant stop to everything. Webster took notes – his pencil scratching on his pad. Risborough listened closely as I concluded my explanation.

'Crikey, Champion,' the general commented after a moment's reflection. He looked over at Webster. 'You've been busy, what? Well done. You have advanced our understanding of the case enormously.' His expression became sombre and he took out a small cigar and paused before he lit it. 'General Troyon must be devastated. He's a good egg, you know. I don't have children myself, but it must be a parent's worst nightmare, and to discover she had become a prostitute.' He shook his grey, tanned head in despair. 'I suppose it was necessary to tell him all that?'

'The general took all the information in his stride, Sir.'

'Well he would,' was Risborough's response, as he pushed himself up from his chair. 'He's very important, you know?' Risborough's wet, cool eyes found me and waited for my acknowledgement which I gave with a nod. 'There are lots of generals,' he continued, his voice sounding more pained than before, 'and some don't matter. Troyon matters a good deal. It goes without saying that this means the case has taken on significantly more importance.' He was pacing now, the dry leather soles of his brown riding boots grinding softly against the parquet floor. He took a slow, thoughtful drag of his cigar. 'So what about this poor demented fellow...' he searched for the name.

Webster chipped in, 'Captain Bradbury, Sir.'

'Yes, what of Captain Bradbury? Is the matter not settled on him? After all, you said he left a suicide note owning up to – what was it? – ah, yes, his "sins", before doing the decent thing, what?'

'Unfortunately I'm pretty sure he didn't do the decent thing, Sir. Not as such. I think it's perfectly possible that the note was written under severe duress, or that the sin he referred to had nothing to do with any of the murders. It is highly ambiguous. What's more he was not known at the Blue Lamp. In my opinion, Bradbury was innocently caught up in the affair and his confession, such as it is, isn't worth the paper it was written on.'

Risborough exchanged a glance with Webster, who cut in, 'What evidence do you have for these brazen assertions, Champion?'

'Among various reasons,' I spoke sharply, because he had piqued me, 'including what I just said, is that Bradbury appears to have no motive. There's also one very fundamental thing missing from the scene of his apparent suicide –'

They looked at me expectantly and I left them hanging a moment. 'Namely the pen he used to write his confession.'

'But he might have written the note hours before, and then lost it later on,' suggested Webster.

'But how would that explain the fresh-looking ink stain on his index finger?'

Webster frowned but I could see the general agreed with me, and checked the major with a flick of a liver-spotted hand. 'Go on,' he said.

'Also, we have established that he was having an affair with the murdered woman next door, a butcher's wife. In addition, as I said, he had never been seen at the Blue Lamp – a fact confirmed by a woman who works there – nor was he known to the women there as far as we have been able to establish. All of which leads me to believe that he was the victim of the same circumstances that led to the murder of his mistress, Madame Fourtier. At the very least, I believe their deaths are only indirectly connected to the deaths of the women at the Blue Lamp.'

Risborough cleared his throat, 'So *who* was responsible, then?'

'I don't know yet. My theory is that Madame Fourtier had the misfortune of observing whoever killed Fabienne Thomas leave the Hotel du Nord whilst undertaking her early morning deliveries.

Certainly the two events – the departure of the killer and her morning rounds, would have occurred at a similar time of day, so it is plausible. I believe that as a result of being seen, perhaps to prevent the risk of identification, the murderer followed her back to her shop and then killed her. It was then during this act that poor Bradbury arrived, only to be dispatched himself and then framed nicely so that he could be blamed for everything that had gone on before. He was the perfect person to blame,' I added, 'because he was dead and couldn't deny it.'

Risborough got up and went to the fire, where he tossed his cigar into the flames. 'That's jolly unfortunate. I'm told he was good officer.' He exhaled, 'And now what?'

'I would like authorisation to visit General Troyon and official sanction to travel through French territory, to ask him further questions about his daughter. This is where it all began and I believe her death holds the key to solving the entire matter.'

Risborough nodded thoughtfully and then said, as though thinking aloud, 'It would at least demonstrate to the general our continued commitment to solving this crime, in concert with the French authorities, of course.'

'He also asked me to keep him abreast of matters, Sir, so this would show good faith on our part.'

Risborough pressed his mouth against his interlocked hands. I exchanged a glance with Webster, then Risborough shifted his position. He had decided.

'Very well Champion, see the general. Reassure him that the matter is being looked after.' He checked me with his gaze, 'But mark me, it's imperative that you don't cause too much alarm.' Risborough sat down at his desk and began to write. 'Whatever happens, you mustn't distress General Troyon. Understand? Now –' He blotted the note and folded it sharply, before forcing it into an envelope. 'This will secure your passage. Go, learn what you can from Troyon and then get back to Béthune and stop this killer at all costs.' He tugged off his spectacles and reached out to shake my hand, his grip surprisingly firm. 'Good luck Champion,' he said keenly. 'I'll telegraph Troyon to expect you.'

Webster showed me out. On the way we paused before a large map of the Western Front hanging in his office. It was dotted with pins of different colours, detailing the deployment of British and Allied units, from Ostend on the North Sea all the way down to Reims. It showed the location of the main field hospitals, including the one outside Béthune where Herbert worked, as well as supply depots.

'Impressive, isn't it?' remarked Webster, evidently pleased with the map. I wondered if keeping it up to date was how he filled his days.

A Union flag with a dangling label marked the location of the new British HQ at Montreuil-sur-Mer, forty miles away on the Atlantic coast.

'What's prompting the move?' I asked.

'It's this new army that being formed under General Rawlinson – the one confirmed last month.' Webster indicated its deployment. 'We're taking on an extra portion of what used to be the frog line to the south, so they can pile more men into Verdun. As a result it makes sense for headquarters to be more centrally located. Montreuil is also closer to the coastal supply lines and, rather conveniently, there's a large frog military college there which they don't need anymore.'

So 'Rawly', as General Rawlinson was known, had been given a whole new army, the best part of a hundred thousand men. Even he would struggle to get through that lot in a hurry. It didn't mean he wouldn't try, of course.

'Was it a surprise that Rawlinson got the command?'

'Not especially.' The major lowered his voice and his eyes shifted towards the double doors connecting us to the next room, 'Mark you, there's not a general in the British Army who wouldn't have given his eye teeth for the job...'

CUT AND RUN

Chapter Nineteen

We left Saint-Omer immediately. Our route took us through the plains of Champagne and on to Reims, where we stopped for a late lunch. We ate bread, onion soup and cold meat in the lee of the remnants of the cathedral, which had been all but destroyed by German shelling in 1914. Its two great towers were now robbed of their soaring windows and one could only imagine the destruction of the gothic interior. Stark photographs of Reims had flooded the press back home at the time, offering a horrifying symbol of the new face of war. It was images like it that had helped rally Britishers like me in their thousands to the flag.

We were now deep inside the French part of the Allied lines, and the columns of green Tommies, topped with cloth service caps, had been replaced by the midnight blue fatigues and oval-shaped steel Adrian Helmets of the French Republic.

After lunch we refuelled the Crossley and were on the home straight for Verdun which lay just seventy miles onwards, roughly, due east. Soon, however, we joined a continuous slow-moving stream of military cars, motor lorries and horse-drawn waggons, mostly carrying troops or crates of supplies. The highway was disintegrating under the weight of traffic, becoming a constant series of cavernous pot holes, each filled with standing water that soaked passengers and threatened to explode tyres or shatter wheels. The going became even slower as the traffic negotiated the craters.

For twenty miles we trailed an open-backed truck carrying French colonial troops. They wore khaki uniforms and matching Adrian helmets. You had to wonder quite what they made of this peculiar European form of orchestrated slaughter. It was bad enough, surely, being British or French in this fight, but dying for the freedom of your colonial overlord struck me as particularly intolerable. I remarked as much to Greenlaw. 'Aye,' he said, 'but they look cheerful enough.'

Before I could answer a deep rumble shook the ground – vibrating the Crossley – and a French plane shot low overhead. Its broad tan wings broke briefly into view between the trees against the grey sky. The Africans in the truck looked out and cheered. 'Vive la France!' they cried, and I couldn't help admiring them.

In the opposite direction came a procession of ambulances, both motorised and horse-drawn. Many of the former category were converted Ford Model Ts, with red and white crosses painted on the canvas sides. Their drivers wore several days' stubble and haunted expressions. The unremitting caravan confirmed what I had heard; that Verdun was bleeding France dry. Occasionally, while stationary, we overheard the cries of the wounded men, packed into the backs of the wagons, before the growl of the engines drowned out the cacophony of pain.

The hills of Verdun were now visible in the distance – the probable destination of the earlier aeroplane, but the tower of that city's cathedral was lost in the low lying cloud, as were the substantial French forts that were said to guard it.

At dusk we reached Souilly, on the outskirts of Verdun. I showed my letter from Risborough to an inquisitive French officer at a heavily guarded roadblock on the edge of the town. The lieutenant eyed my scar again and wasn't happy about my civilian dress but waved us through. As before the Crossley staff car did a lot of the work for us.

A few minutes later we located the local military headquarters, which was set up in the former town hall and festooned with Tricolours and telephone wires. These radiated from its eves to fresh-looking telegraph poles heading off in all points of the compass.

But General Troyon was not there. After a phone call we emerged with directions for another headquarters ten miles closer to the front lines and the sound of war. We passed fields of encamped troops and dense packs of French cavalry patrolling the roads, galloping along the shattered surface with rapidity – and relative comfort. Clearing another checkpoint, we reached a partially destroyed chateau, standing in the midst of series of similarly bashed about out-buildings. A couple of French staff cars – bulbous nosed blue-painted Citroëns – were parked diagonally out the front and horses were being led about. There was also a field hospital in the remnants of a barn. Men were being stretchered in and out. In the distance, bright explosions lit up the dark sky, but fireworks they were not.

Once inside, a stressed captain reviewed the letter and my identification papers. Satisfied, he led me down into a deep cellar and along a narrow damp corridor, its ceiling trailed with electric lights and cabling like bunting. We passed warrens of clustered desks of toiling signallers and soldiers bent over maps or transcribing orders. Telephones rang incessantly, telegraph machines rattled, typewriters cracked like rapid gunfire, the air was heavy with tobacco and sweat; this was the clerical front. Turning a corner I heard Troyon's sharp voice. It grew louder as we approached the end of the corridor. He sounded angry – or perhaps, he was simply bellowing to make himself heard. Then I saw him, standing, telephone receiver held close to his mouth, declaiming, 'Send in the reserves immediately, Colonel.' There was a pause and Troyon began shaking his head. 'No. Do it now...'

He hung up forcefully and in the moment saw me, his expression softening. In his sober field uniform he looked more like the military man that he clearly was and less like a politician in disguise. A sword hung from his belt and his pistol was holstered at the other side. 'Excuse me a moment, Monsieur –' He slipped through a doorway, called out and there followed an exchange with an unseen underling.

When he returned to the room, he offered me his hand and greeting, 'Monsieur Champion,' and smiled. 'No sooner does a telegram arrive telling me to expect you, than you are standing here for yourself. It's going to be a busy night, I'm afraid.'

The general poured two cups of piping hot coffee from a pot that was warming on a cast iron stove. 'Whatever one thinks of the Germans, and I think less than most, you have to hand it to them. They are very determined people.' He offered me a seat and sat down in the chair opposite. 'This must mean you have news for me?'

I held back from the chair for a moment, pausing at the stove, relishing its warmth. 'We are making progress, General. But there is something important I need to ask you.'

He observed me with mild curiosity as I warmed my hands on the fire.

'I have received a piece of information which I am duty bound to confirm with you. I assure you that your anonymity will be preserved. Moreover I have not discussed any of this with the British authorities, nor shall I.' I looked over and looked at his face. 'General, may I ask what the nature of your acquaintance is with a Monsieur Chambord, the mayor of Béthune?'

Troyon's studied expression betrayed no flicker of recognition – though possibly there was something in the shifting of his lips beneath his moustache. I let the question sit longer with him and watched him take out a large cigar. 'Let me think,' he said, as he reached for a box of matches. They were Bryant and May, a keepsake from his recent trip to Saint-Omer, perhaps? The general coughed, 'Monsieur Chambord... ah, yes, he is sympathetic to the political furrow that I plough, Monsieur. I know the man. In fact, we have met a few times, once in Béthune, which I visited some weeks or months ago, I am sure of it.' He inhaled on the cigar, drawing a few peremptory puffs. 'Why do you ask?'

'Because I have been told that you attended a party that Monsieur Chambord threw in Béthune on the twenty-fifth of February this year. Is that correct?'

Troyon paused, and then nodded, an uncertain cast forming on his mouth. 'I could check my diary to be precise,' he said. 'But it would have been about then.' He put the coffee cup to his mouth and watched me as he took a sip.

'Is it true that an unexpected family reunion took place while you were attending this party, General? That is, did you meet Marie-Louise there?'

The question put, I let it stand. From the adjacent room I heard a French voice berating another and the clatter of the telegraph machine intensified. Troyon stared into space, seemingly focusing on patch of air about six feet in front of him, over by the wall. He cleared this throat before replying.

'And what of it?' he pronounced at last. Was I imagining it or were the fingers of his left hand shaking?

'Why didn't you tell me that you had seen Marie-Louise, just eighteen days before she was killed?'

'I think you will know why, Monsieur –' Troyon's voice suddenly strengthened, restored to its customary vigour. I saw the twitching fingers close into a fist. 'I was ashamed to have a whore for a daughter. Is that so unnatural?'

I shook my head at him, and resisted the first reply that came to me, namely that few things were as unnatural as what he himself did that night.

Instead, I lowered myself into the seat opposite him and steepled my fingers thoughtfully in front of my nose and chin.

'I know what happened that night,' I said. 'Everything.'

Troyon's chin rose and a long scar on his lip whitened as his jaw tensed. He blinked and I realised it even if I didn't yet acknowledge it. He was not Marie-Louise's killer. 'I know the whole sorry story,' I continued. 'I'm sorry to say. But what I still don't know, is how precisely it was connected to the tragic death of your daughter.'

It took about a minute, but his eyes eventually found mine.

'I didn't kill her,' he said firmly. 'I know how it looks. You know that, don't you?'

'I believe you, General. But we have to accept that others may struggle to reach the same conclusion if offered a partial version of the story.'

He nodded and got up, pouring himself a tall brandy from a decanter, before standing over by the stove. 'I can see that, Monsieur. But what happened that night was a private tragedy, an unspeakable accident that I will regret to the end of my days. But I did not kill my daughter, nor wish her dead. Far from it.' His chest swelled. 'In point of fact, after that night I arranged for a sum of money to be sent to her through Chambord with a letter imploring her to give up the life she was leading. It was no small sum either, it was two hundred French francs, to be given to her on condition that she leave Béthune and that life immediately, with the promise of more to follow.' He sighed, and looked at me with sincerity bordering on despair. 'I don't know if this was apparent, but I have been told that the compliance of women in such situations is sometimes maintained by the use of addictive drugs, such as opium. They are introduced to the narcotic, encouraged to enjoy it, and then it is used to control them by the same people that employ them. I know that there are establishments in Béthune where British soldiers can obtain opium, too. It is a problem for our army, also.' He picked up his cigar from the ashtray. 'Chambord of course has nothing to do with it, of that I am positive. But as a man of local influence I felt sure that he could arrange for the money and letter to be directed to Marie-Louise. I thought I could trust him. Plainly I was wrong.'

'Presumably the money has gone somewhere,' I offered.

The general coughed into his fist. 'I should tell you that I already knew she was dead when you came to inform me of it. Chambord had written to me. With a heavy heart I thought it best to bury her locally, in Béthune, under her assumed name. I was not happy about it but I supposed it was what she would have wanted.' He bowed his head, 'I, personally, remain deeply unhappy about it and I will visit her grave one day soon and apologise to her. I failed her as a father…'

I heaved myself from the chair and went to the desk, removing a piece of paper and handing him his pen.

'General, there is one thing that you can do to help me find your daughter's killer.'

Troyon looked up me, his eyes momentarily vulnerable looking…

'Write me a list of every man who attended Monsieur Chambord's party in February.'

The eyes resisted for a second, but then he took the paper and the pen and started to write. Then, as the names took form on the paper, I experienced a delicious moment of realisation.

CUT AND RUN

Chapter Twenty

We set off for Béthune that evening, stopping eighty miles to the north of Verdun in Compiègne, not far from Reims. We camped by the car and rose early the next morning, half-frozen, setting off before dawn, Greenlaw stoically at the wheel. He looked exhausted, which he undoubtedly was, but he made no complaint. We both rallied when we recognised a landmark or two that confirmed we were getting closer to Béthune. By now the colours of the military vehicles had changed from blue to back to green and we spoke English at the checkpoints.

To my right I could see the twin high slag heaps outside the coal-town of Lens gradually getting bigger on the broad horizon. In the distance ahead were the roofs and pinnacle of Béthune's belfry.

When we did arrive, Greenlaw went to bed, and I borrowed a bicycle.

Taking the address that Catouillart had given me the day before, I cycled out to the hamlet of Les Chopettes, just a mile and half away. The place was still asleep when I arrived, though I saw a few ambulances dropping off their load of misery at the field hospital. Herbert would be busy, again.

I cycled up several blind alleys and winding lanes before I finding the road that I needed. The sun had appeared at last and was a shining bronze coin above the horizon. The scattered houses of the small village were behind me now and I passed the end of a row of terraced houses. Next there was a row of tall Corsican pines by the road, their thick branches blocking out the morning sunlight. The air carried that lovely, rich tang of damp soil, as well as the honeyed scent of the trees.

Just as Catouillart had promised, there on the right, was a low workman's cottage amidst an ill-tended garden of overgrown grasses and brambles behind a wild, hostile blackthorn hedge. I left my bicycle in its grasp.

The windows and front door were boarded up, so I stole round to the rear, taking care not to alert potential occupants to my presence. There I saw that several windows had recently been freed of these irregular timbers, a fact made apparent by the planks of wood that lay heaped on the ground where they had been discarded, bent nails still protruding from them. At the back of the garden a spade stood in the middle of a cleared area of earth, beyond the old vegetable patch. The soil had recently been disturbed and footprints led from it to a kitchen chair by the back door, which I saw was surrounded in a halo of cigarette butts. I briefly held one of these up and inspected its maker. It was unfiltered and French.

I drew open the back door and peered inside. In the low light, I made out a cast-iron pump looming over the metal washtub. I made out a cold-looking range on the left and the uneven brick floor. Then on the right a dark figure filled a chair, his feet splayed out before him and his head lolled forward. He slept heavily, the note of his slumber even, long and deep.

I trod quietly past the sleeper towards the inner doorway beyond, the spectrum of light narrowing and the world around me losing definition. It was silent in this void and cold. All I could hear was the sound of the breathing from the outer room. Oddly enough there was a spicy, fresh odour of disinfectant in the air. For some reason I experienced an important urge to see what was before me. I looked back to where I had come from, the doorway silhouetted against the garden. The sleeper's breathing stopped – I froze, and then it resumed, exhaling with an unexpectedly shrill call. But I actually didn't care if I woke him. I struck a match.

A young woman lay on the bed, her hair scraped back from her pale face against the pillow. Her eyes were shut, the closed lips almost blue and she was still. Hospital-white bed linen sprung from beneath her chin, where her fingers still clutched it. She was young, probably no more than twenty-five. I lit the candle on a bedside table with the last of my match. She stirred but did not open her darkly ringed eyes. She looked impossibly drawn.

Shifting on my feet, I noticed they were tacky. I lowered the candle... the floor was covered in dried blood. I looked back at the face with its fine features and my mind registered the source of my uneasiness. It was the precise curve of the jaw, not so very feminine you might say, but undeniably so when combined with the gentle arc of the mouth and the eyes. She was ringer for my sister, Dorothy.

I took the candle and went back into the kitchen, and shook the slumberer.

'Nathaniel Kennedy,' I hissed. 'Wake up!'

Kennedy wiped a streak of dirt from his face and looked up from the wooden chair where he sat. His face was haggard, dusted with grey and ginger stubble, and altogether he looked ten years older than the man who had walked into Wivenhoe the Friday before. The back door of the house was wide open and thin light now gave the room its shape.

I had just lit the fire in the bedroom and closed the door on the young woman; her name was Sophie Taylor and she was a nurse at the field hospital in Choques. 'She should make a full recovery,' Kennedy was explaining, his tone quiet. 'We got the doctor out last night.' He closed his eyes reliving the moment. 'It was nearly too late –' His voice fell to a rasp. 'She'd ruptured her stitches… there was so much blood…'

I leaned back against the metal tub, watching him as he broke down. Eventually, he took a miserable drag of his foul-smelling Gitanes cigarette and I met his gaze. I nodded towards the spade embedded in the mound of earth at the back of the garden and let my eyes linger.

Kennedy's voice broke.

'Spare me the lecture, Frank. You're no saint. What's done is done. No one wanted to do it.'

'I think I'll have one of those cigarettes of yours –' I took the packet from him and accepted his box of matches.

As I drew in the rich tobacco, I looked through the open back door at the spade. 'So it was yours?'

'Of course it was ruddy well mine –' Kennedy scowled at me. 'You bastard.'

His voice broke and tears charged down his face. 'I almost lost her, Frank.' His tone appealed for sympathy but I had none for him, not today. 'We couldn't have gone back to Cork and been married there with a baby. We – the child – we would have been outcasts. You know that. Come on man, we're not the first and we won't the last. That's life, Frank.'

And death. I noticed that the shaft of the spade was split and had been bound together with tightly wound string. 'There's no shortage of bastards in the world. One more wouldn't have been a catastrophe.'

He took a drag of his cigarette, 'What do you want?'

I lowered my voice.

'Why didn't you tell me that you'd been a regular at the Blue Lamp – and of both Marie-Louise and Fabienne Thomas?'

He swallowed a looked over the door to where Sophie slept.

'It wasn't germane to the inquiry.'

'Germane? You'd been having sexual intercourse with the two of the victims.'

'It was months ago, Frank,' he addressed me in a hoarse whisper. 'And they weren't victims when I knew them. Plus, as it happens, lots of people slept with them, because that was their job. What's more, I *know* I didn't kill them, therefore whatever I did or didn't do months prior to the case is not relevant. And, yes, it all also helped that I was ashamed of the fact I'd been there, so forgive me if I didn't want to run around confessing it to all and sundry.'

'Is that why you picked me to take on the investigation?'

'Don't be ridiculous.'

'So were you with Miss Taylor on Sunday – and Sunday night?'

He nodded, 'What do you think?'

'And do I take it that you knew who Marie-Louise's father was, before I told you on Monday morning?'

'I didn't, as a matter of fact.' The look he gave me showed he was telling the truth.

'What about Chambord's parties?' I asked.

'What about Chambord's ruddy parties?'

'Do you know that Troyon attended one of them in February?'

His expression hardened, 'I do now.'

'Really?'

'Really!'

'Are you surprised?'

'A little, but not especially.'

'You should have told me about the parties. You know British Army officers attend them, don't you?'

'Yes, Frank,' he sighed. 'I know that. Everyone does. But what you don't seem to appreciate is that the parties *never* happened and, just like the Red Lamp or the Blue Lamp, officially these places are ambiguous. They do and don't exist. Funnily enough, subsidising international prostitution is not an official foreign policy objective of Her Majesty's Government.'

'So have you attended one of the parties?'

'No. Never been asked. Nor would I have gone. It's not my thing.'

I snorted at him and resisted the urge to comment. The good news was that his name did not appear on Troyon's list. I turned towards the door and looked out, considering my next step. It was warming up out there.

'I'm sorry I wasn't entirely truthful with you Frank.' There was a humility in Kennedy's tone now. 'Life is like that sometimes. You pick up secrets along the way, and then you forget you've got them.'

I nodded, showing him I understood, and got up to leave.

'Where are you going?'

'To see General Risborough.' I took a final drag of the cigarette and threw it down into the collection of butts that ringed the wooden chair in the garden. 'He'll know what to do, because I'm damned if I do.'

Kennedy laughed that soft, involuntary Irish lilt of his, one that was normally as infectious as smallpox. But the virus had no effect on me today.

'What's so funny?'

He took a drag of his Gitanes. 'If you go to headquarters and stir up a hornet's nest, no one will thank you, Frank. No one will want to know about General Troyon's unfortunate, dead, whore daughter. No one will want to know about British officers of good standing cavorting with prostitutes and petty municipal officials. They won't want to know about it, Frank. Not any of it.'

'Is that a warning?'

His voice cracked with anger, 'No – but be careful. There's a war on. People have got bigger fish to fry.'

'Fish to fry...' I shook my head at him. 'Don't worry, I'll tread carefully.'

Chapter Twenty-one

First, I trod a path to Herbert Macmillan, to verify the story about Kennedy and the girl. Herbert knew Nurse Taylor and confirmed that he'd seen her with a man fitting Kennedy's description. I suggested he pay her a visit.

I cycled back to the Béthune and went to the Blue Lamp, where the door was answered by a young woman I didn't recognise but who was presumably a replacement for either Marie-Louise or Fabienne. Certainly the lace trimmed-bust of golden dress was cut generously enough to leave me in no doubt as to her contribution to the house of pleasure. I asked for Celine. The woman wrinkled her nose at me.

'She's gone,' she said, her tone implying a degree of permanence, rather than as if she had gone 'to the shops'.

'Where?'

'Who knows?' I noticed the new girl's speech was slurred, a wine glass in her hand swooped into view. 'She'd been stealing, hadn't she?'

'Where's Lefebvre?'

The busty girl sang the name back at me loaded with surprise, and then threw up her eyebrows suggestively at the trio of young officers who sat in the corner. 'Lefebvre, are you quite sure, dear?' she trilled, with a leer. 'Horses for courses, I suppose.' The men, arranged around what I assumed was her vacated seat, liked this and gave it a good raucous laugh. She tittered at me – and I felt rage erupt in me.

'Don't mess me about –' I snatched her elbow. 'What's happened to Celine?'

Her eyes flashed at me – afraid, but fear turned to anger – and she tore her arm free. 'Get out,' she shouted, baring teeth greyed by the wine. She appealed to the officers, 'Throw him out...'

I pushed past her into the next room, where a scantily clad girl in a pink wig, naked from the waist down, danced with a young man as she hummed time. It was the girl called Florence, I remembered. She pushed his hand on to the plump flank of her bottom as it rotated from view. I hurried by and checked in Lefebvre's small study. It was empty. I asked Florence about Celine.

'Dunno. I heard she had visitors this afternoon – her family apparently.'

'Family?' I felt my back tense. 'It was Robecq, wasn't it?'

'Who?' She registered the word and her charcoaled eyes widened, 'No, I never said that –'

'Where is Celine's room?' I pushed past her into the salon beyond. 'Where is it?' I barged into the sitting room, where Kennedy and I had conducted that first interview with Lefebvre on Sunday and then charged into the hallway beyond. I took the staircase that led to the garret where the women had their private rooms.

Snatching open each door I came to, I disturbed the sleep of several women, before reaching the end of the corridor. Here I climbed a bare wooden staircase, erected with a steep rake like a ladder. At the top I pushed open the hatch: light from a tiny window in the steep roof showed a narrow bed and a neat chest of drawers. The room had been stripped of any personal possessions, but I knew at once that this was Celine's room. I got a waft of her aroma of faint… what was it? Turpentine? It was a smell I had noticed but not registered until just now.

These people were thorough. Dreadfully thorough.

I thought of Robecq's cave and my hands closed into fists. I swore under my breath. Bowing my head to stand, I looked out through the window in the direction of the front line – and saw it, or at least the clouds of smoke just above it. The fog of war in the distance. I opened the window and felt the fresh breeze against my face. My heart filled my chest, this was my fault. Somehow I had identified Celine as the source of my information. Perhaps it was inevitable, perhaps they also knew that she was the only person left who could have possessed the information in the first place? I should have frog-marched her to the railway station myself. I cursed myself and stared down at the roof. Self-recrimination would not save her now, not if Robecq had her. I had to think clearly – and fast. He wouldn't have her in his cave, not now, surely?

I noticed one of the tiles was crooked and suppressed an inclination to straighten it. What would he have done with her? I pushed the tile into line and it held there momentarily before slipping away to the gutter and opening up a space between the slates and beams beneath. I took a second look. What was that?

Reaching down, I felt inside – and found something. It was a book, small, like the *Book of Psalms* that my father carried about him. Turning through the pages I saw it was full of beautiful, intricate sketches. Cats, dogs, humans, landscapes leapt out in black ink, pencil and charcoal. These, I knew immediately, were Celine's drawings, confirmed by her handwriting which I recognised from the ledger. And there in the front was her name, Celine Mazarin. I realised that I had never known her surname, nor asked it. I flicked through the book once more, seeing Lefebvre several times – animated, happy, asleep – then Fabienne, looking kind, graceful and Marie-Louise, laughing, her mouth open. I saw Kennedy, I saw McGregor, I saw Bradbury, even – I saw faces that I did not recognise. The last sketch, before the pages were blank, carried yesterday's date and was of me, remarkably lifelike and drawn, it would appear, from memory, presumably like all the rest. So that was why Celine went to Paris, to become an artist. My throat was suddenly heavy. I leafed back through the pages and saw the view that was before me from the window. Clouds scudded across the pencil sky…

I put the book in my pocket and reached inside the cavity once again – locating a further object deep inside. I eased this out with my fingertips, recognising Fabienne's purse. Celine will have placed it there for safe-keeping. I emptied out the coins and counted quickly. It was all there. There wasn't any chance in the world that Celine would have left without these treasures. Not voluntarily anyway. I sighed. My mind was whirring but I knew what to do.

Monsieur Chambord's door was answered by the uniformed butler in the striped waistcoat with the handy fists. I could see his pale face through the plate glass and see it shake at me. I pulled the bell again and saw him go away. I yanked on the bell a third time and saw the servant return, this time with Chambord – and this time I was admitted to small the parlour, where we had met the first time.

'I thought I had seen the last of you,' declared Chambord coldly after he'd sent the servant away.

'I'm looking for Celine Mazarin.'

'If it's a missing person enquiry, I recommend the police.' He offered a smile.

My temper flared, 'You know who I'm talking about, Chambord. You know her: she's one of the young women who works at the Blue Lamp. I know Robecq took her and I know that he won't be stupid enough to take her to his cave because he's already had me there. So where is she? Is she here?' An obdurately blank look confronted me and my voice rose. 'Or is she somewhere else, the same somewhere, perhaps, that you have your dungeon and where you cavort with prostitutes?'

Chambord's gaze was unwavering and his facial expression remained opaque, yet taut and irresolute. I stepped forward and thumped the marble table – causing Chambord to flinch.

'Damn it man, where is she?'

The mayor's inscrutable black eyes worked on my features, weighing me up, trying to divine the line between my knowledge and assumptions. I decided it was time to put my cards on the table, so to speak. Taking my Webley revolver from my pocket I levelled its formidable six-inch barrel at Chambord's face. He raised his hands immediately, and I could see its presence was having quite an impact.

'Now,' I said, 'as you can tell from my appearance, I'm very tired and, not only that, but I've been beaten up much more than is healthy for any man in one week. When you put that altogether with the fact that I've also been privy to things that would make most men weep, then I'll own that I'm feeling a little piqued. Therefore, Monsieur Chambord, I'll ask you one last time; where is Celine Mazarin?'

His chin rose defiantly and his lips set firm – showing a sliver of gritted teeth. I cocked the revolver. The chin bobbed up a bit higher. My finger played on the trigger and I set my mouth into a determined pinch. Still the bugger did not flinch. He wasn't giving in.

'Monsieur,' I hissed. 'I have not led a blameless life. Adding one more sin to my roster of ill-doings will not worsen my standing in the eyes of the Maker.'

The mayor of Béthune swallowed.

'Time is of the essence, Chambord.' I took a deep breath. 'I'm going to count to three. If you don't tell me where I can find Celine Mazarin I will fire.'

Chambord's narrow mouth tightened, his eyebrows lowered, registering bafflement, if anything.

'One!'

His Adam's apple twitched and dipped once more. He swallowed. The fear was kicking in. His mouth narrowed beneath unblinking eyes.

'Two!'

His mouth opened, effecting a combination of respiration and horror – and my heart lifted. After all, I knew I could not shoot this man in cold blood, even if he didn't. But still he said nothing. He just stared at me. I braced my arm for the shot and prepared to utter the next numeral. Was I really going to shoot him dead? I aimed for the space between his black eyebrows.

'Three!'

I heard the pitter-patter of light footsteps approaching – and glanced down towards Chambord's feet, half expecting to see his black Labrador. Instead I saw golden hair in bunches of a girl of about five. She wrapped her arms protectively around his leg. Her angelic face looked up at me and she immediately burst into tears.

I lowered my gun – feeling a crushing sense of shame – as Chambord scooped up the child and got to his feet. Sobbing, she buried her face into his shoulder. 'Go to number seventeen,' he said quietly. 'And then kindly leave us alone, Monsieur.'

Just like Chambord's place, number seventeen was a grand affair. Four windows wide, with navy blue-painted shutters, it was also decorated in a pale shade of yellow, perhaps in fact, the very same paint. I kept walking past it and knocked at the front door of the next house along.

Clutching my left arm I let out a low, pained groan as a young servant girl answered the door. It wasn't very plausible, but I looked a wreck as it was – an unhappy combination of motor-accident and down-and-out. 'Water,' I croaked as pitifully as I could. Fate had rewarded me with a kind-hearted maid and she put her hefty arm around my bowed shoulders and half carried me all the way to the warm kitchen at the back, where fragrant onion soup bubbled away on the broad iron range.

I wailed throughout this performance and then lay back whimpering like a wounded animal in the big kitchen chair as she went off to the larder to find something to revive me. The moment she was gone I slipped through the back door. Outside, I darted to the side of the house bordering number seventeen and climbed a stout tree by the fence.

Once at a good height I scaled the fence and jumped down into the next garden, landing in the soft undergrowth behind a thicket of rhododendron bushes. This was a stroke of luck and for a moment I rested, breathing hard. The whole operation – from the back door to here had taken less than a minute.

I peered out.

Before me was the rear of a very normal-looking townhouse, with a well-kept garden, a good, if slightly long, lawn and rockery at the far end. A table and chairs, with heavy covers over them, stood before a closed set of French windows through which I could see a drawing room in darkness. The curtains in the upstairs windows were likewise drawn. I drew level with the back door. Peeking through the windows, I saw an empty scullery with a red-tiled floor. Everything was neat and there was no evidence of life – no shoes, no waste paper or mess.

If Chambord was sincere and wasn't just leading me down a blind alley, then I might have a few minutes before he changed his mind and alerted one of his associates, such as Robecq or whoever else he had up his sleeve.

CUT AND RUN

I sidestepped along to the next window and looked in: white dust sheets covered chairs, sofas and tables, confirming that the place had was not lived in.

I returned to the back door and stabbed the window beside the lock with the handle of the Webley. The glass shattered across the tiles and I was inside within seconds.

As I listened keenly for any sound, I passed through the kitchen, which was similar in proportions to the one I had just fled. Now in the hallway, my heart thudding again my chest, I crabbed my way along, feeling on guard. From the drawing room I heard the ticking of a long-case clock and I stopped still. If the house was really unoccupied, that clock had no business to be ticking at all. I took out my revolver.

Making every effort to tread as quietly as I could, I followed the hallway to the front of the house and searched the grand reception rooms one by one. They were musty and had evidently not been used in a while. I then surveyed the first floor and then the second and top floors, finding nothing but a study containing cheap French fiction – not in Father Haillicourt's league – and encyclopaedias, and eight plain-looking bedrooms and a bathroom with no soap or towels on each floor. It was all remarkably unremarkable and begged the question – if no one lived here, what was the place for? Who had the front door key? Why had Chambord sent me here? Was it a trap?

At the turn in the stair on the first floor I looked out to satisfy myself that there was no movement in the street below. From here there was a good view of the park with the bandstand at its centre. From this vantage point you saw the structure at a diagonal, so there was the curve of the roof and enough of the side to see the circular, sheltered stage beneath. The hairs stood up on the back of my neck.

Was this the house in which Marie-Louise died? Had her killer stood here and been inspired by this view to make that her final resting place? Was this the yellow house that Celine had spoken of with the dungeon?

But of course it was.

I hurried down the stairs to the kitchen, where I inspected the pantry – empty except for fundamental staples, salt, some calcifying bicarbonate of soda and a tin of China tea. I closed the pantry door behind me, and tried the next one.

Stairs. They led down into darkness. I looked about for an electric light switch but instead found a lantern hanging from the wall, a box of matches left on the shelf by it.

The boards of the stairs creaked beneath my weight, the air turning cold and damp as I descended. At the foot of the stairs, I called out, 'Celine!'

Silence. The lantern showed the corridor leading in both directions, so I went towards the rear of the property, passing through a doorway into a low-ceilinged, room that was completely in darkness. In the middle there was a table, but then I realised it was not a table at all. More like a butcher's block, it was a heavy set, solid piece of furniture, from which dangled chains and manacles. This was Fabienne's dungeon, just as Celine had described. But no one was here.

My heart thudded against my chest as I made for the other end of the corridor – and the door that lay at the end of it. I shouted out.

'Celine!'

The door was locked. It looked flimsy enough, so setting the lantern hastily on the floor, I stepped back and shouldered it. The lock gave way, splintering from the jamb. Taking up the light, I hurried in casting it about, seeing only emptiness in the dancing light. I called out.

The only reply was the faint scuttle of rats.

Then the lantern light fell across the top of a table, which was similar to the one in the far room and likewise adorned with chained manacles. In this second dungeon a pair of iron handcuffs hung at about head height from the wall. But still, no Celine.

She wasn't here, was she? Perhaps I had been too hasty with Chambord. I clenched my fist – I ought to have been more diplomatic. Or perhaps less so. I took a deep breath, my resolve failing me. But I couldn't go back. He would be waiting for me, and if she wasn't here, that meant that Chambord may have alerted Robecq or others, who even now would be coming here. It was unrealistic to think that I could take them all on.

I had to get out – and fast.

Rushing back to the stairs, old floorboards beneath my feet sang loudly. Too loudly. I stopped dead and stepped back, pressing with my toe against the precise spot where my foot had just landed. It gave in to the pressure and creaked. I looked back to the room where I had just come from and the earthen floor, momentarily confused... There was a further space below.

I fell to my knees and searched for a break in the floorboards. And there it was – the outline of a hatch, like the sort that leads to a cellar in a public house. I levered it open with my fingertips and lowered my lamp. A narrow brick staircase led to darkness. The smell of damp and mildew intensified and the temperature fell as I descended. At the bottom of the stairs the soles of my boots met soil, soft and peaty as a freshly dug grave. Something clawing caught the back of my throat and I covered my mouth. Then, unexpectedly, a faint breeze tickled my face, so I followed it.

Hurrying in the direction of the front of the house, the ground turned to brick. In a corner ahead was a pile of blackened debris – rags, discarded offcuts of wood and so on. Brushing my toe through it, I saw fragments of fabric and ash, and then I met a solid object that made my stomach turn – the charred remains of a woman's shoe.

Turning, I cast the light around the rest of the room and saw another dark mass in the far corner. This was bigger and as I approached it took form. I pulled back the blankets... and there was Celine – gagged, bound hand and foot, and quaking with fear and cold. I lowered the lantern so that she could see my face. Her eyes fixed on me – the whites of her eyes already showing around her irises. Then they widened in horror and she let out a muffled cry.

'Don't be afraid,' I said.

Behind me there was a growl and I felt a burning, transfixing pain at my shoulder. I cried out – suddenly frozen, confused almost – and my lantern crashed to the ground. The burning agony suddenly ceased and I dived, rolling across the floor to the wall, gasping. I pulled out my revolver – firing instantly into the middle of the room. In the muzzle flash I saw Robecq's face and his blooded blade in profile standing over Celine. I aimed, squeezed the trigger and he roared – charging at me.

His blade whipped past me – and I fired again. The gunshot illuminated his face, showing wide rageful eyes and the two scars in shadow. His dagger scythed through the air inches from my nose. I lurched sideways, shooting wildly – but nothing happened. It was a misfire. And still he was coming at me. Circling rapidly, I swerved out of the lancing path of the blade. I ducked left and shot out my foot – cracking it against his shin. He flew forwards towards the wall and went down. The knife scuttled from his grasp. There was a moment of silence. I crouched, perfectly still, holding my breath, listening and attempting to make out his dark outline. Then I had him: a low moving shape against the wall. That had to be him. I raised the gun to fire...

From behind a sudden sharp scratch of a boot against brick alerted me. I spun round and thrashed out with my Webley like it was hammer. It struck home – all two-point-four pounds of it, plus what I was giving it – and Robecq growled in pain. I seized the dark mass and struck at him again with the butt of the revolver. There was crack of bone and he yelled. But I hadn't finished with him. I hauled him back and brought the revolver back to strike another blow. This landed with a bone-cracking thud and the Frenchman howled – not of pain but anger. He sprang powerfully at me, smashing the gun from my hand and launched me over backwards. Then he was atop me, his hands on my throat, vicelike on my windpipe. His face was close. Garlic, tobacco and alcohol were heavy on his breath. I struck at his wrists but my energy was draining away. His hands were clamped on my neck. 'Die,' he hissed as he renewed his pressure on my throat. My lungs burned. For a moment I recalled the sensation of swimming underwater and running out of air…

There was a white spark and a match erupted into flame – then a second – and a tethered hand thrust the flaring beacons under Robecq's right eye. I smelled burning flesh and Robecq growled.

CUT AND RUN

He swatted Celine away, sending her tumbling and plunging us once again into darkness. But the pressure lifted from my throat. I gulped down mouthfuls air and started punching, hammering blindly at the mass before me. He fell back and was shouting like a madman – words that I could not understand. In the pitch black I scuttled back to the wall, searching the floor for the knife or the Webley.

There was a gunshot – another deafening explosion and bright white flash – and a bullet skimmed my left shoulder and smashed into the brick wall. I launched myself – half leaping, half diving – towards the vanishing light and smell of cordite and smoke and crashed into him, sending him careering against the wall. He struck the brickwork hard and collapsed to the floor, motionless.

I tore the gun from his limp grip and knelt on him, holding him by the throat and ready to fire, just in case as I caught my breath back. Behind me Celine was moving and I heard her strike a match. She lit the lantern and I saw that Robecq lay perfectly still, a ghost of himself. His right eye was blackened and seeped glistening blood dotted with gross debris. I turned to Celine, whose face I could see was swollen and cut, and I took her outstretched hand.

Chapter Twenty-two

We ran, limping from the house into the park. Celine, wrapped in a blanket from a bedroom, sheltered in my left arm. Her teeth clattered and I think we both shook from shock. My left leg, weakened by overuse, was all but dragging after me. We hobbled like this to the Hotel de Beffroi, and what followed over the course of the subsequent hours was a blur of recovery – the meticulous cleaning and dressing of wounds, the sharp tang of iodine, and then the cleaning and repair of clothing before a long sleep.

In the morning, as these works continued, I sent Greenlaw on an errand, and within an hour he returned with booty, fizzing with excitement – from the Hotel du Nord. 'It was just where you said it was at the leg of the bed,' he declared as he presented his findings to us: a thin gold chain, with a crucifix and a small medallion that had belonged Fabienne Thomas, and which I had seen her wearing on Sunday. I inspected it in the morning light and saw that medallion was in fact a British Army medal of Boer War vintage inscribed with the profile of Queen Victoria and the words 'REGINA ET IMPERATRIX'. I knew it well enough. It had been presented to all military personnel who had served in the campaign for a certain duration and I had even noticed it, for instance, on the chest ribbons on Major Webster's uniform.

The rim, where the name of the recipient was usually inscribed, had been scored through, but there were the remains of what looked like an 'L' at its start, indicating perhaps that the recipient had been a lieutenant at the time of its presentation. I congratulated Greenlaw on his work and we discussed our next step.

'Montreuil-sur-Mer,' I told him, as I reached for my Gladstone.

'Aye? I'll get the Crossley ready. And what about her?'

We both looked over at Celine, who was sound asleep.

'Well, we're not ruddy well leaving her here…'

But first there was someone I wanted to see in Saint-Omer.

When we arrived I gave Greenlaw and Celine money to buy dinner and obtain lodgings, and arranged to meet them later at the agreed hotel. While they saw to this, I took a map, hand-drawn by Greenlaw, and made my way into the maze of Saint-Omer's backstreets and alleyways. Eventually, I found the bar I was looking for. The busy interior was filled with jubilant clouds of smoke and chatter and laughing Frenchmen. I pushed my way to the narrow bar and spoke to the barman, who directed me upstairs.

There was a door at the rear that led to a staircase and the upper storey. As I ascended, the happy burble of the bar diminished and became a distant baritone hum as I continued along the corridor. I stopped at the sound of slow, staccato typing and knocked. A chair scraped against the floor within.

'Who is it?' bellowed an English voice, guarded. 'I'm busy.'

I shouted, 'Thornhill? It's Frank Champion.'

The key turned abruptly in the lock and the door snatched open. Standing before me was the Bowler Hat, still wearing said item along with his ex-Royal Navy greatcoat. The visible portion of the leathery face before me was pinched in disbelieving scepticism. Then the knuckle-like bulge between the eyebrows relaxed and he grinned.

'You'd better come in,' he said, with a slurring emphasis on the 'you'. He locked the door after me and we sat either side of his table, which was crowded with the tools of his trade: a telephone, typewriter, a heap of spent shorthand notebooks, torn newspaper cuttings, an overflowing ashtray and a mostly accounted-for bottle of scotch. This was Anthony Thornhill, veteran correspondent of the *Daily Chronicle*.

'You want a chocolate?' he croaked, reaching back for a box of sundries and lifting them in the air. They were from the same shop in Saint-Omer that had been frequented by Fabienne Thomas's killer. I shook my head. 'Grant's?' he added, lifting the bottle. 'It's all I've got, I'm afraid.' He poured me a stout tumbler's worth without waiting for my response and shoved it over.

'You've stopped following me,' I said. 'Did I do something to upset you?'

He smirked, 'Don't take it personally... Or maybe you've just not seen me, comrade?' He grinned showing several stained teeth.

'Anyway, it's a free country, ain't it? Well it is until the Kaiser comes marching in and we all have to start *sprechening Deutsch*. I don't fancy those verbs much.' He shook his head, 'That'll be me out of a job, no word of a lie.'

Thornhill glanced at the clock on the mantelpiece and reached out to the chocolates. His fingers, which protruded from cut-down woollen gloves, ferreted through the massed confectionary until securing a clutch which he stuffed straight into his open mouth. He chewed them noisily.

'I'm after some information,' I told him.

'Ain't we all, comrade?' he replied, pieces of chocolate tumbling in his open mouth. 'Got anything to give me in return?'

I held his sepia gaze for a moment and took out my pipe.

'It depends on what you're after. Money?'

'Don't besmirch my good name, comrade,' tiny lumps of chocolate flew through the air as he spoke. 'The murders at the Blue Lamp,' he said, smearing a fleck of chocolate from the page in the typewriter before him. 'That's worth more than money to me. Why have you been sniffing around General Troyon? He ain't a suspect, is he?'

'What makes you think that?'

'We haven't time to be coy, comrade. I know you saw him here the other night – and you've been to Verdun. Oh, yes, my monitoring is very good. So come on, play nicely...' he raised his eyebrows. 'How about this, have you ruled him out from your inquiry?'

I weighed up the heavy, veined face before me and took a sip of whisky.

'Come on,' scowled Thornhill. 'Tell me the truth or bugger off. I ain't got all day. I mean it.'

'I'm sorry to disappoint you –' I set a match to my pipe. 'But I'm pretty certain he's got nothing to do with it.'

Thornhill's face fell, but then his eyes lit up. 'So he *was* definitely under suspicion at some point?' His eyes glistened greedily. 'Interesting... And you're sure?' He didn't wait for my confirmation, 'All right, you're sure.' A lascivious smile fell upon his moist lips. 'Now, is that just of the murder of Marie-Louise Toulon, or of all of them?'

'Let's not run before we can walk –' I reached for my whisky. 'Consider that a down payment – an illustration of my good faith. Now, I want some information from you.' I placed the list of officers written by General Troyon on the top of his typewriter, just beneath the expanse of exploded capillaries that comprised his nose.

'What's this?' he asked scornfully. He pushed another chocolate into his mouth as he read the names and started patting his pockets for matches. He frowned, shaking his head as he lit a cigarette.

'Don't know them... Faversham will be Colonel Faversham, he's not over here much. Normally he's in Aldershot, see?' Thornhill's eyes lit up. 'Ooh, Hooky Horace,' he beamed.

'Hooky?'

'On account of his 'ook,' he croaked. 'General Horace. Vice-Chairman of the Imperial General Staff, lost his right hand at the Battle of Omdurman when he fought off three crazed Dervishes single-handed, so to speak.' He grinned over and then returned to the list, thinking. 'They gave him another medal for that. Anyway, he's apparently fallen foul of the French high command. From what I hear they can't stand him.'

Fabienne had told Celine that one of the British guests at the party had a metal hook or prosthesis in place of a hand.

'I'm afraid I don't know any of the others, not off the top of my head anyway. So,' the journalist laid the piece of paper down and I gathered it up quickly. 'What is this list?'

'Before I tell you, tell me more about General Horace.'

Thornhill shot me a sore look. 'Very well –' He topped up his glass to the brim, 'in the interests of good Christian sharing. As you may be aware, there's been a certain amount of excitement of late among the British Army's finest, ahead of the establishment of this new Fourth Army – and, more's the point, who was going to command it. Now, as you probably know, they announced that Rawlinson was getting it on the sixth of February. What you probably don't know, comrade – because very few people do – is that just days before this, on January twenty-sixth to be exact, while every British general officer from Dublin to Delhi was jostling for the job like a bunch of nags on the start line at Newmarket, Haig received an anonymous communiqué purporting to express the sanctioned viewpoint of the French general staff, no less. It made it clear that they would not tolerate the appointment of certain individuals of whom they did not approve. They included a black-list of brass and, apparently, Horace's name was at the top of it.'

'Do we know why they opposed him?'

'No, but it's the only credible explanation for why he didn't get the job. That and the fact that he mentioned it in a conversation at the hotel here that was overheard by yours truly.' Thornhill smiled. 'Crazy old world, ain't it, comrade? So there you go, off to India for poor General Horace.'

'And who else, apart from Horace, was on the list?'

'Persons unknown, alas comrade, meaning I couldn't tell you even if I wanted to.' He played his fingertips together under his nose. 'And believe me I've tried my hardest to find out. As far as I can tell, no one outside of an uncharacteristically small circle of persons of great importance, who I imagine to be limited to approximately Mr Haig, the person what wrote it and Hooky himself, actually knows who is on the list.' He shook his head, 'Highly unsatisfactory state of affairs, I'd say.' He slurped at his whisky. 'But rumours are flying and I'm sure the truth will out sooner or later.'

'Horace must have been furious.'

'Somewhat more than that, I'd have said, comrade. But what choice does Haig have? He's desperate to keep the frogs sweet because he knows that if he loses their support, then the French little birds will twitter away into the ears of the King and the British Cabinet. And then he'll be out on his coiffured ear, before you can say *Entente Cordiale*!'

With Thornhill's words still ringing in my ears, the three of us set off early the following morning for Montreuil-sur-Mer.

CUT AND RUN

Greenlaw sped us through neglected-looking French hamlets and sprawling fields under a leaden sky. Dieval, Brias, Croix en Tournois... the villages were a blur against the backdrop of the Crossley's stately forty-five miles per hour. All the while military traffic came the other way – sodden lorries with troops and supplies, vans of horse fodder, staff cars like ours loaded with officers. As we got closer, rather like the approaches to Verdun, so the way became more congested until we formed part of a long snake of slow-moving military traffic.

The outskirts of Montreuil-sur-Mer were marked by a vast field of innumerable round tents. The flags told me it was a division of Australians and New Zealanders. We then passed a sprawling depot of mechanised vehicles with railway sidings and a station beyond. A tumult of activity was taking place with voices shouting this way and that. High derricks unloaded wagons of goods. We stopped several times at checkpoints but gained passage, thanks to my letter from Risborough, Greenlaw's authentic uniform and our impressive staff car. Even, I would hazard, the presence of a badly beaten young French women – Celine – helped create a sense of extra-military urgency.

At last, shortly after lunchtime, we entered a thronging archway that led into the walled medieval city of Montreuil-sur-Mer, where I explained our business once again.

The town was a moving landscape of field green British Army uniforms, like Aldershot on a Saturday afternoon. Occasionally I saw the bush hats of the Anzacs or the tall turban and broad whiskers of Indian Army havildar major. Shopkeepers had erected signs in English over their windows, and there were even one or two in Hindi.

The Army headquarters occupied the town's sixteenth-century citadel, which overlooked part of the town on one side and the sea on the other. It had formerly been a military academy, as Webster had said. It was here that our journey terminated, this time at a brightly painted barrier that looked like it had been pinched from a gymkhana in Bagshot. After an exchange with a tiny but ferocious Welsh Colour Sergeant of the Honourable Artillery Company we were in.

I left Greenlaw and Celine to mind the Crossley in the cobbled courtyard and went inside, taking the double doorway directly underneath the very broad Union flag that I'd seen them take down at Saint-Omer. At the desk, I asked to borrow a copy of the latest *Army List* from a suspicious-looking second lieutenant whose duty it was to administer to the needs of arrivals. He took one look at me and obviously concluded that I was an audacious thief, so watched me closely as I reviewed the tome, seated on one of the benches. Likewise he was gratified and rather surprised when I then announced that I would like to see General Risborough.

'Is he expecting you?' he asked archly.

Several minutes later I was sitting with the man himself in the middle of his large bare office, one corner of which was filled with unpacked tea crates. A portrait of a beautiful woman hung over the black marble fireplace, however. Major Webster sat by us to take notes. His gilt chair was pulled in close, keeping him central to the dialogue, which he was not.

I adjusted my weight on the narrow, highly stuffed chair. Every muscle in my being ached and my joints felt like the corroded working parts of a bicycle recently rescued from a canal. It was Thursday morning. I had arrived on Sunday, and since then enjoyed perhaps twelve hours' sleep, three of which occurred in the Crossley, in transit. I waited for General Risborough to settle in his chair and give me a nod to tell me that he was ready.

'Go ahead, Mr Champion,' he said.

'I'm afraid I've have come to ask for your help again and for your advice, on a rather sensitive matter that may well require your intervention.'

Risborough smiled encouragingly, 'Go on.'

'First, I will summarise my findings thus far into the case of the murder of Marie-Louise Toulon, real name Troyon, as I think this will be my last report to you on this matter.'

I cleared my throat and nodded as Risborough signalled for me to continue.

'On February twenty-fifth Marie-Louise Toulon attended a party given by the mayor of Béthune, a Monsieur Chambord, for the benefit of prominent British Army officers, some stationed in the area. Also attending were two other local prostitutes, Fabienne Thomas and Suzette Emmolet.'

Webster and Risborough exchanged a doubtful glance. The general nodded distastefully at me and I continued.

'What is not commonly known is that among the guests was a prominent French soldier, General Maximilian Troyon.' Webster shifted uneasily on his seat. Risborough leaned forward.

'It was at this party that General Troyon became acquainted with his daughter's profession after a period of some two years' estrangement. The general was distressed, as you would expect, and offered his daughter a substantial sum of money and all available assistance to help her give up her life at the Blue Lamp. I won't trouble you with all the details.'

Webster cleared this throat, 'Get on with it, Champion. Get to the point.'

Risborough raised his hand sharply, silencing the major.

'Take your time, Mr Champion.'

I bowed my head respectfully to Risborough.

'Perhaps equally astonishing is the fact that among the other guests at Monsieur Chambord's soirée, was one General "Hooky" Horace.'

'Horace?' Webster gasped. 'Ridiculous!'

'Major, enough!' Risborough turned to me. 'Nothing would surprise me about General Horace...'

As I spoke I took out my pipe and its accessories, my leather pouch of tobacco and matches.

'I have discovered an interesting connection between Horace and Troyon, General, which I now wish to ask you about.' He signalled his approval as lit my pipe, prompting the flame to dip and flare at the bowl. 'The recent move of the British Army HQ is integral to a more substantial deployment of British Forces to the south, I gather, permitting the French to concentrate their forces around Verdun, in particular, as we take up more of the front elsewhere.'

'Just doing our bit to give the Hun a whipping, Champion,' grunted Webster.

'Quite so, Major.' I turned by my attention back to Risborough.

'Central to this deployment has been the formation of the new Fourth British Army under General Rawlinson, to stand alongside the three existing British Army formations already in the field.'

Risborough acknowledged this with a tight nod and I continued, my attention momentarily distracted by the playing card-sized mass of vividly coloured decorations on his chest.

'In the days prior to Rawlinson's appointment I have learned that an anonymous communiqué purporting to be from an officer of the French general staff was sent to General Haig spelling out certain French objections to various candidates for the post of commanding officer of this new formation. I have information that General Horace was named in this memo, along with one or two others, whose identities have not been shared.'

I allowed the statement to stand for a moment, waiting to see if either Risborough or Webster would acknowledge the existence of the communiqué. Neither did; in fact their expressions remained rigidly impassive, which confirmed the truth of the matter since otherwise it would doubtlessly have been roundly rubbished.

'Since learning of this communiqué, it has occurred to me that author or co-author of this anonymous document could well have been General Troyon, who, as we now also know, will have been in General Horace's company not long before at the aforementioned party in Béthune. Even if he wasn't an author of it, since it's been effectively sanctioned by the French general staff, we know it has his approval. Or it wouldn't have been sent.'

Nodding, Risborough shifted in his seat.

'And?'

'The communiqué, Sir, has led me to make several challenging deductions which I wanted to share with you.' I smiled at him and saw that they both looking at me keenly. 'Gentleman, I believe that Marie-Louise Toulon was murdered because of the communiqué, by someone who knew her real identity – namely the daughter of its likely author, General Troyon.'

Webster got his outrage in first. 'Preposterous!' he exclaimed. 'That would mean...'

A raised hand from Risborough silenced this objection.

'Let Mr Champion continue, Major.' He cleared his throat with a dry cough. 'It would useful to know on what basis you make this "challenging deduction".'

'Certainly, General. The answer to the puzzle, I realised, was staring us in the face,' I paused, letting them hang a moment. 'A British Army condom was found in Marie-Louise Toulon's hand when her body was discovered. And what is a condom, Sir, in common parlance at least?'

Webster scoffed, 'A French letter!'

'Precisely, Sir.'

Webster roared but again Risborough's hand quietened him. The general's hazel eyes shone at me.

'So, Mr Champion, you believe that General Horace murdered Troyon's daughter because Troyon impeded his promotion?'

'Well I did think that, but I'm not so certain now.' I leaned back in my chair – it creaked loudly – and drew on my pipe.

Webster exhaled sceptically, 'What are you talking about, Champion?'

The general glanced irritably over at Webster. 'Do be quiet, Major. Go on Mr Champion…'

'General Horace had the motive, the relevant information and indeed, from what I'm told, the temperament to carry out the crime. But there's a but.'

I produced Fabienne's necklace from my pocket and handed it over to Risborough.

'It is my belief that Fabienne Thomas was having a relationship with a senior British Army officer. It is my belief also that she revealed the secret of Marie-Louise's parentage to this man and that he, now armed with that knowledge, killed her in revenge for Troyon's supposed authorship of the so-called French letter.'

Risborough shook his head despairingly at my statement, before turning his attention to the necklace.

'You'll see, Sir, that the small medallion is in fact the Queen's South Africa Medal. I believe it was a keepsake from this officer to Fabienne Thomas. Unfortunately, I can't make out the holder's name, which as you can see, appears to have been deliberately defaced.'

'But it can't be Horace,' said the general. 'Because Horace was safely tucked up in India for the duration of the Boer war.'

As he spoke Webster pulled an *Army List* out from one of the packing cases and started leafing through it quickly. 'You're spot on, General. Horace was in the eleventh Highlanders in Puna at the time. It's not him.' He clamped the book shut in triumph.

'Quite right, Major. It can't be Horace –' I nodded at Risborough and received the necklace back from him. There was the shortest of pauses. 'But it could be you, General.'

In the seconds of stoney silence that followed this statement, Risborough's tanned, wizened face showed shock, outrage but not indignation. Webster, meanwhile, was already turning the pages of the *Army List*…

'You'll discover, Major, that General Risborough was a lieutenant-colonel when he received the Queen's South Africa Medal in 1902. That's right, isn't it, General? Which is consistent with starting the initial 'L' on the side of the medal.' I cleared my throat, and met Risborough's hard eyes. 'You killed her, didn't you, Sir? And then you killed poor Fabienne Thomas when she found you out. How devastating that she was carrying your unborn child…'

Risborough moved quickly. In a split second he was on his feet and had his Webley trained on the space between my eyes.

'That's enough,' he barked, his chest heaving. 'How dare you accuse me. God damn your impertinence...' His eyes flitted to Webster but the revolver remained locked onto my eyebrow line. 'Restrain this man, Major. Gag him, if necessary. Stop him breathing another word of this absurd calumny. We shouldn't have trusted Captain Kennedy. Where is Kennedy? Major?'

Beyond the infinite black circle of the revolver's chamber, beyond the angular blade of the front-sight, Risborough's eyes were wild. A bead of sweat chased down his forehead and dripped from the eyebrow onto his cheek. If he pulled the trigger it would punch a half-inch wide ball of lead towards me at six hundred feet a second with more than two hundred pounds of pressure behind it. The only consolation was that I wouldn't know much about it.

Then I heard a metallic click and looked over – Webster, quicker still than Risborough, had drawn his Webley and levelled it at the general. His revolver was cocked, giving him a split-second lead over Risborough. The lightest of pressures from the Major's fingertip would redecorate the far wall with the general's grey matter. I took a deep breath. That squared things up a bit.

Risborough's focus pivoted to Webster and back again, now looking straight at me down the barrel of the gun.

'Thank you Webster,' he whispered, his mouth twitching erratically. His voice surged, flashing panic and anger. 'Guards!' His eyes scanned me and Webster again, this time the revolver switched between the two of us. He took a step back towards the fireplace, his finger caressing the trigger. Webster's aim was unwavering.

'Put the gun down, General, or I'll be forced to shoot.'

As Webster's threat hovered in the air, I reached out an open hand towards Risborough. 'General, please…'

'To hell with you Champion,' he spat. He braced his arms for the shot and I stared into the trembling black abyss of the barrel of his Webley, and swallowed hard.

'Champion!' He was half shouting at me, spittle flying from his mouth. 'What sort of name is that, anyway? I expect you think you're some sort of hero, don't you?' He laughed, his nostrils flaring, and words started to tumble from his mouth more rapidly. 'If I'd got command of the Fourth Army, I'd have helped end this dreadful war sooner. Yes, mark my words. I'd have saved lives. Damn Troyon. Fewer men would have died pointlessly, but because of Troyon – and people like you, Champion – more innocents will die. And they will, in their thousands if Haig and Rawlinson continue to wage this war as they see fit. Attrition, he calls it. That's one way of putting it. Damn you Champion, I could have saved lives…'

His hand stopped shaking, the black dot fixed on me and I saw the creases in the skin of his trigger finger stretch as he applied pressure. His gaze flicked to Webster, 'To hell with you all…'

In a rapid blur, Risborough jammed the barrel of his revolver to his temple and pulled the trigger. The sound of the shot was muffled but it spewed a hideous geyser of skull, brain and blood from the other side of his head. Momentarily the lifeless body was stationary and then it collapsed, slumping all at once to the floor, where it fed a rapidly expanding pool of dark, viscose liquid.

I picked up my pipe, which I had dropped in the mêlée, and looked down at the encroaching tide as Webster holstered his pistol. So that was that.

CUT AND RUN

Chapter Twenty-three

The rain fell in an unremitting drizzle, just as it had all morning. About two dozen mourners, including several army officers, gathered at the side of the open grave not far from a small white-painted chapel with a slate roof and steeple, which had an even chance of being pretty on a sunny day. Madame Lefebvre wore black along with several of the women from the Blue Lamp. Among their number were one or two new faces but I recognised Rebecca and Florence. Beyond the huddle a ploughed field stretched down and then up into the distance, eventually terminating in a strip of grey-looking woodland. On the far side of the woodland was the war.

Portly Father André Haillicourt officiated. It seemed appropriate. There was a good breeze and I saw him pushing his snowy white hair back from his eyes. I was standing well back, along the lane leading to the entrance. I no more wanted to talk to Lefebvre nor the others than they did to me.

The coffin was brought in on a hand-cart painted white, drawn by six men, dressed sombrely in black, who walked in step. They wore black bicorn hats, traditional here, with white gloves, white bow ties and short capes of black velvet. Six more of their number, similarly attired, led the procession two abreast in front. They passed close by me and drew up to the edge of the grave. The priest bowed to them.

Catouillart arrived at my side and bobbed his head courteously. Father Haillicourt was speaking now, I saw, his hands swept apart, a thumb enclosed by the Bible. He addressed the heavens as much as the people, words lost in the rain and wind.

'They're the Charitable Brothers of St Éloi of Béthune,' declared Catouillart into my ear. He nodded toward the bicorn-hatted figures. 'They have buried the poor of Béthune since the twelfth century when the plague first arrived here. They are a secular fraternity and honourable men.' He nodded meaningfully. 'The story goes that were founded by a pair of blacksmiths. St Éloi appeared to them one day and told them: "The scourge shall never reach you nor your house." And it didn't. They eat turnip even to this day to ward off the plague.'

The coffin was now being lifted to the open grave and drawing level next to it. I saw Chambord among their number. Honourable men indeed.

Father Haillicourt's face was now florid. He wiped his cheek with his white cuff as he spoke. I caught only an occasional word in the breeze. The word 'Fabienne' drifted across the abyss between us again.

'I hear that congratulations are in order,' added Catouillart as I saw Lefebvre blot her eyes with a black handkerchief.

'After a fashion,' I replied. The plan had been to keep news of Risborough's death quiet; as quiet as the grave. Clearly, they had failed, but they always would. When someone dies like that the truth comes after them.

The priest's mouth opened but I could not discern the words. They were borne away by the harsh breeze. The Charitables had lined up behind the coffin, presumably to be ready to do their duty. Catouillart leaned in.

'You did well, my friend.'

'Perhaps. What about Robecq?'

'Unfortunately, he lives, which is more than he deserves. But he still isn't walking, which is something. He'll never be a crack shot either, but he'll live…' Catouillart coughed into his fist. 'The search of his farm turned up nothing. There was no opium, no contraband cider, so whatever was there has been moved on. We'll monitor it. We could find no more evidence of Suzette Emmolet either. Robecq denies knowing anything about her. I hate to say it but I think he may even be telling the truth.'

As I watched the six lead Charitables arrange themselves with military precision around the wooden coffin an unerring sensation of failure gripped me. I watched them lift it over the grave with neat, synchronised movements.

God, I thought, I've been slow.

The Frenchman read my expression. 'What is it?' he asked.

Fabienne's coffin sunk from view, fast like sunset in the tropics. The rain splattered against my hat. The Charitables began to shovel dirt on top of her. I closed my eyes and said a prayer, one of apology for failing to help her. It was my first prayer in a long time and I doubted it would do any good. None of the others had.

I saw Chambord move forward, lift a spadeful of earth and sombrely twist the handle, allowing the soil to slide onto the coffin. And then, it happened. The unerring sensation curdling my stomach blossomed into a realisation. I nudged Catouillart's elbow.

'We need to talk.'

The Frenchman caught my eye and the waxed tips of his moustache lifted optimistically. In the distance I saw Haillicourt cross himself. I crossed myself.

It was coming up to noon the next day, Sunday, as I climbed the stairs of the tall belfry in Béthune. The individual sandstone steps were bowed by long centuries of use and the thirty-six large bells at the top began to chime their midday song, a prelude to deep long toll of the hour. It was deafening.

By the end of the melodious orchestration, I had reached the top, and was on the balcony surrounded by the medieval crenulations, not unlike the battlements of well-preserved Norman keep in some damp cinque port. I took in the view, looking from the four sides of the tower, relishing all the points of the compass.

From the east I could hear the thunder of the daily bombardment quite clearly, a crash of artillery carried on the stiff, moist easterly breeze. In the town below, where you were more sheltered from the wind and had the hustle and bustle of life to contend with, this sound of war didn't carry, but not up here. The distant battle lines were several blurred scars on the dark horizon. It was stranger still to think that the land I could see beyond was in German hands.

Doubtless it would change hands again before all this was over. The back and forth turned my mind to the tides of the River Colne on the east coast of England, where there would be no end of it until kingdom come.

Down to the right, in the south-west, were the broad open fields between the villages of Loos and Hulluch where I had fought the September before. I could see the flat top of Hill Seventy where so many Cameron Highlanders died on the day of the German counter-attack, in the main because of the decision by senior officers not to support them with the reserves. I remembered the flashes of their guns as they defended, utterly overwhelmed and completely unsupported. It was like the lights going out in a distant town, one by one. I was too far away to be of any help...

Just then, I heard blunt, short footsteps and turned – turning in time to be hailed by that distinctive voice – the dusty, dry sound of corpse being dragged through gravel. It was the Eagle.

'Greetings Hornbeam!' I had not seen him in daylight before, and it was not an improvement. He stopped no more than three yards from me, his hands buried in the side-pockets of his leather trench coat. He expertly appraised my various injuries as well as my face, now liberated from the thatch.

'You looked better with the beard,' he stated, as he sidled over to the battlements. He took in the view, his hungry eyes curious and sucked in the air, drinking in the cold and the notes of cordite and sulphur from the coal fires.

'They're busy today,' he said, nodding towards Germany.

We both looked across the horizon – seeing the battlefields and then the tall, twin slag heaps of spoil outside Lens, whose hinterland was rich in coal, just as Béthune's was.

'I heard you'd left town,' the Frenchman said, snatching the words through the air. 'I had feared that you had intended to provoke my displeasure by breaking your side of the bargain.' He grinned, showing those lonely teeth. 'I'm pleased to see that my faith in you was not misplaced, or at least I hope it isn't.'

In this glum daylight his skin had a bluish tint and looked like it had been rubbed in flour; an aridity which reflected the vocal cords. His pale complexion, I noticed, accentuated the gross colours of the aquiline tattoo, which looked sore or infected. He shivered through his coat, his shoulders shaking, and then spat his words out at me, like a sadistic games master springing a cricket ball at an unprepared boy. 'So come on Hornbeam, I've not got all day. You gave Robecq a thorough seeing-too, just a pity you didn't finish the job properly.'

He noticed the decided look of reluctance on my face and chuckled, 'Trust me, Hornbeam, you would have done a fine public service, and you almost did.' He lifted the corners of his mouth in an expression that resembled a smile. 'Now, what about Suzette Emmolet?'

His dark foxhound eyes scrutinised me, extracting the spirit of my response from my features, before I'd given it. I looked away, out over the sea of steep roofs and countless smoking chimneys, to the grey-coloured fields beyond. But there was no inspiration there – the truth was I still didn't know. We had searched everywhere and come up with nothing. The poor woman had vanished without trace, all except for that grisly artefact that I had chanced upon in Robecq's cave.

'I'm afraid, Eagle, I'm going to have to let you down. As far as I know the rest of her could be anywhere – likely buried in a cellar in one of these houses, under six foot of earth anywhere out there, or weighted down in the canal. One day she'll turn up, of that I'm certain. Or, perhaps, you could just tell me yourself?'

He wheeled round slowly, a dry frown on his forehead. He was amused rather than angry.

'What makes you think I've got anything to do with this?'

'Because you were the only person to notice that she was missing.' I let this stand. 'Then you made a point of mentioning the missing finger, which turned out to be a vital clue in identifying her. Your intervention led me to investigate Robecq. I can't help feeling that it's too much of a coincidence.'

He laughed.

'What if I said that you had arranged for the hand to be left in the box in the cave, so that Robecq could be blamed and removed as a rival – but not by you, rather by the authorities, thereby allowing you to take over the Blue Lamp, not to mention a thriving opium business?'

'I'd say it all sounds too good to be true, Detective Hornbeam,' he grinned malignantly. I had no proof, just a combination of suppositions and coincidences that I felt made an unarguable case against him.

'I'm here to offer you a bargain, Eagle. If you tell me where to find her then this need go no further. I give you my word that I'll not pursue it. But at least her body could be returned to her family and laid to rest. That would mean a lot to them.'

'I'm sure it would, Hornbeam.' He sighed as if losing patience with me. 'If only you had hard evidence Hornbeam, then I expect I could be worried. Of course, the authorities would still need to do their duty, which they don't show much lust for. It's a pity they're so spineless, isn't it?' He paced over to the wall and looked down over the parapet. 'If even a corpse – or part of it – isn't enough to stir them into action, what hope do we have? The Eagle pulled his trench coat around him tighter. 'Do you ever wonder what the world coming to, Hornbeam? I do. *Constantly*.' He broke into hard laughter, 'You give someone a helping hand…'

'Stop it!'

His eyes shot to me with sudden ferocity.

It was a warning which I ignored.

'Tell me where she is, otherwise I will make sure you take responsibility for her death.'

His face softened.

'Oh, Hornbeam. You hopeless romantic. I don't think you're going to get on in the twentieth century very well at all. It's not a place for nice people, you know? You need sharp elbows for this century.'

As he spoke I experienced a premonition. I pushed my right hand into the pocket of my overcoat and found the cold metal grip of my Webley. I heard the creak of the cogs in the belfry immediately beneath us and guessed that the set of smaller bells in the narrow pinnacle were about to add their siren to the big bell beneath our feet.

There was a giant metallic crash as the main bell chimed.

The Eagle lunged – seizing me with his powerful hands and flung me at the battlements. I slammed into the stonework, the wind knocked from me. The great hands gripped me again and hurled me up, onto the embrasure.

'If you want Suzette so badly,' he growled, as he lifted me over the ridge of the wall. 'I suggest you start down there.'

I found myself looking down at the square below, seeing the

stallholders and people milling about like ladybirds on the leaf of shrub. My hands scrambled for a grip on the stone ledge... I lost my hold and now my arms wind-milled.

'Happy landings, Hornbeam!'

The ladybirds suddenly looked a lot closer. I shut my eyes and cried out...

The sound of a gunshot was buried by the second chime as the bell sounded the quarter hour. The Eagle collapsed forward, a dead weight pinning me to the wall. In that split second a hot pain seared through my left leg and I felt a firm grip seize the back of my trousers and haul me back to safety.

It was Greenlaw. Catouillart stood by the top of the steps, a pistol still smoking in his grip. Finding my feet, they immediately gave way and I was falling, gasping, hitting the stone floor slowly, my head spinning. I found myself gasping for air, the pain in my leg all consuming. I looked over and saw the Eagle's feet; he wore leather boots with thick wooden heels like a Spaniard. And he wasn't dead. His foot moved. I saw it. He was still moving, crawling. Quickly. And now he was drawing a snub-nosed French Ruby semi-automatic pistol from his trench coat pocket, pulling back the slider, cocking the pistol and taking aim at me. I shouted out.

Flame and smoke spewed from Ruby semi-automatic, like a volcanic eruption in my face, renting my eardrums. I heard a cry and saw Catouillart dive. Another shot boomed out and Greenlaw spun round gripping his side.

The Eagle fired again and then was up on his elbow, training the gun on my head. I was helpless as the pain gripped my leg. Beneath the floor of stone I could feel the great mechanism moving and I knew the mighty bell was about to toll. He would time his shot for the bell, I knew. I saw the neat black dot of the end of the barrel. I saw blood on his teeth. My hand now in my pocket remembered the cold Webley in its grip.

He fired again. The black dot of the Ruby burst into flame and smoke.

And everything went black…

Chapter Twenty-four

I was aware of the sound of a whistle, of rapid footsteps and hushed haste. Finally my eyes opened and I saw Catouillart kneeling by me, a bloody handkerchief in his hand and his face grave. Next to him was Greenlaw, bleeding, but looking relieved. There was a doctor, too, doing something I could not see with a bandage. I turned my head and saw the heap of the Eagle, the tattoo on the side of his head shattered by a bullet hole. His facial expression in death was as in life, scornful. His eyes were still open and filled with contempt. Quite so.

Catouillart prised my fingers from the Webley in my right hand and rubbed the metalwork clean with a cloth.

I stopped seeing anything for a while after that and presently I realised I was dreaming. I was floating through time and space, arriving in the Cheshire twenty years before in the 1890s. It was late summer and lush greenery was sprouting up between the brick houses of Northwich in the gardens, the cracks in the lanes, the alleys and the greens. My sisters, in white Sunday tea dresses, play in the meadow behind the rectory, running through the tall grasses with forget-me-nots and dog rose in their hair. I'm flying above them, like a spirit. Below I see Dotty's face, mid-rapture, laughing innocently and looking up without seeing me. A cloud passes over the afternoon sun and there's my father's rocking chair – it's occupied by Lieutenant Murray, still caked in the grey, brown mud of Loos, and looking young, tired, embittered, his holster empty. He doesn't look up at me and, my heart sinking, I remember why and how it is I come to have his Webley revolver.

Later still, I stirred. I was conscious that much more time had passed. The first thing that alerted me to my surroundings was the cleansing whiff of disinfectant. I had always rather liked the smell and treasured its associations with order and calm. That was interesting. There was a glow and slowly I opened my eyes. I was exhausted.

Directly above me, I saw an elderly man with long white hair, streaked with grey and a white beard twisting down to his waist. He was attended by winged cherubs, lute and lyre to hand, and ethereal mists shrouded his legs. He was pointing. My field of vision tracked down. There was a dove, its wings outstretched, and below that the hallowed figure of Jesus on the cross, his torso pierced with arrows and beneath him, the apostles.

Underneath the Holy gathering was a high altar screen in filigree gold, panelled and shut. And before it were beds, a couple of dozen of them in three rows and covered in neat, white bed linen. Directly opposite was a bed with a bandaged figure.

I was back in the British field hospital at Choques. Home sweet home.

Greenlaw, seated in the chair next to my bed and his arm in a sling, was smiling at me.

'Well done Champion,' he said, tears appearing in the soft sod's eyes. 'Good to see you.' He grinned, showing me his dimples.

A few moments later Herbert Macmillan arrived at the bedside. He inspected a clipboard that hung from the end of my bed, before perching besides me.

'I'm won't tell you how long it took me to get that lead out of your leg, you ungrateful bastard.' He smiled. 'And then we took a lump out of your side – did you know about that? You're lucky to be alive Frank. Again.' He placed his hand on my shoulder. 'And would you credit it? You even managed to break your pipe during this fracas. I don't know…'

He pressed his beloved meerschaum clay pipe into my hand. 'No – take it, old man.' He waved off my protests and as he moved off I saw the pipe was ready to be lit and that he had slipped a box of matches onto the bed without my noticing.

I clamped the stem between my teeth – it felt good, weighty, a pipe of substance – and got myself up to a sitting position. Lighting up, I watched a bandaged chap being brought in on a gurney. The orderlies started lifting him onto a bed. As I got the first flavour of the meerschaum's hot burn I remembered the last moments in the belfry. I got a flash of it. The Eagle, the fight, the bells, the gunshot. But most importantly I suddenly remembered what he had said about Suzette Emmolet. It all came back in a mad, pell-mell rush.

I reached out, grabbed Greenlaw's arm and sprang as quickly as I could from the bed. I ignored the pains in my body. 'Come on Greenlaw, I need my clothes…'

It was a Monday and the main square of Béthune was filled with stalls and market goers. Knots of eager shoppers and traders hurried to and fro with baskets of produce or pushing trolleys of goods. A throng of children ran past us, shrieking with excitement. Greenlaw and I moved purposefully through the crowds. We carried lanterns, even though it was not yet ten o'clock in the morning.

We stopped over a large cast iron drain cover and, between the two of us, levered it off. We were confronted with a dark hole, smelling strongly of effluent. One of the stallholders barked at us to stop but a grim glance from Greenlaw told him not to interfere. 'You shouldn't be going down there,' the Yorkshireman told me, 'not in your condition.'

That from the man with an arm in a sling.

'Come on –' I lit the lantern and climbed down, lowering myself awkwardly into the cobbled drain, my boots landing in stagnant drain water. I gritted my teeth as the fresh wound in my left leg reminded me of its presence with a steely pain. I landed and took a deep breath. It was sore.

A look back and forth told me the low tunnel continued east–west along the hundred yards length of the square. Greenlaw's legs came into view and he lowered himself in.

We headed along the tunnel in the direction of the belfry. I didn't know what I was looking for, as such, but I hoped I would know it when I saw it. We soon passed under another large drain cover, followed by second after another few minutes. There was nothing to be seen, so we stopped and went back the other way. 'Bear with me,' I told Greenlaw as we doubled back.

We reached our starting point and then pressed on, the gradient of the drain steepening. We were going down now slightly and the water began to move more quickly past our ankles. The smell got worse too. Greenlaw, his nose and mouth covered in a rag, started barking at murky shapes washing past us in the low stream.

We reached a crossroads. Greenlaw cast this lantern in the three directions confronting us. Where now, he was asking?

I pointed left, 'Towards the belfry.'

We were now walking against the flow of the sewer water and it splashed dark and murky against our shins. Rats scampered along the water's edge around us, screeching and scuttling into the darkness. Greenlaw kicked out at one, which squealed.

'What are you looking for?' he growled, more to the rat than me. I was about to say again that I didn't know, when I saw it.

I lifted the lantern to illuminate a section of the brick wall of the sewer.

'Here –'

The cement had been all picked away, but the bricks put back in place to close up the gap. 'They dug caves in the thirteenth century, during a siege for people to hide in. If you don't mind,' I said, indicating the wall.

Greenlaw's good shoulder went to it and he burst through, tumbling into the dark abyss beyond, swearing as he splashed into the water. I raised my lantern and saw her – a shrouded figure laid out on a brick pedestal, like a knight's tomb on a cathedral plinth. 'There she is,' I said.

The Yorkshireman was on his feet, hurrying towards her.

'Tread carefully,' I said. 'There's no need to hurry.'

Epilogue

The shadows of evening were lengthening on the shingle foreshore of Mersea Stone and on the far side of the river, the town of Brightlingsea had lost its afternoon lustre. I flicked the rod and gave a great cast and saw the almost invisible line flick out through the glum white sky in a great unfurling heap. The sound of it landing was lost to the surf and frothing wave crests. With still two hours to go before high water, the tide was ripping by up to the point, deluging the mouth of the River Colne with its twice daily dose of salt and sea life.

My baited hook now sat over the second break where the shingle meets the sand. As I waited for a bite my mind pondered anew the events of the previous fortnight.

A postcard had arrived from Knaresborough from Greenlaw on his well-deserved leave. He was to be married next month, he said. I had also received word from Celine; a letter, explaining that she had returned safely to her parents' place in Brittany. She said I would be welcome if I ever fancied visiting, which was a surprising offer, though one I was unlikely to take up. But you never knew.

A seagull dived towards my baited hook and its claws plunged into the water. In a moment its head flashed and twisted through the white spume and then it launched off, my worm fluttering in its beak. I reeled the line back in.

Behind me I heard the crunch of footsteps on the shingle. The footfalls were deep, heavy and purposeful, and becoming louder. I recognised the tempo.

'It's late in the season for whiting,' said the singsong voice that I expected behind me. It was Kennedy. 'Oughtn't they be on their way to Africa by now?'

I cast him a glance before recovering the last yards of line and then snagged the hook off on one of the eyes of the rod and locked it off.

'What do you want?'

The mild hostility in my voice took him aback, momentarily.

'I thought you'd be interested to know,' he said. 'General Troyon was found dead last night. He hung himself.'

Kennedy's moustache closed sombrely over the sides of his mouth.

'Good,' I said, picking up my bucket of whiting. I ignored Kennedy's expression of mild consternation and started to trudge up the breach.

Our footsteps laboured in the subsiding stones and we stayed silent until we reached the sandy track. This followed the river all the way to Fingrinhoe, where I had tied up the tender to my Essex trawler, *Nancy*. As we walked I updated Kennedy on what I had learned of the case before I left France, culminating in the discovery of Suzette Emmolet's body.

We arrived at the low wooden jetty to which I had tied my dinghy and climbed in. As I rowed across the river, I told Kennedy the full details of what had transpired at Chambord's party. 'The misfortune of it was that this same girl, Fabienne Thomas, happened to be friends with both Marie-Louise *and* included Risborough among her more wealthy clients. With her naturally curious inclination, she will have wanted to know what General Troyon was like, so who better to ask than the British general who knew him better than most and whose pillow she regularly shared?'

I heaved on the oars.

'So why did General Troyon hang himself?'

I smiled.

'I can only assume that he felt guilty for killing Fabienne Thomas, an act he took in revenge for the murder of his own daughter.'

'But how could he possibly have known it was Risborough who killed Marie-Louise in the first place?'

I delayed my explanation of the details until we had boarded *Nancy*, at whose steep stern we had just arrived. Kennedy handed the bucket up to me and then we settled in the cockpit. I took out a sharp knife and started to gut the fish.

'It's my belief that Troyon didn't know at first who was responsible, but he was no fool.' I sliced the head off the first whiting, taking the sharp blade carefully around the fin. The bright eye glinted as I swept it into a spare bucket, so as to stop it dirtying the cockpit. 'He had the clue that Risborough had left, namely the British Army condom, making it clear to anyone who knew that the man responsible was one of those maligned in the 'French letter'. That narrowed it down. There had also been Chambord's party. So Troyon did some digging, which included arranging to see Fabienne on the night of his speech in Saint-Omer, which I suspect was sorted through Chambord. I believe that Fabienne realised that she had identified Marie-Louise to Risborough and for whatever reasons was suspicious of him. That, in part, was why she agreed to see Troyon. If only she had known what his intentions were...'

I had cut the tail and other fins off the whiting and now slit along its narrow, smooth belly. 'Troyon wanted both to hurt Risborough, but also to use the murder as an opportunity to subtly point the finger back at him – for both murders. So, he copied the essential wound that had been inflicted on Marie-Louise to suggest that same individual was responsible for both murders. Then he dressed the scene for a deliberately British seduction – the negligée from Capet and Carr on Piccadilly, the chocolates from Saint-Omer, and left us to do the rest. Unfortunately Madame Fourtier was unlucky enough to see him and, whether she recognised him or not, he was not prepared to take the chance. As for Captain Bradbury, I realised Troyon's guilt in the case when I discovered that the fountain pen used to write Bradbury's bogus suicide letter was in fact his own. That successfully undermined the cleverness of the rest of the ruse.'

I pushed my finger into the interior of the fish, yanked out its green, brown and bloody innards, and flung them into the bucket. One of the fish's eyes stared up at me.

'I assume that Risborough's actions have been hushed up?'

'Absolutely,' declared Kennedy with relish. 'Officially speaking, he cracked up.'

Which wasn't too far from the truth, for a change. I ran the blade of my knife along the inside of the fish's spine, freeing any last debris of its guts, and then rinsed the whiting out in the bucket, sluicing the water inside and rubbing my finger along the ranks of bones abutting its flanks.

I pressed the fish with a rag and laid it one side on a piece of newspaper to dry out. By now I had the head, tail and fins off the second whiting and was gutting it. My hands and the floor of the bucket were stained red. Kennedy's nose was curling up but he remembered what he had come for.

'So what caused Troyon to top himself?'

I sent the guts from the second whiting over the side and they sloshed into the water. 'In all honesty, I wasn't sure about him until a few days ago. But I kept coming back to the pen… and the precise shade of rather bright blue ink which he had used – and which made Captain Bradbury's note quite so distinctive. So I decided to fly a kite. I was queuing up at the butchers and the boy took a telephone call before announcing that a certain Mrs such-and-such wanted a repeat order on account but wanted it sent to a different address. That gave me an idea. I immediately contacted Capet and Carr in London posing as General Risborough, and asked for my last order to be repeated immediately – but for it to be dispatched to a new name and address. The name I gave was that of General Troyon, along with his address in Paris, provided to me by the ever resourceful Catouillart.

'So at some point last week, a negligée identical to the one found in the room at the Hotel du Nord, where Fabienne was killed, would have arrived at his apartment in Paris?'

'Quite so. And I can only assume that when Troyon discovered it, he must have been rather non-plussed.'

'Non-plussed?' gasped Kennedy. 'He topped himself.'

I laid down the second gutted and cleaned fish, and wiped my hands on my soiled leather waistcoat, before taking out my pipe. 'Oh well,' I said, striking a match and drawing the hot, drowsing tobacco down into my lungs. 'It was probably for the best.' Smoke billowed from my mouth like the funnel of a decrepit trawler.

Kennedy went below and returned clutching a bottle of Tobermory whisky, one I kept for special of occasions. He yanked off the cap and offered me the bottle.

'What are we celebrating?' I asked. I took a deep swig and handed it back to him.

'You got Troyon. You should be glad.'

'I'm not glad. The French are going to miss him. He was probably one of their best.'

'Yes,' sighed Kennedy. 'I'm sure they'll try to keep a lid on his death for the time being for fear of damaging morale.'

Kennedy looked pensive for a moment, then he put the bottle to his mouth and took a good drink.

'How's Nurse Taylor?'

'Very much better, thank you.' He brightened and passed the bottle back to me. 'We're going to be married in August.'

'I'm so pleased –' I gripped his hand and shook it warmly. I took a steep tilt of the bottle and felt my smile fade as grim thoughts once again oppressed me. I looked up at the frayed pennant that flew from the top of the mast. Its point was threadbare and snatched back and forth in the stiffening breeze. I emitted a long sigh that I hadn't see coming, not unlike the rain that the wind shift portended. 'What's tragic is that more Frenchmen will now end up dead because Troyon is gone. His replacement will almost certainly be less effective. He was a compassionate general.'

'You can't think like that Frank.' Kennedy took another glug of the bottle. He clapped me on the shoulder in an act of friendship that took me by surprise. 'Come on, let's eat some fish. Whiting doesn't like to hang about.'

I took the bottle, stared dismally down at the deck, noticing a crack in the wooden plank and sighed. I raised the whisky in a salute to the heavens, and recited something that I'd committed to memory a long time ago. 'Observe, in short, how transient and trivial is all mortal life,' I declared. 'Yesterday a drop of semen, tomorrow a handful of ashes. Spend therefore these fleeting moments on earth as Nature would have you spend them, and then go to your rest with a good grace …'

I put the bottle to my mouth. As the rich, kind potion descended I reminded myself that Celine had escaped and, to an extent, justice had been done. Some of it, at least. With that, I looked down at the two green-silver-coloured fish with renewed gratitude.

'Very well,' I said to Kennedy. 'I'll light the stove.'

ALEC MARSH

Author's note

The origins of this book go back many years to a conversation I had with my then agent, Antony Topping, and his suggestion that I consider writing a story set against the backdrop of the First World War. I was immediately taken by the idea and several years of research and work followed as I created and built up the life and character of Frank Champion and the world on the Western Front that he was going to inhabit in 1916.

As you will now know, with the exception of a few pages – when Frank Champion and Private Greenlaw venture out to the front line in search of a suspect – the war itself plays almost no part in this story. Yet it looms large over the damaged cast of characters who populate the narrative, as well as the whole organisation of the society waging the war. Among those most directly influenced by the war, of course, is our protagonist, an ex-infantryman who fought and was injured at the battle of Loos (pronounced 'loss', appropriately enough) in 1915. That was the first major engagement involving Kitchener's volunteer army – all those patriotic young men who joined up in heady months of 1914 when everyone hoped that the war would be over by Christmas.

For details of the battle of Loos and that part of Frank's back story I am grateful to Alan Clark's *The Donkeys* – a book that will make you rageful even as it brings you to tears – and *1915: The Death of Innocence* by Lyn Macdonald. Among the more than fifty thousand British men killed in that battle was John Kipling, the son of Rudyard Kipling. He was eighteen.

As you are probably aware, the red and blue lamps, as they were called, did indeed exist. In *Goodbye to All That*, Robert Graves's memoir of fighting in the trenches, he mentions the red lamp brothel in Béthune and seeing a queue of men a hundred and fifty deep waiting outside, a scene which is brought to life somewhat in *Cut and Run*. As a matter of fact, in each town where British Army stationed men there would indeed be red lamps for rank and file soldiers and blue lamps for the officers, and, I understand, when towns changed hands between the sides in the conflict, the German army would conform to this practice too.

I've drawn on another aspect of his book. where Graves described the effects of what we would now term post-traumatic stress disorder, to inform Champion's character. While recovering after being injured, Graves recalled experiencing flashbacks. 'In the middle of a lecture I would have a sudden very clear experience of men on the march up the Béthune-La Bassée road,' he wrote. 'The men would be singing, while French children ran along beside us, calling out: "Tommee, Tommee, give us bullee beef!" and I would smell the stench of the knacker's yard just outside the town…' Then after explaining several more vignettes he concluded, 'The scenes were nearly always recollections of my first four months in France; the emotion-recording apparatus seemed to have failed after Loos.' A close reading of *Cut and Run* will show that I have drawn upon these too.

Other aspects of the background of the story are accurate too, including the movement of the British Army's general headquarters to Montreuil-sur-Mer 1916 and the creation of the Fourth Army on 5 February under General Henry Rawlinson. These men were the ones who would go on to fight and die at the Somme.

Aside from the research and the reading for this book, it naturally enough sits against the massive cultural freight of the Great War. It's an unavoidable part of our national landscape, albeit one that is moving further away, like a tectonic plate shifting a once dominant landmass. As well as the reading and films and plays such as *Journey's End*, and inevitably, the BBC's *Blackadder Goes Forth*, there are several individuals who have brought the war closer to me who I would like to remember. One of these was a maiden aunt, Olive Greenlaw, who lost her elder brother in the war. There was a very proud photograph of him on the wall of her house that she would show us when we visited as children. Then there was the recollection of my grandmother, Irene Spouse, who was just old enough to remember seeing the Tommies going off to war on the trains. I could see them reflected in her eyes. Next, there's the connection with my father's father Frank Marsh, who joined up and fought for king and country in the Great War. His experience left him with no doubt that the primary task of a junior officer was to protect their men from the senior officers. He survived the war and died when I was one or two. Finally, there was a Great War veteran named Smiler Marshall who I interviewed more than twenty years ago when he was 104. Smiler joined up in 1914 after shaking hands with Kitchener at a recruitment event and would go on to fight at the Somme. I will never forget what he told me about going into no-mans-land, nor his very profound sense of the waste of war.

There was a real Frank Champion, too, a man I met once or twice, whose name I've borrowed, that I must thank. He also smoked a pipe and served his country with distinction, though during the Second World War. I would like to thank this grandchildren David and Thalia for giving me permission to borrow his name. I hope they don't disapprove, too much. I would also like to thank my proofreader Stephen York. Finally, I thank my publisher, Richard Foreman, at Sharpe Books, for deciding to bring this story to the world.

Alec Marsh
October, 2024
Manningtree, Essex

Printed in Great Britain
by Amazon